ENIGMA

ISAAC'S STORY

SHANDI BOYES

COPYRIGHT

ALSO BY SHANDI BOYES

Denotes Standalone Books

Perception Series

Saving Noah *

Fighting Jacob *

Taming Nick *

Redeeming Slater *

Saving Emily

Wrapped Up with Rise Up

Enigma

Enigma

Unraveling an Enigma

Enigma The Mystery Unmasked

Enigma: The Final Chapter

Beneath The Secrets

Beneath The Sheets

Spy Thy Neighbor *

The Opposite Effect *

I Married a Mob Boss *

Second Shot *

The Way We Are

The Way We Were

Sugar and Spice *

Lady In Waiting

Man in Queue

Couple on Hold

Enigma: The Wedding

Silent Vigilante

Hushed Guardian

Quiet Protector

Enigma: An Isaac Retelling

Twisted Lies *

Bound Series

Chains

Links

Bound

Restrain

The Misfits *

Russian Mob Chronicles

Nikolai: A Mafia Prince Romance

Nikolai: Taking Back What's Mine

Nikolai: What's Left of Me

Nikolai: Mine to Protect

Asher: My Russian Revenge *

Nikolai: Through the Devil's Eyes

Trey *

The Italian Cartel

Dimitri

Roxanne

Reign

Mafia Ties (Novella)

Maddox

Demi

Ox

Rocco *

Clover *

Smith *

RomCom Standalones

Just Playin' *

Ain't Happenin' *

The Drop Zone *

Very Unlikely *

False Start *

Short Stories - Newsletter Downloads

Christmas Trio *

Falling For A Stranger *

One Night Only Series

Hotshot Boss *

Hotshot Neighbor *

The Bobrov Bratva Series

Wicked Intentions *

Sinful Intentions *

Devious Intentions *

Deadly Intentions *

Coming Soon

Nanny Dispute *

WANT TO STAY IN TOUCH?

Facebook: facebook.com/authorshandi

Instagram: instagram.com/authorshandi

Email: authorshandi@gmail.com

Reader's Group: bit.ly/ShandiBookBabes

Website: authorshandi.com

Newsletter: http://eepurl.com/cyEzNv

DEDICATION

My dedicated readers who inspire me to continue writing.
I hope you enjoy Isaac's story.
Our enigma.

Shandi xx

1

———

A frigid breeze bristles the hairs on my arms and dots my neck with goosebumps. It isn't solely the plummeting evening temperatures causing these prompts to my body.

It is fear.

When I wring the railing keeping me upright, the coolness of the steel offers relief to my sweaty palms.

"You can do this, Isabelle," I chant to myself. "Millions of people do it every day."

I've spent most of today at airports. To say I'm fearful of flying would be an understatement. I'm petrified. My flight this morning was on a Boeing 777 from San Francisco to New York. I gripped the armchair so tight for the eight-hour trip, my French-tipped nails nearly snapped off.

There's no logical reason for my fear. I've never been on a plane that plunged from the sky or lost loved ones during a disastrous flight. My distress is merely embedded deep inside me.

I'm generally fearless, an adventurous person who takes calculated risks on a regular basis, but when it comes to flying, I'm a quivering bundle of nerves.

Before I chicken out, I push off the railing and collide into a wall of hardness. The collision knocks me onto my ass, and my wrist jars with the rigid marble floor.

I wince in pain, but it's a forgotten memory only seconds later when a deep voice above says, "I'm used to people falling at my feet, but not quite as undignified as that." Although his tone is stern, it also has a hint of amusement behind it.

Mortified, I raise my eyes, drinking in polished black dress shoes, an impeccably tailored three-piece suit, and the most exquisite eyes I've ever seen.

The pain zinging my wrist no longer exists as I drink in the magnificent creature in front of me.

More features come into focus—plump lips, powerful jawline, thick, luxurious hair long enough to run my fingers through but not long enough to be classed as unkempt, and an ideally placed dimple in a chiseled chin.

The definition of a man is standing in front of me, and the visual is riveting.

After angling his head, the stranger assesses me as vigorously as I perused him. His prolonged gawk has me wishing I'd taken my room-mate's advice on dressing more professionally instead of for comfort.

Alas, when your backside is going to be planted in a seat for a minimum of sixteen hours, you want it encased in comfort, and there's nothing more comfortable than my black Juicy Couture sweatsuit.

No, I didn't pay two hundred dollars for sweatpants. I found these beauties at the thrift shop in San Francisco nearly two years ago. They've faded, now more of a charcoal gray than their original black, but they get the job done. I've removed my jacket, and my white fitted shirt has risen to my stomach during my tumble.

Once I've yanked my shirt to a respectable level, I return my focus to the mysterious stranger. His mouth is etched in a firm line, and his unique-colored irises are barely visible since his eyes are narrowed.

Clearly, he's a man who prefers class over comfort.

I shouldn't be shocked. His apparel screams wealth and superiority, not to mention his composure, which exudes authority.

Grimacing, I scamper from the floor. I almost slip again when the stranger grips my elbow to assist me with steadying my footing.

"Thank you."

The woes keep coming when I notice the contents of my satchel spilled during our collision. My bag is full of the necessities a girl needs for traveling—lip gloss, a Snickers chocolate bar, loose change for snacks, a Kindle loaded with my favorite books, and tampons.

Oh god...

In a scurry to grab my possessions, I bob, the stranger dips, and we headbutt.

"Fuck," he cusses, his voice vibrating.

Even with it feeling like I've suffered a grueling left swung hit from Oscar De La Hoya, I keep my cuss inside my head.

As I move for the plastic chairs lining the corridors of the airport, I rub the sting. My vision is blurry and signs of a headache are forming.

I plop onto a chair as the suit-clad man gathers my satchel contents from the floor.

Tampons included.

Great.

Once he's collected my items, he places my bag on the chair next to me, then crouches in front of me, engulfing me with his manly scent.

Seeing him displayed directly in front of me has the depths of his eyes hitting me full force. It isn't solely their unique coloring that has my brows scrunching. It is their intensity.

"Are you okay?" The rasp of his voice causes butterflies to take flight in my stomach.

Unable to establish words through my suddenly dry mouth, I nod.

When he runs his index finger along the area pulsing with pain, instead of feeling the sting of our head knock, I experience the buzz of his touch.

Once he's assessed my eye, he raises two fingers in the air and then asks, "How many fingers am I holding up?"

"Two," I say through the smile dying to break free.

His handsome face is contorted with strictness, but his remorseful eyes give away his genuine concern.

He's worried about me.

"What's your name?"

I can't hold back my smile for a second longer, so I let it free while answering, "Isabelle."

The stranger returns my smile, which makes the situation between my legs worse than a bump to the head. "I don't think you're concussed, but you need to ice your eye. A bump is already forming."

"I'm fine, really." *Totally embarrassed, but fine nonetheless.*

A cufflink is exposed on the sleeve of his business shirt when he stands before holding out his hand in offering. "Let's go."

"Where?"

When his brow cocks, wordlessly requesting me to follow his seemingly bossy demand, I swallow the lump in my throat before slipping my hand into his well-manicured yet still manly hand.

After snatching up my satchel, he guides me deeper into the airport. His hold is firm enough to indicate his superiority, but not tight enough to cause pain to my wrist still throbbing from my tumble.

When we arrive at the first-class business lounge, I dig my heels into the carpet, lessening the stranger's fast pace.

The air sucks from my lungs from the sheer closeness of his handsome face when he abruptly turns to face me. Most people would feel threatened by his complex gaze, but my body heightens with anticipation.

With silence prominent, his brow cocks again. If I hadn't heard him talk earlier, I'd assume he's a mute.

Realizing the ball is in my court, I gesture my free hand to the luxurious-looking lounge. "I can't go in there."

My voice is so weak, I almost roll my eyes at its naïveté. Yes, this man standing before me is entrancing, but I've had plenty of eye-catching men in my life, and my composure is usually more composed.

This stranger, however, has me flabbergasted like a teenage girl meeting a member of a popular boy band.

"I'm underdressed." This time, I sound how I usually do—friendly, but not a total pushover.

When he scans my body, I suck in my stomach. I could never be accused of being shy, but even a Victoria Secret model would feel like a troll while standing across from perfection.

The stranger's perusal is long, and when his eyes return to my face, his smirk is panty wetting. "You look perfectly fine."

Unsure of a reply, I issue my gratitude for his compliment with a smile.

His eyes snap to my lips for the quickest second before he once again makes a beeline for the business class lounge.

"Mr. Holt," the doorman greets him without fault.

When we arrive at a bar that's so well polished my wide-eyed expression reflects in it, Mr. Holt lifts me to sit on a high-backed barstool. His effortless lift makes it seem as if I'm as light as a feather.

After snagging a midnight-black napkin from the counter, he leans over the bar. When his tailored suit strains against his back, it grants me a glimpse of a spectacular backside.

I didn't realize I was an ass girl until now.

Oblivious to my gawk, he opens a cooler flap nestled in the bar, then removes a handful of ice. The bartender doesn't bat an eyelid at Mr. Holt helping himself to their supplies. He continues watching the game, not at all bothered.

After wrapping the ice in the napkin, Mr. Holt raises it to my throbbing eye. "Hold that."

Once I do as asked, he snags two glasses from a wired rack, then signals for the bartender to join us. He must be a regular at this lounge, because the bartender doesn't ask what drink he'd like. He grabs a bottle of whiskey from a glass shelf behind the bar and then sets it in front of him without a word escaping his lips.

Mr. Holt dips his chin in thanks before pouring two generous nips of whiskey into the glasses. He then hands one to me.

"It will help with your headache," he explains to my bemused expression.

When he downs the shot without a shred of hesitation, my mouth becomes parched from the sensual way he swallows the flaming liquid so effortlessly.

Desire surges through me when his tongue removes the remnants of liquor from his lips.

My deviant mind was pondering doing the same.

Needing something to soothe the dryness, I drink the generous helping in one hit.

While grimacing through the burn setting my throat on fire, I slam the glass onto the counter before locking my watering eyes with Mr. Holt.

"Another?" he asks, his smirk unmissable.

Not waiting for a reply, he fills my glass again before sliding it across the ebony counter. Due to the overgenerous serving, whiskey splashes over the rim and puddles on the glistening countertop.

He watches me cautiously, his expression neutral even with his lips curving when I ask, "Are you trying to get me drunk, Mr. Holt?"

The veins in my neck strum when he replies, "Would it make it easier to get into your panties?" Loving my flaming cheeks, he winks as cockiness oozes out of him. "I'm joking."

I sigh in disappointment. Upon hearing my shameful response, Mr. Holt's eyes return to my face. His gaze is primal, commanding, and strong, and it heats my face even more than the whiskey.

My brazenness surprises even me. I'm not usually so bold, but with his self-assuredness and grace, I have no doubt he'd be extraordinary in bed—sheet-clenching, multi-orgasms, can't-walk-straight-for-days sex.

My hand holding the ice trembles as I shift my focus to anything but Mr. Holt's sinfully handsome face.

We sit in silence for several minutes, but my awareness of his closeness is paramount. Even without looking at him, my pulse won't weaken, because I can feel him studying my profile.

Once the ice has melted, I dump the napkin onto the bar, then drag my hand down my thigh to remove the inky stains smeared on my fingers.

I gulp when Mr. Holt licks his thumb, but I stop breathing altogether when he uses that spit-covered thumb to clear away the mess under my right eye.

As if hardwired into the responses of my body today, he stiffens before flaring his nostrils. His eyes are more dilated now, and even more lusty.

I'm about to assure him nothing is as it seems, but the shrill of a cell phone saves me from making a fool out of myself for the third time this afternoon.

With his eyes darting between mine, Mr. Holt slides a sleek phone out of his trousers pocket, then squashes it to his ear. "Yes."

His tone exposes his superiority, but I'm too busy taking in the time on his Rolex to work out who he's bossing around.

I only have twenty minutes before the check-in for my flight closes.

"Thank you for your assistance, but I must go or I'll miss my flight."

I snag my satchel off the countertop, then push off my barstool, eager to get away, but before I can, Mr. Holt seizes my wrist.

After advising his caller to wait, he lowers his phone, then asks, "Are you sure you're okay?"

"Yes, I'm fine, thank you."

After slipping out of his hold, I hotfoot it to the exit doors of the business class lounge, not once glancing back at the mysteriously captivating Mr. Holt.

2

As I splash water on my face to calm the heat spread across my cheeks, I take in my reflection. My eyes are wide and bright even with my dilated pupils making them darker than usual.

Sunbathing for hours has given my skin a vivid glow, meaning my hued cheeks are less illuminating, and my lips are plump from the sting of whiskey.

I want to say my rouged appearance isn't entirely based on the enthralling Mr. Holt, but that would be a lie.

At least my clumsy display in front of the most assured man I've ever met warranted a moment of reprieve from my panic.

I've barely thought about my fear of flying over the past thirty minutes.

After exhaling a big breath, I hook my satchel over my shoulder, then pull open the weighted door of the ladies' restroom. I rush toward my departure gate, hustling to avoid being late since my run-in with Mr. Holt has left my time stretched thin.

I swerve, dart, and weave between thousands of commuters who appear as frantic as I do.

By the time I arrive at my departure gate, my neck is drenched with sweat and my cheeks are blemished.

After blowing an unruly hair out of my face, I hand my ticket to the gate attendant.

Her top lip snarls when she takes in my flustered appearance. Although I don't owe her an explanation, I can't help but murmur, "It isn't as it seems."

She *tsks* me as her slit-eyed gaze lowers to the ticket scanner on the gate counter. My bright-eyed expression could be mistaken for someone who recently tumbled out of bed after a night of rigorous activities, but she doesn't need to be rude.

Though I wouldn't mind being reprimanded if sex was the cause of my late arrival.

It's been a while since I've seen my sated face in a mirror, but alas, that isn't the reason I'm arriving at the departure gate without a minute to spare. It was my disastrous run-in with the most strikingly handsome man I've ever met that has me scampering.

Once my ticket is thrust back into my hand, I head down the gangway. My knocking knees become more apparent with every step I take, so I focus on the male flight attendant at the end of the corridor, hoping his light-blue eyes that pop off his face will distract me enough to board without incident.

They do—somewhat.

My hand tremors when I give him my ticket.

"Good afternoon, Ms. Brahn."

I fleetingly smile since I've lost the ability to speak. Fear has once again rendered me mute.

"Today you're seated in 1A." He hands me back my ticket. "Upon entering, take a left at the second corridor."

Nodding, I take a hesitant step. Loud pounding thuds in my ears with every step I take.

As I walk through the galley, a flight attendant clipping back dark-blue curtains asks, "Can I help you?"

"I'm looking for Seat 1A."

She scans my ticket before returning her eyes to my face. "Seat 1A is this way, Ms. Brahn."

After gesturing behind me, she skirts by before walking through another set of curtains.

I apprehensively shadow her. My brows furl as I take in the elegant space. Luxurious, well-spaced black leather reclining chairs, elegantly dressed men and women sipping on flutes of champagne, and the piquant aroma of wealth filtering in the air announces there must be a mistake.

I don't belong in business class.

When I scamper down the wide corridor, I don't miss the disdained gasps when my rhinestone-embedded Juicy backside sashays by.

"This can't be my seat," I inform the flight attendant when I reach her.

"1A." She highlights the 1A marked on my ticket with her long, skinny finger. "1A." With the same finger, she points to the 1A displayed on the overhead compartment two seats down.

After rubbing my arm like my daftness is nothing out of the ordinary for her, she saunters back down the aisle. I stand mute, frozen in both fear and shock until the Fasten Seat Belt sign illuminates only seconds later.

I shove my jacket and satchel into an overhead compartment, then skedaddle to my assigned seat. I may not belong in business class, but I refuse to fly without a seat belt, and these belts are the biggest I've seen on an aircraft.

When I lift my eyes from the fluorescent lights lining the aisle, I'm confronted by an intense gaze that has me tripping over my feet.

"A beautiful woman falling to my feet twice in one day. This has to be a new record," Mr. Holt banters when I crash into his thigh.

I return his greeting with a grin before diving past him to take my seat, which is next to his.

When I plop into my chair, I search for my seat belt. My nerves have me jittering so much I struggle fastening the silver clips together.

Sensing my struggle, Mr. Holt stills my shaking hands by placing his hand over them before he buckles me in. A spasm bolts through my pussy when he tugs on the light-gray strap so firmly it digs into my waist.

"Thank you," I stammer out, suddenly hot.

He smirks before dropping his focus to my white-knuckled hold of the armrests. "Scared of flying?"

"Is it that obvious?"

His lips curve again. "You do know recent studies have shown—"

"Traveling in a car or a truck is one hundred times riskier than flying. Yes, I'm aware of that. It still doesn't help."

"Actually, I was going to say..." —I could kill him for the delay— "recent studies have shown the endorphins released during sexual activities can overtake cortisol and other fear-induced chemicals." His eyes are back on me, hot and heavy. "Perhaps you should consider testing their theory?"

My pulse quickens. Is he propositioning me?

Before I can form a response, we're interrupted by a radiant voice above. "Can I help you with anything, Mr. Holt?" When I break my intense stare-down with Mr. Holt, I'm met with a beautiful blonde flight attendant who is staring at him as if he is dessert. "Perhaps I can take your jacket?"

When he stands to remove his suit jacket, I lick my suddenly dry lips. His suit-covered crotch—that's straining to hold in the enormity of his manhood—is shoved into my peripheral vision.

I shouldn't be looking, but I can't tear my eyes away.

When my eyes finally follow the prompts of my brain, the heat in the airplane worsens. Mr. Holt's smirk reveals he noticed my gawking stare.

Mortified I was busted staring at a stranger's crotch, I divert my eyes, catching the mad glare of the flight attendant in the process.

She plays the part of a scorned woman well.

"Would you care for a drink, Mr. Holt?" Although her eyes are narrowed, her tone doesn't allude to her anger. Her performance is remarkable—a genuine ten out of ten.

Mr. Holt hands her his suit jacket while replying, "Teeling 30-Year-Old Single Malt Irish Whiskey."

"Excellent selection."

When Mr. Holt retakes his seat, the flight attendant attempts to walk away. I say "attempt" because she barely gets two feet away before Mr. Holt snatches up her wrist. "Are you going to ask Isabelle if she'd like something to drink?"

I can't see his face, but if the flight attendant's pupils are anything to go by, his expression is furious.

The flight attendant drifts her eyes to me. "Would you like something to drink?"

I shake my head. With the somersaults my stomach is doing, I can't trust it to keep anything down. "No thank you."

"Are you sure?" Mr. Holt twists to face me. The intensity of his eyes has me swallowing harshly, but unlike the flight attendant, I'm not scared by his glare. I am stupidly turned on.

Unable to speak through the lust curled around my throat, I answer him with a nod.

Upon spotting my agreeing gesture, Mr. Holt relinquishes the flight attendant's wrist. She scurries down the aisle, her steps as erratic as my surging heart rate.

After offering Mr. Holt a grateful smile for his assistance, I lean my head on the leather headrest, then suck in a big breath, hopeful it will settle my nerves. A strong, manly aroma overwhelms my senses. Expensive cologne, body wash, and a smell I can't quite identify make an enticing scent I'd happily spend hours smelling.

When the plane jerks toward the runway, I snap my eyes shut.

Here it comes.

The main part of flying I fear the most.

After tightening my grip on the armrests, my teeth gnaw on my bottom lip. I bite it so painfully I'm anticipating the tangy flavor of blood to flood my taste buds at any moment, so you can picture my shock when another sensation steals my devotion from my fear of flying.

A jolting buzz sends a current from my clenched hand to my heart. Glancing down, I spot a long, elegant finger tracing the veins protruding in my hand.

My breathing lengthens when I lock my eyes with the finger's owner. Mr. Holt is staring at me, his gaze penetrating and utterly consuming—even more so when he asks, "How about we test the theory?"

Too terrified to form words—and perhaps a little horny—I once again nod.

Every fine hair on my body bristles to attention when his finger leisurely glides up my arm, stopping at the throb in my neck. When he grips my throat, my pupils widen. His hold is tight enough to cause some discomfort, but not firm enough to stop me from releasing a husky moan.

It is more thrilling than worrying.

After loosening his grip, he saves my lip from my menacing teeth while saying, "I'm going to bite that lip."

When his thumb slides over my lips before dipping between them, wetness pools between my legs. Brazenly, I nibble on the tip of his thumb before curling my tongue around it and gently sucking it.

I've never been so bold, but his attentive stare is making me reckless.

My body temperature turns excruciating when his hand curls around the back of my neck. His groping fingers amplify the tingling in my pussy and turn my breathing ragged. His eyes skim my face before darting to my famished mouth. He stares at me for several long seconds before his head tilts like he's aiming to align our mouths.

I snap my eyes shut and lick my lips, preparing to taste his perfectly structured mouth.

When a whoosh of air hits my cheeks, my eyes pop back open again.

Mr. Holt isn't advancing toward me.

He's retreating.

Ouch.

Once he is again sitting on his side of the plush leather seat, he downs a hefty serving of whiskey. Even disappointed, my pussy spasms when his Adam's apple bobs up and down.

Something so simple shouldn't be so sensual, but it is—without doubt.

When his glass is void of liquid, he returns his eyes to me. They still display his hunger, but something in them has altered.

After slanting his head, he nudges it to the window next to me.

I gasp when I follow the direction of his gaze. Nothing but puffy white clouds reflect back at me.

"I'd say the theory has been proven," he mutters aloofly.

Though grateful he distracted me long enough I survived takeoff without a meltdown, disappointment still hits my chest.

The touching, the rush of excitement, the desire, was it all a game?

A ploy to lessen my panic?

I hope not, but things aren't looking good for me right now.

3

———

After pressing my palms on the vanity of the business class bathroom, I suck in a big breath. This washroom is larger than the economy bathrooms I'm accustomed to, but I still can't extend my arms without hitting a partition wall.

While exhaling, I lift my eyes to a gold-encrusted mirror. My face is flushed, my lips are swollen and red from Mr. Holt's thumb rubbing along them, and the undeniable glint of lust is brightening my usually dark eyes.

This look doesn't belong on my face.

It isn't me.

That woman who nibbled on a stranger's thumb isn't me.

I have rules.

Morals.

Morals I'd happily forgo for one taste of Mr. Holt's sinfully delicious-looking mouth.

What? Jesus, Isabelle, get a grip!

I've been hiding in the washroom for the past twenty minutes, trying in vain to reel back the dignity that eluded me when I sucked on a stranger's thumb.

It's been a woeful waste of reading time.

I'm jittering with so much excitement that I look like a child on the verge of peeing her pants.

Thankfully, there is only an hour and twenty-three minutes until we land.

Yes, I'm counting.

Unfortunately, that means I have an hour and twenty-three minutes left seated next to a man who makes me want to disregard all my standards with nothing but a smirk.

I'm not generally like this. At the very least, I expect to be wined and dined before allowing any man to get close to my panties, but one glance from Mr. Holt's piercing gray eyes makes me want to tear them off and hand them to him on a shiny silver platter.

An urgent knock on the door startles me away from dangerous thoughts.

"Just a minute."

I shouldn't be surprised by the interruption. I've been hogging the only bathroom in the business class section since the Fasten Seat Belt sign was switched off.

Once I'm semirespectable, I swing open the door.

My breath hitches halfway to my lungs when I discover who's knocking.

Mr. Holt's well-formed six-foot-plus physique fills the doorway.

As his eyes roam my body, he steps into the washroom, hogging the remaining space with an undeniably strong aura. My thighs touch when his enticing scent rids the space of its offensive sanitizer smell.

His lack of remorse about the intrusion exposes he's a man who knows what he wants and won't back down until he gets it.

From his smirk alone, I can tell he wants me.

Since I am pleased by my inner monologue, a moan vibrates my lips.

Don't judge. I may be in a washroom thirty thousand feet in the air, but I haven't had sexual contact with a man in months, let alone with one as devastatingly gorgeous as Mr. Holt.

His voice is as tickling to my lips as my moan was when he asks, "Why are you hiding in the bathroom?"

"I'm not hiding." My tone hints at my deceit, but he doesn't call me out as a liar. He merely stares, and it sets my skin on fire.

Seconds feel like minutes when we undertake an intense gray-eyes-versus-brown-eyes, lust-driven staredown. We're close enough for the hum of intimacy to be felt, but far enough apart I still hold a shred of composure.

A victorious smile tugs my lips high when he surrenders first. While scrubbing a hand over his head, he shoves his other into his pocket, then says, "I don't have time for relationships."

Brazenly, I reply, "That's okay, neither do I."

In my industry, I can't have a pet, much less a relationship.

Mr. Holt's eyes lock with mine. Shock from my blasé response is covering his face. "If we do this, you need to be aware it's a one-time-only deal. There won't be any calls in the morning, no dates next week. One. Time. Only."

I nod without pause for thought.

Even if my shrewdness is being blinded by lust, I appreciate his frankness.

I hate the false promises most men give to get in your panties. Don't get me wrong, I'm an old romantic at heart, and one day, I hope to have my fairy tale ending, but for now, I'm happy to participate in what I'm sure will be mind-blowing sex with another consenting adult.

Mr. Holt smirks at my agreeing gesture before stepping closer. When he places a business card for a nightclub called The Dungeon into my palm, my brows furrow.

"Meet me here Saturday night at ten o'clock." My thighs shake when he adds, "Make sure you wear a dress. Panties are optional."

I'm shocked when he heads for the door. Upon hearing the shameful protest I tried to hold in and failed, he spins back around.

His hooded gaze is ruthless, and it pins me in place with desire. "There's nothing more I'd like to do right now than find out what you look like under *all* those clothes, but if I start, I won't stop."

Who said I'd want you to stop?

He arches a brow, announcing I said my statement out loud instead of in my head. "Are you on your period, Isabelle?"

It takes everything I have to stutter out, "Wh-what?"

His assumption deserves credit, but I'm too embarrassed to articulate a better response. His unexpected attention has riveted me so much that I forgot I'm smack-bang in the middle of red week.

Seeing the forlorn look on my face, he mutters, "That's what I thought." A pulse throbs through my pussy when he growls out, "There's no way I'll only be able to sample half of you, Isabelle. I want to taste *all* of you."

My body temperature intensifies when he ensures I can't miss the honesty in his eyes before he exits the restroom faster than he arrived.

After gathering the minute smidge of dignity I have left, I exit the washroom and head back to my seat.

The flight attendant's eyes narrow as I walk by, but I don't attempt to refute her accusation.

My flushed face alone warrants her allegation.

Mr. Holt's eyes lift from his whiskey glass when he notices my approach. He smirks, and just like that, my insides purr like a kitten.

"Isabelle."

I try to act unaffected by his ravishing roar. "Mr. Holt."

I take my seat, where I strive to keep my focus on the brilliant blue sky beaming through my window, but my need to know everything gnaws at my insides until I eventually blurt out, "How did you know I was on my period?"

His lips brace the rim of his glass before his eyes flick to me. "Other than the two empty chocolate wrappers in your satchel and the fact your Kindle was open on a sappy romance book, the *tampons* were the biggest indication."

I smile at his unease from saying "tampons" out loud before saying, "They could have been my emergency stash."

"Like guys who carry condoms in their wallets?" When I nod, he tilts closer. "Any guy who tells you he's carrying a condom in his wallet in case of an emergency is full of shit. We only put a condom in our wallet with the intention of using it the night we put it in there."

"Let me guess... the first thing you do when you wake up is place a condom in your wallet?"

He chuckles a scrumptious laugh that awakens my libido that I tried to bury in a shallow ditch in the bathroom. "Not every morning." He winks. "Just every second morning."

Ignoring the bitter taste his tease caused in the back of my throat, I continue my interrogation. "Did you put a condom in your wallet this morning?"

Before he can answer me, a cough sounds from above. The flight attendant is once again interrupting us, and she appears as unhappy about our conversation as I am her interruption.

Mr. Holt acts as if we're still alone. "No, I didn't. That's why it took me so long to join you in the washroom."

His reply is loud enough for the flight attendant to hear, but I'm too far gone to care about her nosy-nancying. "So even if I weren't on my period, we wouldn't have done anything?"

Excitement melds through me when his whiskey-laced breath flutters my lips from him motioning his head to a gentleman seated in 3A. A white napkin is tucked in the front of his ivory business shirt, and since he is oblivious to our appraisal, he continues munching on a marinated chicken dish.

My jaw drops when Mr. Holt announces, "He'll need to replenish his wallet before he goes on the prowl tonight."

"You didn't... You wouldn't... You can't ask someone to borrow a condom, can you?"

I'd never have the gall to ask someone to borrow contraception, and although Mr. Holt doesn't lack confidence, I'm still astounded he's confident enough to do that.

My shoulders slump when he admits a short time later, "I'm joking, Isabelle." I struggle not to writhe when he leans in intimately close and whispers, "You would have just had to ride me bareback."

Oh god, I think I just had a mini orgasm.

He snickers at my reaction before turning his attention back to his whiskey. I focus on the blue sky, hoping to calm the heat in my veins.

Even after numerous lung-filling gulps of air, an intense pulse still rages through my body, only dampening when it's time to land.

For the rest of my life, I'll be indebted to Mr. Holt. During landing, he once again used his irrefutable sex appeal to divert my panic. His groping fingers and the low rasp of his voice prove sexual endorphins can overrule fear-induced chemicals.

I never thought I'd be a fan of flying, but if every flight follows today's path, my fears will soon be nonexistent.

Mr. Holt remains quiet as we walk down the gangway side by side, but I feel his watch most of the way.

When we reach the end of the departure gate, I twist to face him. "It was a pleasure meeting you, Mr. Holt."

I thrust my hand out in offering, but instead of shaking it, he kisses the side of my palm. "Until Saturday, Isabelle."

Seriously, his voice alone could bring me to climax.

While struggling not to show my excitement, I nod before heading toward the departure lounge.

Every step I take amplifies the stabbing pain in my chest. That is terrifying to admit, even more so since he was a stranger only hours ago.

Just outside the frosted glass double doors of the departure lounge, I freeze.

"Don't turn around, Isabelle. Just keep walking," I chant to myself, not wanting to be disappointed if Mr. Holt isn't at the gangway, watching me.

After rolling my shoulders, I lift them high before hustling through the double doors, only glancing back for the tiniest glimpse.

A broad grin hurts my cheeks when my eyes lock with Mr. Holt for the quickest second. He's still lingering at the end of the gangway, tracking my every move.

Yes!

4

My sluggish eyes scan the crowd at Ravenshoe Airport, seeking my ride. After an intense final flight, I'm exhausted, both physically and mentally.

When I fail to find Regina, I remove her photo from my satchel and run my eyes over her profile to ensure I'm searching for the right person.

While holding the faded Polaroid picture in front of me, I walk through a gathering of people ecstatic their loved ones have returned home or arrived for a visit.

Several minutes later, my eyes flick between the Polaroid and a lady at the side of a baggage carousel. I'm reasonably sure she's a match for the woman in the photo. She has the same black afro hair, high, illustrious cheeks, freckles dotted across her nose, brown eyes, and a broad smile.

Although I'm now skeptical this image was snapped in the last decade.

When the lady I'm hoping is Regina notices my curious gawk, she cautiously strolls my way. She's shorter than expected and a little rounder, but she has a friendly aura.

"Isabelle Brahn?"

I return her stare while asking, "Regina?"

When she nods, I squeal before throwing my arms around her neck and hugging her tight. Regina was a dear friend of my uncle Tobias. By dear friend, I mean *close* friend, though Uncle Tobias would have never admitted that in public.

He was an extremely reserved man.

Regina seems uneased by my friendliness. I don't mean to make her uncomfortable, but it's rare for me to meet any friends of my uncle.

I'm also notorious for being a little overfriendly.

When Regina inches back, she scans our surroundings, making sure no one witnessed our exchange.

Once she's satisfied no one is watching, she jests, "I don't see the family resemblance."

Smiling, I slap her forearm. She grins as if pleased with herself before collecting my suitcase from the floor and making a beeline for the exit.

I promptly shadow her.

When I spot her car parked in a tow-away section at the front of the departure gate doors, I smile. The red and blue lights beaming out of the rear window ensure it will never be towed.

"There has to be some perks to the job." She shoves my over-stuffed suitcase into the trunk of her unmarked police car before gesturing for me to enter.

Two miles from the airport, I'm grateful I didn't forgo my seat belt.

Regina drives like she's in pursuit.

When the afternoon commuter traffic becomes dense, she flicks on her sirens, making the backed-up traffic part like the Red Sea.

Once we emerge from the populated roads, she rummages through a bag of donuts sitting in the console. I giggle over the cliché that a well-decorated police officer appreciates a good donut.

"Don't laugh. Once you try these bad boys, you won't be able to stop. Pure. Heaven."

After digging her hand back into the greasy bag, she thrusts a massive cinnamon donut in my face. My stomach grumbles when its sugary aroma invades my nostrils, but I wordlessly deny her offer with a headshake.

I'd have to run ten miles to work that baby off.

Regina shrugs before ripping her teeth through the donut she was offering me. She attacks it with unbridled fury, her assault only ending once every last smidgen is devoured.

I fight not to laugh when she pops her thumb into her mouth to ensure not one speck of cinnamon sugar remains on her finger. She consumes carbs like my uncle—with the tenacity of a shark.

Her fingers are spotless by the time she asks, "Can you grab me a napkin?"

When I open the battered glove compartment she's hooking her spit-covered thumb at, numerous manila folders and a handful of napkins fall into my lap.

I toss Regina a napkin before collecting the folders so I can return them to the glove compartment.

"Keep the gray one out," Regina instructs. "I color-coordinated that one just for him."

After shoving the non-required folders back into the overflowing "filing cabinet," I peruse the extensively noted documents inside the gray folder.

Eagerness is clear in Regina's tone when she suggests, "Page two."

My heart lurches in my throat when I do as instructed. Piercing gray eyes, high, defined cheekbones, soft, plump lips, and a dimple in his chin ensures the very definition of a man is displayed in front of me.

Oh no.

"Can anyone say gorgeous?" Regina squeals, scaring the living daylights out of me.

She avoids a near head-on collision she almost causes from inspecting Mr. Holt's photo more than the road before saying, "That unbelievably handsome man is Isaac Holt, a twenty-seven-year-old businessman who is unmarried, has no kids, has lived in Ravenshoe the past six years, and has one sibling named Nicholas Holt." She sucks in a big breath like her lungs are as desperate for air as mine.

"He owns a handful of highly successful nightclubs within the state, and his current estimated worth is forty-three million dollars."

My stomach rolls when I stare into the eyes of the man who had me mesmerized mere minutes ago.

There has to be a mistake. That incredibly captivating soul can't be the same person Regina is investigating.

Needing answers, I ask, "Why is law enforcement interested in him?"

"He's twenty-seven and already a multi-millionaire. And those figures are only estimates. Rumors far exceed the digits in his multiple bank accounts." She twists her lips like our conversation isn't as serious as it is. "That alone warrants an investigation."

Unsure of a reply, I return my focus to the documents.

The more I read about the elusive Mr. Isaac Holt, the more he piques my interest. He wasn't evasive today, but he indisputably exudes mystery and intrigue, so I can understand the interest being bestowed on him by my colleagues.

Shock echoes in my tone when I murmur, "He made his first million before his twentieth birthday. Before he'd even left college."

Regina nods. "We've had nothing on him for years, but an under-cover agent has spotted him numerous times the past year entering an underground fight ring. Usually, those types of functions don't gain the attention of law enforcement, but this particular circuit has some notorious members."

When she nudges her head to the file, announcing it will answer the questions forming in my head, I continue perusing the documents inside.

Isaac is pictured numerous times with two extremely large men. One looks like he was recruited from the military. His hair is still the military-issued crew cut. He's ruggedly handsome but lacks the mysteriousness that makes Isaac so intriguing. The other guy's blond hair is clipped close at the sides but longer on top. His eyes are ocean blue, and he's smiling in nearly every photo. He's also handsome but in a humble, boy-next-door way.

"The brown-haired man remains anonymous, but the blond is

Jacob Walters," Regina informs me when she notices the images I've stopped on. "We believe the brown-haired man is either an associate of Isaac's or his bodyguard. Jacob is his fighter. Isaac owns him."

My eyes rocket to Regina's. When she nods, my stomach churns.

How can you own someone in the twenty-first century?

I thought slavery ended years ago?

In silence, I flick through the extensive collection of Polaroid photos.

"Col Petretti and Vladimir—"

"Popov," I interrupt.

"You've done your research."

Regina seems impressed by my knowledge.

She shouldn't be.

Vladimir Popov and Col Petretti were two names frequently exploited by my superiors during case studies while I was in training.

"What does Isaac have to do with the mob?"

My heart pounds my ribs as I wait for Regina to answer.

Mercifully, she doesn't keep me waiting long. "He's one of them."

"Who am I here for?"

I pray for her not to say Isaac's name.

My prayers are left unanswered.

"The bureau's focus is Isaac. If we get anyone else, it's a bonus."

5

———

"During surveillance you're supposed to be incognito among the rest of the population."

When Regina arches a brow, I glance down at my white short-sleeved shirt, black linen pants, and cropped boots. "What's wrong with what I'm wearing?"

I grimace when her eyes dart to the top of my head. I instinctively put on my black FBI cap. It's become a habit the past two years to brush my hair into a low ponytail and use my bureau-issued cap to hide the wispy strands wanting to frame my face.

My pants are the standard government-issue black trousers all rookies get, and my shirt is now plain instead of having "Trainee" emblazoned on the front in thick black ink.

"Much better," she mumbles when I remove the cap and put it on the mantelpiece. "Your uncle would have been proud of you, Isabelle."

Tears well in my eyes. My uncle raised me from a small child. He was killed six months before I applied to join the bureau.

He had initially been a police officer, and that was how he met Regina. He took her under his wing and taught her everything he knew about the local beat, even though he was ten years her senior.

A few years later, he became a detective, and then he was recruited by the FBI.

My uncle is the sole reason I decided to join the Bureau. I want to make him proud, and I want to help people the way he helped me.

I can still accomplish that. I just have to go against a man who makes my heart race with only a sideways glance.

I try to keep my focus on the task at hand and not on the man who invaded my dreams every night this week. "Have you ever worked with Alex Rogers?"

Alex is my superior officer. He's four years older than I am and was the talk of the town at the academy. He was the golden boy, the beloved "adopted" son of the trainers.

He started his career like all rookies—at the bottom of the rankings—but he soon climbed to a lucrative position.

He's now the head of his department and has a handful of staff underneath him.

It's inspiring considering he's only twenty-eight.

"No, but he's a pretty little thing."

I grin. When I saw Alex's photo on the wall at headquarters in San Francisco, my first thought was that he is pretty. He looks like he spends more time in front of the mirror than I do each morning.

I'm not saying he is ugly—he most certainly isn't—but he has that plastic Ken doll look.

A camera flash blinds me as Regina says, "Smile."

Once white dots clear from my vision, I learn the source of my sudden blindness.

Regina is holding an ancient-looking Polaroid camera.

She smiles while placing my half-exposed picture alongside two similar images on her refrigerator. The only difference is that I'm in plain clothes, and she and Uncle Tobias are wearing police officer uniforms.

"It's tradition." After wiping under her eyes to ensure no tears have fallen, Regina flurries around her eat-in kitchen, gathering her purse and keys.

The year before my uncle died, he shared many stories about

Regina and him. He loved Regina, but their work kept them apart. Their interracial relationship already raised eyebrows, but a rookie officer dating her superior was also frowned upon.

Tobias thought once he became a detective, he'd no longer have to hide his relationship with Regina, but he did. Not because it was frowned upon anymore, but because he had gone undercover.

He had to keep his entire life a secret, not just his relationship status.

"How come you never married and had your own family?"

Regina's coffee mug freezes halfway to her mouth. Her watery eyes shift to the Polaroid picture of Tobias on her refrigerator before they stray to me.

She doesn't say anything. Everything is relayed by her eyes. They reflect not only pain but love as well.

Just like Tobias, there was no one else for her either.

I often asked Tobias the same question, and he replied, "Why do I need anyone else but you, kiddo?" But I could see his heartache in his eyes.

He was a good man who sacrificed his own happiness for the sake of others.

He passed that trait on to both Regina and me.

"Are you ready?"

After exhaling my nerves with a big breath, I nod.

"Excuse me," I interrupt.

I've just entered an office on the third floor of a brick-and-mortar building across the street from Isaac's eighteen-plus dance club, The Dungeon.

Considering there's only a handful of people milling around, the atmosphere is surprisingly bustling.

The middle-aged lady I addressed ignores my introduction.

"Hello," I greet again, this time to a blond gent ruffling through a stack of papers.

His eyes glide over my body before they settle on my face.

Just as he's about to speak, a profound voice booms across the room. "I need that document now, Brandon."

Brandon smiles a lopsided grin before his focus shoots down to the documents he was tousling through before I disturbed him.

Enthusiasm beams out of him when he locates the item he's seeking. I track him when he bolts to the other side of the room. I recognize the man he's sprinting for. It's Ken from the bureau wall.

Shit! I meant to say Alex.

At least I didn't call him Ken to his face. Imagine how embarrassing that would have been.

The room plunges into silence, amplifying my quiet giggles.

I mask my laughter with a cough, but my gesture doesn't fool Alex.

His eyes narrow, and his lips set in a hard line.

Great first impression, Isabelle, I chastise myself while making my way to the man glaring at me in disdain.

Alex studies my body like Brandon did, except when his eyes land on my face, he doesn't smile. He is as pretty in person as his photo shows. Every strand of his dirty-blond hair is faultlessly placed, though it does look like he drags his fingers through it several times a day, giving it that sexed-up look. His eyes are light-blue, his nose flawlessly straight. His cheeks are well-defined, and his jawline is razor-sharp.

He's preppy and pretty at the same time. I might have said deliriously handsome if he wasn't glaring at me. An angry scowl never looks good, no matter how gorgeous you are.

"Hi, I'm Isabelle Brahn, your new agent."

"Michelle!" he screeches, making me jump. "I thought I ordered a blonde?"

My eyes bounce between Alex and a middle-aged lady who has joined us. Michelle is also attractive, mid-forties, and has sandy-blonde hair cut to sit just above her shoulders.

"Does she look brunette to you?" Alex asks Michelle.

When Alex's slanted eyes snap to me, I square my shoulders,

remembering what my uncle always quoted. *Don't let them scare you. Never show your fear.*

"Umm, yes, she does appear to be a brunette."

Alex seeks Michelle's gaze, which has darted to the floor. When he gets it, he asks, "In the past two months, have you ever seen him with a brunette?"

Too curious for my own good, and also hating that Michelle seems to be in trouble for something that has nothing to do with her —genetics are no one's fault—I ask, "What does my hair color have to do with my placement?"

I balk when Alex spits out, "Isaac Holt fucks blondes. You're a brunette."

"Excuse me?" I hiss out, my tone harsh. I know what he's saying is untrue, but anger outweighs my wish to dispute his false claim. "I wasn't brought here to sleep with Isaac Holt. I was assigned here to help with your investigation."

"You were brought here as eye candy," Alex interjects.

The room no longer bustles with activity. Instead, my colleagues eyeball the altercation between Alex and me.

I'm shocked by his blatant disrespect, but I can't express my outrage since my anger is so firm.

I didn't train for months to be a piece of eye candy. I trained to become an agent—a *good* agent, just like my uncle.

"We could bleach her hair," suggests Brandon, assuming my silence is in rumination for Alex's dilemma.

"Not happening."

When I fold my arms in front of my chest to strengthen my denial with an aggressive stance, Brandon's and Alex's eyes snap down to my breasts.

I snarl, but it does little to lessen Alex's scowl as he murmurs, "Once you're in a dress and a pair of stilettos, Isaac won't care you're a brunette."

"Once you have a personality transplant and a plastic groin inserted, nobody will care you're a Ken doll."

When chuckles erupt around the room, it dawns on me that I said my retaliation louder than planned.

Alex's growl forces the diminutive office back into a hive of activity.

Once everyone's focus is no longer on us, Alex joins me at the side of a glass "fishbowl" office. Since he's a few inches taller than my five-foot-seven height, my heelless boots mean he can look down at me as he says, "I know who your uncle was. I know his reputation, but you need to learn your place. You were only brought here as a distraction for Isaac. He never lets anyone in, and you're supposed to be our way in."

I maintain a strong stance, not once backing down or showing my fear. I plan to make my uncle proud, but I can't do that by losing my morals.

"I am an agent for the Federal Bureau of Investigation. I am *not* a prostitute."

6

———————

"**S**tupid, arrogant, pompous prick. He probably has a plastic groin, and that's why he's so cranky. You can't have sex if you don't have a dick."

When the man at the front of the line eyes me curiously, I smile at him before returning to scrutinizing the menu boards above his head.

I'm once again doing the team's early morning coffee run. It's been the sole focus of my position over the past month—that and filing.

The instant I refused to don a skimpy dress and pimp myself out for the bureau, Alex put me on desk duty.

I spend my days twiddling my thumbs, filing useless reports, and doing coffee runs.

Who would have thought months of grueling training would land me a job as a glorified coffee girl?

I place my order with the barista before collecting the mountain load of sugar packets the agents request.

"Do you have any Splenda?" I ask a staff member who's been preparing my coffee order every morning this month.

Harlow is a ball of mischief bundled into a bakery uniform. Her humor is a little on the crude side, but she keeps me on my toes with her wittiness.

Harlow hands me a handful of Splenda while saying, "Sugar won't kill you."

I try to think of a comeback but am left a little speechless.

I have a slender build, but I wouldn't say I'm skinny. I have a runner's body, but with more boobs than Olympic athletes have.

I work hard to maintain my weight, but by skipping sugar in my coffee, I won't feel guilty devouring the blueberry and chocolate chip muffin I ordered with it.

It's all about getting the balance right.

Instead of giving a comeback to Harlow's taunt, I stick out my tongue.

She retorts with the same level of immaturity, "Earlier this morning, I licked the muffins."

When she hands a customer his order, I tug open the bag holding my muffin to inspect it for lick marks.

It doesn't appear to have been compromised, and in all honesty, with how hungry I am, I'd still eat it even if she did lick it.

Harlow's chuckles echo around the bakery when she notices me inspecting my muffin. "I was joking about licking the muffins." She hands me the two crates of coffee I ordered while asking, "Same time tomorrow?"

After rolling my eyes, I nod, though I'm certain I'll be visiting this bakery again this afternoon.

A black Mercedes-Benz town car halts my hasty departure of the bakery. I don't need to see the occupant to know who's inside. The personalized license plate is all the indication I need.

Isaac.

From the nook of the bakery, I stalk the car that has come to a stop at the corner of First Avenue and Welsh Boulevard. My chest thrusts hard when Isaac glides out of the back passenger door of his shiny black car.

Just the authoritative way he walks will add an exciting element to the nightly routine I've been undertaking the past few weeks.

It's been over a month since our flight, yet he still invades my dreams every night.

Since I am anticipating to see the blue surveillance van that tracks Isaac's every move, I scan the street.

I'm surprised when I fail to locate them.

My chest stills as an exciting prospect swamps me.

This is it.

This is the opportunity I've been waiting for.

This is my chance to prove my worth to Alex's team.

After dumping the coffees into a waste bin, I creep closer to Isaac. Years of training activate in an instant. I maintain a safe distance and stay on the opposite side of the road to ensure my pursuit goes unnoticed.

Today, Isaac is wearing a tailored dark-blue suit with a light-blue dress shirt. He's minus the tie he usually wears in most of the surveillance images I've perused, and his dress shoes are so polished they gleam in the sunlight.

When he enters a flamboyant-looking restaurant, I cross the street.

As I weave between a steady line of cars, I once again scan my surroundings.

There's still no blue surveillance van in sight.

When I stroll up to the restaurant, I expect the doorman to welcome me with open arms.

He doesn't.

He snubs me, and the door remains closed.

I eye him peculiarly, wordlessly demanding an explanation for his rudeness.

With his lips quirked in amusement, he drinks in my low-end pants, fitted ribbed shirt, and black ballet flats.

To further prove his point, he nudges his head to the patrons seated inside the restaurant.

They're dressed far more elegantly than I am.

"There's a public restroom one block over," he announces, his tone snobbish.

Masking the urge to knee him in the balls, I smile sweetly before heading to the far corner of the restaurant.

Peering through the paned glass windows won't cost me a damn cent.

Seconds later, I witness Isaac kissing the cheek of a lady with shiny black hair. Once she returns his greeting, her lips hovering closer to his lips than his cheek, Isaac removes his suit jacket and hooks it on the back of a chair before sitting across from the chair she vacated to welcome him.

When Isaac hands her a sealed envelope, she smiles cunningly. Her unusual response to a greeting card exposes the surveillance team is missing a prime opportunity to survey Isaac in his natural habitat. They've only ever captured him in work environments. This appears more personal than business.

Over the past few weeks, Isaac's meetings have been with reputable business associates or his fighter, Jacob. This lady has never popped up in the hundreds of surveillance images I scan into the bureau's database every day.

Realizing I need to match brains with brawn, I yank my cell out of my pocket. My hands grow clammy when I snap a sneaky picture of Isaac's companion while the doorman is distracted by clientele entering the restaurant.

After hiding behind a potted hedge, I check the quality of the image I just snapped. I sigh when the early morning sun reflecting on the window covers half of Isaac's companion's face.

I snap another pic.

Its quality is as bad as the first.

"Think, Isabelle, think."

My eyes bulge when the perfect plan smacks into me.

It takes me scrolling my short list of contacts twice before I remember Alex never gave me his cell phone number.

He'd hate to make me feel like I'm a part of his team.

Instead of contacting Alex, I dial a number I know by heart.

"Federal Bureau of Investigation, how may I direct your call?" questions the switchboard operator.

"My name is Isabelle Brahn. My agent number is 5586718. I need you to patch me through to Alex Rogers, head of the Ravenshoe Division," I inform her as my eyes flick between the doorman and Isaac.

"Patching you through now."

Alex's phone rings several times, making me worried he won't answer.

I'm about to disconnect the call and try again, when the call finally connects.

"Alex Rogers," he snaps down the line.

"Alex, it's Isabelle—"

"Did you mess up my coffee order again? Black with two sugars. It isn't that hard."

Anger minces up my words. "No, I didn't mess up your order." But if he keeps speaking to me so rudely, I may fish it out of the bottom of the garbage bin and serve it to him without a napkin. "Why isn't the surveillance team following Isaac?"

Alex grunts. "He's still in bed."

My brows furrow as my eyes snap back to Isaac sipping coffee in an overpriced restaurant. Even with his unique eyes hidden by aviator glasses during my initial surveillance, I couldn't mistake him. He's too striking not to notice, and we won't mention the insane response of my body.

"He isn't in bed. He's right in front of me having breakfast with a lady at a restaurant on the corner of Welsh and First Avenue."

While Alex summarizes a reply, Isaac's focus suddenly shifts to the restaurant window. He appears to be staring straight at me.

With my heart in my throat, I sink into the alleyway while praying like hell that he didn't spot me spying on him.

I remember that my cell phone is attached to my ear when Alex asks, "Are you sure it's him, Isabelle?"

"Yes," I assure him, my pitch as high as my heart rate. "I'm one hundred percent certain it's him."

The flurry of activity I've witnessed every day the past month barrels down the phone when Alex barks out a handful of orders.

Once his team is moving like a well-oiled machine, he says, "We'll be there in five minutes."

After disconnecting our call, I flatten my back against the outer wall of the restaurant and take in some big breaths.

I'm clutching my phone so tightly, my knuckles are white, and my heart appears seconds from breaking out of my chest cavity.

I never knew surveillance could be so thrilling. I envisioned hours of eating donuts and busting to use the bathroom, but it's much more exciting than that.

Or maybe it isn't undercover work that has my heart spasming. Perhaps it's seeing Isaac again?

I'm drawn from my thoughts when a voice I immediately recognize says, "Bring the car back around."

After becoming one with the brick wall, I peer around the corner. A potted hedge helps to keep me concealed, but my watch could be busted at any moment.

Isaac stands mere feet from me.

Even from a distance, his commanding aura is notable. It isn't scary or threatening. It is more alluring than anything.

Suddenly, he yanks his cell phone away from his ear before he scans the faces of the people lining the street.

He stops seeking the eyes he feels on him when the lady he greeted in the restaurant joins him on the footpath.

When she stuffs a cigarette between her painted lips, Isaac lights it with a gold lighter.

Ignoring the jealousy forming in my chest, I attempt to snap another picture of her.

This may be the FBI's *only* opportunity to capture her face.

In the silence of our unusual situation, my camera click is easily audible.

Shit!

Again, I splay my back to the wall. The roughness of the brickwork scratches my skin, but it has nothing on the pain of my stupidity.

How could I have been so stupid to forget to turn the sound off on my phone during surveillance? I'm confident they heard the click. It was as loud as my thrashing heart.

After many calming breaths—and a few more expletives—I peer back around the corner. Isaac's Mercedes is parked in front of the restaurant. His acquaintance is already seated in the back, and he has one foot in.

Before he fully slips in, he slings his eyes in my direction. I'm sure he's spotted me through the green hedge, but I can't cowardly retreat this time.

I'm trapped, captivated by his entrancing eyes.

Several tension-riddled seconds pass before he shakes his head and slides into the back of his town car.

I wait for it to vanish into traffic before crumbling onto the ground and cradling my head in my hands, aware without a doubt that I'm in way over my head.

7

A gasp parts my lips as I dive for the computer mouse. I click anywhere and everywhere on the screen, praying my manic clicks will stop my personal photos being uploaded to the FBI's database.

Realizing my excessive clicking isn't alleviating the situation, I cover the images flicking across the monitor with my hands, meaning only portions of my skin are on display for the world to see.

"I'm so sorry," I apologize, mortified.

Except for a rare grin tugging his full lips high, Alex's expression remains neutral.

Brandon's response isn't as reserved.

I kick him in his shins when he attempts to pry my fingers away from the screen, hopeful for a more in-depth preview of my risqué vacation snaps.

"I had a two-week vacation at Del Mar before I was assigned here." I give them any excuse I can as to why there are several images of me in a skimpy bikini being uploaded into the bureau's database.

Darn selfie sticks have made it too easy to get full-body shots when vacationing alone. I do love that bikini, though. I shouldn't. It took months of grueling workouts for me to feel confident enough to wear a bikini like that.

After a few margaritas and a stern lecture on body image, I reluctantly slipped into the scraps of material society classes as a bikini.

Knowing I'd probably never wear it again, I got a little excited about taking photos from multiple, and what I was hoping at the time, appealing angles.

"It was hot in Del Mar," I murmur when neither Brandon nor Alex reply to my admission.

A genuine smile morphs onto Alex's face. Although I despise him and call him several crude and accurate names under my breath multiple times a day, I still relish his true smiles.

Brandon playfully tugs on the collar of his shirt. "That wasn't the only *hot* thing there."

I try to hide my gratitude at his compliment. Only the smallest smile creeps on my face, but it's enough of a response for him to notice.

"No," I inform him delicately, stealing his chance to ask me on a date for the tenth time in the past two weeks.

"Who said I was going to ask you out?"

Arching my brow, I stare into his hazel eyes that are a little greener today than usual.

He caves two seconds later.

"One date won't kill you."

Brandon is cute, but our personalities are too similar for us to be anything more than friends. I don't agree with the whole opposites-attract notion, but I believe your partner should bring qualities to a relationship you don't already have.

If you like sweet foods, they should like sour. If you're a live-your-life-on-the-edge type of person, they should be more reserved and prefer taking their time to consider their options. That way, over time, you eventually get a perfectly balanced relationship.

Well, that's been my logic. I could be wrong since my theory has yet to be proven. I'm single and living with my uncle's old flame and her two cats.

Oh god. I'm going to become one of those crazy, dressing-gown-wearing, chain-smoking, hair-a-ratted-mess cat ladies.

"Our next weekend off, we should go out," I suggest to Brandon. "As friends. And just drinks... no dinner or movies, just drinks."

When he nods, a stern cough demands my attention. Alex's brows are furrowed, and his lips are thin. His stance projects anger, and if I'm not mistaken, a smidge of jealousy.

"If you have time to date, I need to increase your workload."

When he shoots daggers at Brandon, Brandon mumbles, "Sorry."

After a handful more tension-riddled minutes, I hesitantly drop my hands from the computer monitor. Relief washes over me when I notice my bikini photos are no longer filtering across the screen.

Barely breathing, I scroll to the photo of Isaac's companion I captured this morning.

A shocked groan vibrates Alex's lips at the same time remorse stabs my chest.

"Run facial recognition," requests Alex, slapping Brandon on the shoulder three times.

Brandon nudges me out of the way with his elbow before he rolls in close to the desk and runs his fingers over the keyboard.

While Brandon sets to work on unearthing Isaac's companion's name, I switch my focus to Alex, hoping some commendation will lessen the guilt I'm experiencing for spying on Isaac.

Alex scans my face, but not a word seeps from his lips, so I try to settle my guilt myself.

You're just doing your job, Isabelle, I silently justify.

As we watch the facial recognition software scan potential matches for Isaac's companion, Alex inches closer. He's so near I can smell what he ate for breakfast. I never picked him as a blueberry-pancake-with-maple-syrup type of guy, but there's no denying the aroma—sweet and sickly at the same time.

My stomach grumbles. Not only did I dump the coffees into the trash, my blueberry muffin went right along with them.

"I bet you wish you didn't ditch your muffin now," Alex whispers in my ear.

I stare at him, confused.

I'm confident I kept my mumblings to a bare minimum this time.

When he notices my perplexed expression, he smiles—not a genuine, heart-fluttering smile, but a sly grin that makes me wonder what he's concealing with his pretty-boy exterior.

"Bingo," shouts Brandon, breaking the uncomfortable stare-down between Alex and me. "Facial recognition has a match."

I scan the information displayed. Delilah Anne Winterbottom, thirty-six years old, publicist and divorcee, spouse of Henry Theodore Gottle III, before their divorce settlement was finalized eight months ago. She lives in New York City, has no siblings, no children, and no criminal history.

"Looks like another dead end."

"A dead end?" Alex's eyes bore into mine as if he's a parent reprimanding a child for failing an exam.

"She's a publicist..." I attempt to reply before catching Brandon shaking his head.

He points to something on the screen, but with the overhead lighting reflecting on the monitor, I can't see what he's referencing.

"Please continue, *Isabelle*." Alex spits out my name as if it's venom. "I'd love to hear your reasoning as to why this is a dead end."

My eyes shoot to Brandon to silently plead for assistance. When Alex follows the direction of my gaze, anger reddens his face.

Recognizing that our ruse has been busted, Brandon's finger slips from the monitor as he swallows several times in a row.

"Henry Theodore Gottle III," Alex informs sternly. "Son of Henry Gottle, suspected mob boss of New York City."

"Just because he's the son of a mob boss doesn't automatically make him part of the mob."

Alex laughs, seemingly amused by my reply. His chuckle doesn't match his looks. It's a scary, witch-like laugh that has everyone in the office stopping what they're doing to stare at him peculiarly.

It takes several tedious minutes for Alex's laughter to die down. When it does, he says, "You surely can't be that stupid." When I fail to respond to his taunt, he stops grinning and steps closer. "And here I was thinking you made it through the academy solely by using your brain. I guess today proves what I'd originally suspected." He keeps his voice loud enough that the agents watching his charade can hear him. "You weren't brought here for your academic abilities." My arms fold over my chest when he leisurely assesses my body. "But since you're so determined to utilize your brain instead of your other more *desirable* assets..." —his eyes drop to my breasts—"be a good girl and fetch the coffee you failed to produce this morning."

With a flick of his wrist, I'm once again downgraded from a respectable field agent to a glorified coffee girl.

8

___

"You have a stalker." Harlow's face is animated as she waggles her brows. "A total drool-in-the-corner-of-your-mouth tall drink of water, but a stalker nonetheless."

When she gestures to the corner of the bakery, I bleakly swallow. Isaac Holt is peering at me from behind the morning newspaper.

When he realizes he's captured my attention, he smirks before folding the newspaper in half and placing it on the table. His eyes never once detour from mine.

Although my first response is to run, it would look mighty suspicious if I fled now.

For the past two weeks, I've successfully avoided another run-in with him. The establishments he dines at are far fancier than this humble bakery that's become my second home, but if I were honest, I knew this run-in would eventually happen.

Ravenshoe is large, but it isn't big enough to get permanently lost in the crowd.

"He's been here over half an hour and has never paid anyone any attention until now." Harlow hands me the whole grain and rye toasted cheese sandwich I ordered for lunch.

Once I have a mug of coffee filling my empty hand, Isaac motions for me to join him.

My heart wants to say yes, but my brain knows better. It seeks a spare chair I can use to conceal my wish to flee.

I groan when I discover no empty tables in the entire bakery before shooting my eyes back to Harlow, hopeful she'll offer me an out.

I get nothing but more stupidity added to the giddiness clustering in my stomach. "Go on, he's hot."

After rolling my eyes, I give in by gingerly pacing toward Isaac. Harlow can look at him for his irrefutable sex appeal, whereas I must look at him through the eyes of an agent.

Ruthless, cunning, heartless, and unlawful were the first thoughts that popped into my head when I read his file, but when I look into his gray eyes now, they disclose an entirely different story.

The closer I get to Isaac, the more I can absorb every impressive feature of his face—sculpted cheekbones, plump and full lips on a mouth that could have me toppling into ecstasy just from hearing him speak, and a pair of exquisite eyes.

No photo will ever do his eyes justice because they can't capture how intense they are in person.

"Hello, Isabelle." Even with his tone angry, my name still rolls off his tongue seductively.

"Hi," I reply as my heart violently flips.

A smile sneaks onto my face when he pulls out a chair for me, and then air snags in my throat when he sits next to me instead of the chair opposite me.

Trying my hardest to ignore his manly scent, I dump my satchel under our table, then pull out my toasted sandwich.

Isaac remains quiet, but just like at the departure gate, his eyes track my every move.

The air is suffocating, riddled by the thick stench of awkwardness.

I hate it, but since I can't fix it, I take a sizable bite of my sandwich. I'm famished from not eating since breakfast.

A moan rumbles up my throat when the gooey, cheesy goodness infiltrates my taste buds.

When a string of cheese snaps off and lands on my chin, my tongue darts out to clear the residue from my face.

Isaac groans a low and menacing growl that forces my knees together and my eyes to his. My cheeks heat when I bust him staring at my lips.

Even though his watch makes me hot all over, I dart my eyes away before I become trapped by his alluring stare.

I peer out the window at the front of the bakery as panic engulfs me. If anyone in the surveillance team witnesses our exchange, Alex will force me into a skimpy dress and parade me in front of Isaac by this evening.

I refuse to be treated as a commodity.

I'd rather gather coffees for narcissistic, self-centered assholes than be forced into prostitution.

With my mind made up, I say, "I have to go." I shove my half-eaten sandwich back into its bag, then snatch my satchel from the floor. My coffee is in a ceramic mug, so much to my dismay, it will remain untouched. "I forgot an important deadline."

I race for the entry as quickly as my shaking legs can take me.

Harlow is shocked by my hasty retreat, but the priorities of her customers remain in the forefront of her mind. "Do you want me to pour your coffee into a takeaway cup?"

I shake my head while continuing for the door.

Cool air blasts my face when I emerge onto the footpath, but only a few brisk strides later, someone clutches my elbow and drags me to the corner of First Avenue.

When my angry eyes lift to accost the person manhandling me, I am met with the stern profile of Isaac. His lips are thin, and his jaw is twitching.

Not looking at me, he pulls me into the alcove of a pub that looks like it hasn't opened its doors in the past century, then crowds me against a paint-peeled door.

My pussy tingles from his closeness.

Stupid, traitorous body.

He's technically the enemy, yet my body still gets excited about his attention.

"I assumed you must have left town when you failed to arrive for our date, but lo and behold, here you are, *months* later."

I remain quiet as his eyes—full of turmoil and uncertainty—dart between mine.

"Are you going to at least attempt an excuse?"

Remorse claws at my chest as I shake my head. Trying to fool a man who can see through to my soul would be stupid and ineffective.

Teeth grinding together fills the silence between us when Isaac clenches his jaw.

"That person you met on the plane isn't me. I'm not usually like that," I reply, deciding honesty is the best policy. "I don't do random hookups with strangers."

"And you think I do?"

"Yes," I answer without a smidge of hesitation.

Isaac's eyes snap to mine before the most wicked grin creeps onto his face.

I try not to return his smile, but I'm defenseless. Someone as gorgeous as Isaac would have an extensive list of women vying for his attention, so I'm somewhat surprised—and a little excited—that my failure to arrive for our date ruffled his feathers.

The air shifts from tense to teasing when he mutters, "I still want to bite that lip."

My pupils widen when he caresses my cheek. I should be pulling away, but I can't. I'm frozen with desire.

When he runs his thumb along my top lip before his head tilts, my knees meet.

There's no doubt he is going to kiss me this time around.

Not a single iota of rejection is felt.

Just before Isaac's lips brush mine, a raspy voice interrupts. "Sorry, boss, but we've gotta go."

I sigh when Isaac yanks back, leaving only his expensive cologne lingering in his wake. Upon hearing my pathetic response, his lips furl as if his rake of the street isn't filled with worry.

Following his gaze, I spot the man I've seen in numerous surveillance images in the driver's seat of Isaac's town car. Just a few blocks down from the Mercedes is the blue surveillance van that tails his every move.

When Isaac's focus returns to me, I gulp. If I thought his eyes were intimidating before, now they're downright dangerous.

"Meet me at the bakery tomorrow," he requests, his tone stern and to the point.

"I can't."

Seeing the surveillance van is the only reminder I need that I can't associate with him, no matter how loud my heart screams at me to ignore my rational-thinking head.

"It wasn't a request, Isabelle."

He runs his index finger over the cupid's bow of my top lip before striding to his awaiting town car.

Before he slips inside, his head cranks back to me. "Tomorrow," he instructs before he glides into the back of his car.

The instant it rolls down Welsh Boulevard, the surveillance van commences its pursuit. I shadow myself in the darkness of the alcove to ensure none of my colleagues spot me as they zoom by.

While leaning on the peeling-paint door, I strive to calm the erratic beat of my heart.

I can't believe I was so senseless I nearly kissed Isaac Holt.

Isaac. Holt!

A man currently under investigation by the FBI.

A man who has half of the county following his every movement.

A man who smells so delicious I want to run my cheek along his jaw just to capture his scent.

After reprimanding my lack of judgment, I emerge from the niche of the pub and walk back to my workplace.

Approximately halfway there, my phone dings with a text message. When I yank it out of my jeans, I notice the message is from an unknown number.

My excitement intensifies, wondering who the message could be from.

It vanishes when I read the text.

UNKNOWN NUMBER:

You're late.

I jog down the bustling street, weaving in and out of the heavy foot traffic.

My quick strides halt when another message dings on my phone.

UNKNOWN NUMBER:

Pick up coffee on your way back.

9

"You can stop hiding, you know," jests Harlow. "He hasn't returned here since he left you that card on Monday."

I've been eating lunch at a local burger joint every day this week to lessen the chance of another run-in with Isaac.

I can't trust myself to be in the same room with him. Just one look at his deliriously handsome face, and my inhibitions fly out the window.

When I returned to the bakery bright and early Tuesday morning for the agents' morning caffeine fix, Harlow handed me Isaac's business card. On the back of the card, he wrote:

When you stop denying what your body wants.

His cell phone number was at the bottom.

I crumpled the card up and tossed it to the floor, but no matter how hard I tried to pretend it wasn't there, I couldn't tear my eyes away from it.

By the time Harlow finished preparing my order, the card was in my jeans pocket, where it has remained for the past four days.

Harlow hands me two crates of coffee while asking, "Do you work seven days a week?"

I struggle to think of a reason why my cover as a secretary would be collecting so many coffees on a Saturday morning, so I settle for a half-truth. "Umm... no. It was a big night for my friends and me last night. I was the designated driver, which means I'm also responsible for the morning-after caffeine fix."

I cringe, certain my excuse is about to be busted, but when Harlow smiles, I realize she's accepting my explanation.

"Do you work seven days a week?" I ask, since I've just realized she's here every morning right alongside me.

"It's kind of a requirement when you're the owner," she answers, staring into space. "But I sure miss late nights and long sleep-ins."

I gawk at her in surprise. She seems around my age, which is young to already own a business.

Noticing my shocked expression, she laughs. "I've always loved to bake, and this has been a dream of mine since I was a girl." She gestures her hand around the bakery. "But I'm slowly realizing dreams don't always turn out how you envisioned them."

I nod in understanding. I was so excited when I was accepted into the academy. I thought I'd live a life of suspense and intrigue, but I'm learning what I visualized as an agent varies a great deal from what I do every day.

I have nine months, two weeks, and one day left on my contract with Alex's department. Then, hopefully, I'll be reassigned to a better unit, and the dreams I've envisioned might transpire.

I offer Harlow a sincere smile before I head for the exit. I'm about to exit when my name is called.

Harlow waits for me to face her before asking, "If you have any more exciting nights planned, can you throw a dog a bone?"

Smiling, I nod again.

Only once I'm in the alcove do I remember I'm going out with Brandon tonight. I invited him out under the strict understanding it's a friends-going-out-for-drinks-night-only invitation.

No assumptions, no false promises, just friends.

He readily agreed.

When I dart back inside the bakery, Harlow's head lifts from the cash register.

"Do you have any plans tonight?"

She shakes her head as excitement beams out of her.

"It isn't a raging party, just a friend and me having some drinks, but you're more than welcome to tag along."

We hash out the details remarkably quick, but by the time I walk back into the office building across from Isaac's nightclub, the coffees I purchased are stone cold.

Alex grumbles under his breath as he reheats his brew in the microwave in the galley kitchen, but his grouchy mood can't dampen my excitement.

I haven't been out dancing in months, but even more thrilling than that's the fact I've made a friend.

I miss having the close connection of a girlfriend. As much as I love Regina, she mothers me too much to be considered a confidant. I need a female companion to discuss the conflicting emotions I'm currently feeling for Isaac Holt.

Hold on, what?

I'm a federal agent. Any feelings I'm considering need to be squashed. I can't even befriend someone like Isaac, let alone develop feelings for him. I need to crush the idea of a relationship with him and treat him like the bloodsucking leech his FBI file wants to lead me to believe.

But, my uncle always said you should never judge anyone by other people's opinions. He'd often quote, *Until you have a legitimate reason not to like someone, you should treat them how you wish to be treated.*

Isaac hasn't done anything to warrant me disliking him.

He may be crude and a whole lot cocky, but I'd be lying if I said his vulgarity didn't turn me on.

I haven't stopped thinking about how he smelled when he cornered me in the rundown pub's alcove, let alone the scenes from the plane playing on repeat in my dreams every night.

When a hand slams down on my desk, I jump in fright. I'm so startled, I spill my now iced coffee down my shirt.

After grabbing tissues out of my desk drawer, my furious eyes lock with Alex's unamused face. "I've been calling your name the past five minutes," he informs me. "What has you so intrigued you can't follow a simple command?"

"I was just thinking..." —I scan the photos on my desk, trying to think of a reason why I failed to respond without mentioning I was once again fantasizing about Isaac—"that I don't believe he is an associate of Isaac's." I lift a photo of the man I saw driving Isaac's car earlier this week. "I think he's his bodyguard."

He appraises the image while asking, "What makes you think he's not an associate?" For the first time in the past two months, his tone sounds neutral.

"Anytime he's been photographed with Isaac, he's either driving his car or completing surveillance of the area." I gather the images of Isaac's bodyguard I've printed over the past few days. "An associate wouldn't drive the car while Isaac sat in the back seat. He'd sit in the back right along with him," I continue, impressing myself with my ability to think on the spot.

A grunt rolls up Alex's chest as he flicks through the photos. "I guess we could cross him off our list and focus our attention solely on Isaac."

"No," I shout, probably a little too loud as Michelle lets out a squeal. "There's something about this guy that has me intrigued." I snatch the photos out of Alex's grasp to find the picture I was researching yesterday. "I can't for the life of me work out why he hasn't come up in any of the facial recognition searches I've completed on him the past two days."

His brows squeeze, apparently unimpressed I've been undertaking searches without permission.

"He's worked in a government department before, which means he should be in our database," I advise, pacifying his scowl. "This tattoo is a symbol of an air force squadron. That squad only returned from Afghanistan two years ago. Only squad members can get that tattoo." I hand him two photographs. One is the original picture of Isaac and his bodyguard jogging, and the other is zoomed in on the tattoo I'm referring to.

I bring up the information I found on the tattoo yesterday afternoon on my computer.

Once the squadron member tattoo on the screen is enlarged, I turn my monitor to face Alex. He holds the photo against the computer screen mere seconds before a smile tugs his lips high.

"Brandon, I need you to get me someone high in the US Air Force, now!" He practically jogs to Brandon's cubicle. His hasty retreat stops halfway before he turns around to face me. "You did good, Isabelle." A mammoth smile spreads across my face when he adds, "See if you can find any members of his squadron. Maybe they can help us identify him."

My heart gallops with excitement at being assigned my first official task as an FBI field agent.

10

When Harlow picks me up at nine, excitement beams out of me. I've spent most of my day searching for ex-squadron members. I secured a reliable source that may assist me in discovering the identity of the man who works with Isaac. I scanned his photo to my contact earlier tonight. He will show it to a tattoo parlor owner who has previously tattooed that squadron symbol. He may be able to assist me in tracking down an ex-squadron member who's willing to talk to me. Most hang up the instant I advise them I'm from the FBI.

Obviously, there's no comradery amongst colleagues.

"Wow, you scrub up nice," praises Harlow when I slip into the passenger seat of her car.

Smiling, I roam my eyes over her fitted black dress. "As do you." A wolf whistle sounds from my lips.

Besides her big, beaming smile, she looks completely different out of her work attire. Her hair is no longer pulled back in a low ponytail, instead hanging loosely down her back.

This is the first time I've realized her auburn-brown locks are curly. Her lips are glossed with a vibrant red sheen, and her eyes are done in a dramatic Cleopatra way.

She's gorgeous, and she'll no doubt give any woman a run for their money tonight.

"Here." Harlow offers me a tube of lipstick before pulling her car away from the curb. "It matches your dress perfectly."

The bold red lipstick will pair well with my tight strapless dress, so I place it on before handing it back to her.

"Wow, we won't buy a drink all night," she predicts.

She isn't joking. We're inundated with requests to buy us drinks the instant we enter the nightclub.

After wrangling our way through a mass of sweat-drenched, heated bodies, we locate Brandon in a private booth next to the dance floor.

He must have arrived early to secure a prime spot. The brown button-pressed leather booth has a sense of intimacy, with thick, red velvet curtains hanging off black metal A-frames. A stream of purple LED strip lights running along the roof reflects on the sheer curtain draped down each booth, giving the illusion of privacy.

The nightclub is packed to the brim. Most of its patrons appear to be of college age. The interior is lavish but outdated. It isn't usually the type of club I'd hang out at, but it was the closest in our area that didn't have an association with Isaac Holt.

After greeting Brandon, I introduce him to Harlow, and then over the next two hours, we sample a range of fruity cocktails and accept a handful of invitations to dance.

When one dance partner gets a little handsy, I head to the bar for a bottle of water. I've been downing cocktails like they're soda, and they are rushing to my head in quick succession, making my footing a little unsteady.

Brandon must spot my troubles, because he curls his arm around my waist to lessen my stumbles. "Are you okay?"

"Yeah," I slightly slur. "I think I downed too many drinks too quickly."

"Lucky for us, we have tomorrow off." He winks before requesting a double scotch on the rocks from the bartender.

I understand his eagerness. Alex is a slave driver. Tomorrow is my first day off in two months, so it's probably been even longer for Brandon.

After grabbing the bottle of water the bartender set down for me, I twist to face the dance floor, slipping out of Brandon's grip in the process. I like Brandon, but I don't want to give him the wrong idea.

We're only here as friends.

I smile when I spot Harlow at our booth. She also has a bottle of water and a tired expression.

I giggle to myself. We've only been out for two hours and we already want to go home. Can anyone say grandma?

Not ready for our night to be over just yet, Brandon replaces my water with a colossal cocktail full of a frothy pink liquid. "Who knows when we might get another day off?"

He downs his double scotch on the rocks in one hit, his nose scrunching as he slams the now-empty glass onto the countertop.

He looks like he's about to puke.

I giggle when he groans out, "I forgot how much that burns." Upon hearing my laughter, he raises his brow. "Oh, you think you can do better?"

His riling mock gains the attention of the college students surrounding us. "Chug... chug... chug."

When the clubgoers get in on the action, I down the pink concoction as dared.

I never back away when challenged.

The cocktail is delicious and slides into my empty stomach smoothly.

When I consume every last drop, the crowd erupts into a roaring chant.

I attempt a curtsy but bump into Brandon when I trip over my feet.

Brandon seems oblivious to my almost intoxicated state. After waggling his brows, he asks, "Another?"

Cringing, I shake my head. I'm already stumbling, so once the alcohol from the cocktail makes its way into my bloodstream, I'll be well over an acceptable limit to be drinking in public.

It's time for me to call it a night.

While Brandon places another order with the bartender, I head for Harlow to check if she's ready to go home.

Halfway across the dance floor, my elbow is clasped in a tight grip. I don't need to look up to know who's grasping my arm. The jolts bolting up my arm are all the indication I need to unearth the identity of the man veering me away from Harlow.

Quicker than I can blink, Isaac drags me into a peeling-paint hallway that houses the outdated bathrooms. He scans the urinal-scented space for half a second before he walks us toward the manager's office at the end.

I should be pulling away from him, but with my pulse tripling from his closeness, my inhibitions evaporated the instant he touched me.

A middle-aged gentleman wearing a knock-off Ralph Lauren polo shirt with slicked black hair lifts his head when we enter his office, but before he can get a word out, Isaac says, "Get out."

The manager's confused gaze bounces between Isaac and me before he hurries out of the office as demanded.

Once he leaves the room, Isaac releases his hold so he can lock the door. When he spins back around, I stiffen and my pulse intensifies.

His expression is furious, but it's what he's trying to mask with an unyielding gaze that has me pinned in place. It exposes unbridled jealousy and lust.

"Did you get my card?" he questions in his sexy-as-hell voice.

Striving to portray that my body has no desire for him, I cross my arms over my chest, strengthening my stance. "I'm not sleeping with you—"

"I never said you'd get any sleep." Butterflies flutter in my stomach when he steps closer. "Well, not for at least a few days."

I attempt a rebuttal, but I'm rendered speechless, my mouth only capable of opening and closing.

"Still trying to deny what your body wants?"

When he takes another step, my senses are engulfed by his intoxicating scent. As he watches me like a hawk, he brushes his thumb over my top lip.

A moan vibrates in my chest when he dips his thumb into my mouth. I'm not solely excited to have *any* part of his body in my mouth. The smears of the cocktail he removed from my lips are as inviting as his manly scent.

I suck them off his thumb like I haven't been fed in months.

When his eyes flare from my unexpected brazenness, I sway toward him, craving his closeness.

Regretfully, I lose my footing in the process.

Isaac's brows curve as suspicion builds in his eyes. "How many drinks have you had tonight, Isabelle?"

I shrug. I stopped counting over an hour ago.

"How many drinks have you had?" he questions again, sterner this time.

"A few," I huff. "Who are you, my dad?"

He takes my stab at his ego in stride by ignoring it. "Are you drunk?"

A playful grin curves my lips. "Maybe a little."

He groans when I hold my thumb and index finger an inch apart, indicating how drunk I think I am.

In case you're wondering, an angry Isaac is sexy as fuck.

He is either a master taunter or skilled at acting ignorant because he barely balks at my jeer before asking, "How are you getting home?"

"I wasn't planning on going home alone." With my intoxication making me more daring than usual, I add, "But you just ruined my chances of finding a suitable companion for the night."

I'm lying. I have a minimum three-date rule to get into my panties.

Well, I usually do.

My rules seem null and void when it comes to Isaac Holt.

My ego gets bitch-slapped when Isaac snaps out, "I don't play games, Isabelle, so if you're attempting to make me jealous, you are wasting your time."

Huffing, I skirt past him, eager to return to my friends so I can continue enjoying my weekend off.

I chose this nightclub because Isaac didn't own it, but here I am, having my confidence trampled by the very man I was trying to avoid.

As I dart toward the door, a rush of dizziness causes me to lose my footing for the umpteenth time tonight.

This is what I get for wearing pretentiously high stilettos.

Isaac saves me from stumbling to the floor like a drunken fool. He grips the tops of my arms before pulling me into his well-carved chest.

Shamelessly, I take a deep whiff of his scent before I lose the chance.

"You smell so good," I slur, my praise incapable of being held back for a second longer.

The cocktail must be hitting my bloodstream quicker than anticipated. Otherwise, what excuse do I have for my stupidity?

When Isaac's lips brush my ear, the hairs on my neck prickle.

Please God, grant him permission to let go of the reins for one night.

My prayer goes unanswered. "Tell your friends you're leaving. I'll wait for you out front."

My eyes snap to him so fast nausea floods my stomach. "I can't leave with you."

I may be tipsy, perhaps even on the verge of drunk, but I'm still coherent enough to know I can't risk my career by leaving with him.

Isaac acts oblivious to the tension hanging thickly in the air. "It wasn't a suggestion, Isabelle. Tell your friends you're leaving and meet me out front."

He moves for the office door, his strides long and effortless. Once he unlocks it, he turns to face me. His beautiful features are constricted with anger, and I hear the same angst in his tone when he warns, "If you're not outside in five minutes, I'll come find you."

11

____

A moan erupts from my throat as I snuggle deeper into a smooth and soft texture. I don't know what thread count these sheets are, but they're the softest I've ever lain on. I'll have to thank Regina for replacing my bedding, as it makes me feel like I'm sleeping on a cloud.

After pulling my arms out of the quilt, I have a leisurely stretch. My muscles feel exerted, but that's expected when you dance for hours in four-inch heels.

When I sluggishly open my eyes, I come face-to-face with my disheveled reflection.

I quickly sit up, causing a rush of dizziness to cluster in my head. For several minutes, I circle my temples, easing the pounding that makes it feel like my brain is escaping my skull.

Once the urge to vomit passes, I glance around the apparent bedroom. The space is vast but cold and sterile. I'm on the right side of a king-size four-poster bed, and other than the two mahogany nightstands bordering it, the room is empty.

No photos or knickknacks are on the bedside tables that would indicate whose room I'm in, and no paintings adorn the walls. Other than the mirror on the ceiling, it is as basic as they come.

When I peel the dark sheets away from my body, I gulp. I'm wearing *nothing* but a white V-neck shirt. I don't need to run my hands down my chest to know I'm braless. I can feel the heaviness of my breasts, but I also didn't have a strapless bra to wear with my dress last night.

If it isn't already concerning I've awoken braless, I'm also sans panties.

After diving out of bed, I throw open the top drawer on the bedside table, hoping it may give me some hints as to whose residence I'm in.

Other than an open box of condoms and a bottle of lubricant, the drawer is empty.

I tug on the hem of my shirt, vainly trying to cover my bare butt as I rush to the other drawer.

Its contents aren't as obvious as its predecessor. It takes me a second to realize what the scraps of lace and silk are.

They're an extensive collection of ladies' panties—*used* ladies' panties.

Yuck!

Bile rises from my stomach to my throat as I slam the drawer shut. I'm already on the verge of being sick, but the odds double when a door opening creaks through the room.

I jump back into the bed to cover my naked derriere with the super-soft comforter and sheets with only a second to spare.

My heart pounds louder than my head when Isaac enters the room wearing nothing but a towel. I balk as memories of last night filter back in.

Isaac pulling me into the manager's office.

Me sucking on his thumb like it was my last meal.

My shameful pleads for him to take me on the desk we were standing next to.

Just one glance into his eyes had me throwing caution to the wind.

I remember Brandon's disappointment when I said I had to go. I told him I'd been sick in the bathroom stall and was too embarrassed to stay.

Harlow offered to drive me home, but she'd been drinking as much as I had, so I asked Brandon to call her a taxi.

My stomach rolled as I walked toward the exit of the nightclub, but it wasn't from nerves—it was from excitement.

Isaac was waiting for me at the entrance door. His lips crimped when he spotted me. It was raining, so his bodyguard sheltered us with an umbrella as we hopped into the back of a waiting four-wheel drive.

Hugo.

That was what Isaac called his driver when he instructed him to lose the tail.

Lose the tail.

Does Isaac know we are following him? And did the surveillance team capture me with him last night?

I flick my eyes to Isaac, who's watching me curiously. I try to keep my focus fixed on his face, but the urge to scan his glistening pecs and the firm bumps in his midsection is too strong, and I give in to temptation.

In nearly every photo I've scanned of him in the FBI database, he's wearing a suit. Although there's been the occasional photo of him in gym shorts and a shirt from when he goes jogging, I've never seen him like this, so up close and personal.

His body is perfect.

Out of this world delicious.

When my eyes return to his face many minutes later, I realize I'm not the only one categorizing desirable assets. Isaac's hooded gaze is locked on my chest, his gaze so molten it activates every one of my hot buttons.

Confused, I yank up the comforter to cover my budded nipples.

Amused by my attempt at modesty, Isaac laughs. "Don't you think it's a little late to be shy, Isabelle?"

Although petrified I've thrown my career down the toilet by

sleeping with this man, my body still shudders from my name rolling off his tongue.

Once Isaac reaches the side of the room, he presses his palm on the white wall. A hidden door pops open two seconds later, piquing my interest.

I'm so intrigued. If I weren't half naked, nothing would stop me from discovering what is hiding in that secret room.

Plastic ruffling filters into the room a second before Isaac exits the hidden nook with a dry-cleaning bag in one hand and polished black shoes in the other.

I sigh.

I was anticipating something more extravagant than a hidden closet.

My disappointment doesn't linger for long. Who could be disappointed when the man from their dreams commences dressing in front of them?

Against the screamed demands of the naughty devil on my shoulder, I dart my eyes away when Isaac drops his towel, only glancing back for the occasional peek at a body too perfect to ever justify with words.

Holy. Fuck.

I'm not a fan of swearing, but no other words could describe Isaac's... umm... *package.*

When he catches me staring at his cock, he winks but doesn't twist away to discourage my gawk.

Mortified he busted me ogling him like a virgin who's never seen a penis before, I return my eyes to the wall.

I've seen penises—plenty of them.

Well, not heaps, but I can't be classified as a virgin, either. I've just never seen one as handsome as Isaac's.

Can you call a penis handsome?

"No, you can't," Isaac says with a hint of amusement.

I dart my eyes back to him, equally confused and horrified.

How did he know what I was thinking?

His expression exposes the truth.

I need to learn how *not* to babble out loud.

Once Isaac finalizes the last button on his blue business shirt, he joins me on the bed. "I have a meeting I must attend this morning. Your dress was sent to the dry cleaners, but there are spare clothes your size in the closet." He gestures his hand to the hidden room.

I cringe while wondering if the clothes in the closet are cleaner than the panties in the drawer.

I freeze when Isaac says, "They've never been worn. Catherine purchased them specifically for you this morning."

Can he read my thoughts?

When he tilts in close, my pussy tingles. I wish I hadn't drunk so much last night. Not solely so I could remember what happened but so I could recall what his kisses taste like. Then, I won't need to waste more hours fantasizing about them.

"Stop looking so worried, Isabelle." Isaac's minty breath settles my swishy stomach. "You wouldn't have any doubts if I'd fucked you, no matter how many drinks you had."

My brows scrunch as my eyes bounce between his. "We didn't have..." My words trail off, unable to articulate the word "sex."

Locks fall across his brow when he shakes his head. "No, we didn't."

"Why?"

Does he not find me attractive?

Am I not his type?

My eyes lift to the mirror above the bed. Even though my hair is a mess, and mascara is smeared under my eyes, I am still half presentable. I'm not a complete wreck.

When I return my focus to Isaac to silently demand an answer, he says with a growl, "I like my women not comatose."

My thighs press together when he licks his thumb before he rubs it under my eyes, removing the mascara smears.

Once the mess is cleared away, his eyes lock with mine. "You passed out within ten minutes of sitting in the back of my car."

Since he seems angry about my lack of control while drinking, I try to work on that fact first. "I generally handle my liquor a lot better than I did last night, but I was drinking on an empty stomach."

Even I grimace about my piss-poor excuse. Most people would happily use that for their inebriated state, but it's a weak excuse.

I know it, and so does Isaac.

"What would have happened if I hadn't arrived at that club when I did, Isabelle? What if it were another man who carried you into his apartment and undressed you?" His livid expression grows as his eyes wander over my face. "Do you think he'd have slept next to you all night, smelling your enticing scent without touching your seductive curves and skin?" The pulse in my neck strums when he sucks in an unashamed whiff of my scent. "I could smell you all night, but I couldn't do a damn thing about it." The reason for his anger is exposed when he snarls out, "A lesser man wouldn't have resisted."

I was already horny just thinking about us sleeping in the same bed, so you can imagine how bad things become when you throw his protectiveness into the mix.

My breathing shallows as my body tingles with anticipated excitement.

Two years of training, Isabelle. Are you willing to throw everything away for one night between the sheets with this man?

Even though I should be screaming no, a resounding yes is the first word that pops into my head.

Ruthless, cunning, lawless, I chant over and over, willing myself out of a possible dangerous situation. *Ruthless, cunning, lawless.*

My chant is silenced when Isaac removes himself from the bed and gathers his suit jacket from the stack of dresser he got dressed next to.

Once he's put it on, he advises, "Hugo will return after dropping me off. He will take you home." His demeanor is prickly, almost violent, and it has me panicked I said my silent chant out loud.

Although confused by the swift change in mood, I reply, "I can take myself home."

After a beat, Isaac nods before walking through white wooden double doors. Upon exiting, he turns his head to face me. He studies my body for several heart-clenching seconds before his attention turns to my face. His expression is unreadable when he demands, "If you go out drinking with your friends again, only go to my clubs."

With my shrewdness blinded by the horniness his protectiveness instigates, I nod.

His lips curl, seemingly pleased by my agreeing gesture, before he exits the room.

Groaning, I flop on the bed and throw an arm over my eyes. I swear I'm not usually this senseless. There's just something about Isaac that upends my levelheadedness and throws it out the window. It's more than just a sexual attraction, too. I've known plenty of eye-catching men, but none of them have made my body react the way it does when Isaac is near, which is scary considering he hasn't touched me sexually yet.

Imagine how explosive it will be when he does.

What?

I need to leave before I make another stupid mistake.

My mouth drops open when I enter the massive walk-in. Several dozen dry-cleaning bags housing expensive suits line one wall. Two-dozen dress shoes hog the floor underneath them, and an extensive collection of ties hang on a display rack.

As I head to the far corner of the room that houses a selection of women's clothing, I run my hand across the dry-cleaning bags. I smile when I notice white running shoes next to the black pumps I wore last night.

I've never seen the sense of wearing heels during the day. I've always preferred comfort over appearance.

I grab the sneakers and yank down a pair of jeans and a short-sleeved shirt before leaving the closet.

When my curiosity gets the best of me, I dart my eyes to the bedside table containing women's underwear.

Did Isaac place the underwear I was wearing last night in there?

Although the temptation is healthy, I can't stomach the idea of having my panties collected like a trophy along with many other women, so I put the jeans on sans undergarments.

I'd rather go without panties than believe the tension firing between Isaac and me isn't as strong as I hope.

After pulling the short-sleeved shirt over my head, I tug my unruly hair out of the neckline and run my fingers through it to get the frazzled pieces under control.

Once the laces on the Converse sneakers are tied, I enter a living area as sparsely furnished as the bedroom. Two leather sofas and a coffee table are in the middle of the room. A white marble kitchen sparkles with cleanliness, and its appliances look like they've never been used.

Needing something to absorb the alcohol still sloshing in my veins, I help myself to a bottle of cold water from the refrigerator before making a beeline to the closest exit.

As I mosey to the front door, I spot my cell phone and purse on the entryway table. My phone is on top of several open envelopes. From this distance, they look like personal correspondence. The addresses are handwritten.

My pulse increases as I ponder if they could hold something invaluable for our investigation. Even something minute could be imperative in an inquiry like ours on Isaac, but I can't break his trust, can I?

He hasn't done anything to justify me snooping into his private life. I'm here at my own choice. I didn't go home with him because of my job. I left with him because I wanted to.

He intrigues me enough I risked my job by leaving with him last night, so no matter how hard I try to justify that I should snoop on his personal affairs, I can't bring myself to do it.

After snatching my clutch purse and cell off the table, I exit the apartment.

The first thing I spot when leaving the foyer of the building is Isaac's Mercedes town car parked across the street. The back window is rolled down, and his stern eyes are locked on my purse that doubles as a filing cabinet for my work expenses.

I hesitantly wave.

Isaac doesn't wave back.

He glides the tinted window back into place before requesting his driver pull into the Sunday morning traffic.

12

———

"I thought I gave you the day off," Alex remarks from the corner of the office, startling me.

He's lurking near the window that overlooks The Dungeon. From the padded box seat, there's an uninterrupted view of the dance club and the parking lot below.

Alex shifts on his feet to face me. His unshaven chin and the dark circles plaguing his eyes make him appear guarded.

They also expose what I've always known.

He never leaves the office.

"You did, but I have a lead, so I thought I should get a head start on it."

After storing my satchel in the bottom desk drawer, I fire up my computer. Half of me is here to pursue answers as to why Isaac is so mysterious, whereas the other half doesn't want to be alone with a woman who can read me as well as my uncle once could.

Regina never removes her detective hat, either.

My mind shifts to Isaac's coldhearted dismissal this morning when I plop onto my seat. I could be wrong, but his demeanor seemed off-kilter.

Isaac is an enigma. He only allows people to know what he wants them to know. I don't believe anyone truly knows the real Isaac Holt, not even those privileged to be on his close-knit team.

"What's your lead?" Alex props his hip on my well-organized desk. It is spotless because between coffee runs and filing, I have a lot of time for tidying.

I'm tempted to tell him I've unearthed Hugo's first name, but my intuition is advising me to keep that snippet of information to myself until I get more concrete evidence of who Hugo is.

For all I know, he could be using an alias. Furthermore, there's no way to justify how I unearthed his name without disclosing I went home with Isaac last night, so I need my mouth to remain shut to keep my job and my private investigation into Isaac.

I surprise myself with my quick thinking. "The tattoo parlor owner said he'll email me back this morning. He might have a squadron member willing to talk to me," I reply, half-deceitful. I have a contact, but they haven't agreed to talk to me yet.

Alex watches me for several awkward seconds before he nods.

"Did you have any luck with the Department of Defense?" I question, prying him for any information that may contribute to my private investigation of Isaac.

He groans before shaking his head. "I'm filing them under a dead end."

My lips curve high. This is the first time we've held a normal conversation in the past two months.

"I'm impressed with your dedication, Isabelle," he commends me. "Keep this up and you may get off coffee duty sometime next year."

His chuckle echoes when he enters his barren office space. I wring my wireless mouse, fighting like hell to keep it on my desk and not at the back of Alex's arrogant head.

After squandering four hours at my desk, I'm no closer to discovering if Hugo is his real name. Although a Hugo was part of the American

Hornets Squadron, there are no pictures of Isaac's Hugo in any squad photos, and no records of him exist in the air force database.

The only information I've located on any Hugo in this half of the country is a death certificate for a Hugo Marshall, who died two years ago.

Frustrated with my lack of progress, I scan one of Hugo's surveillance photos into the facial recognition database and then expand my search to include social media sites. If his face is on something, I'll find it.

Well, I will in a few hours, as the expanded searches take hours to run through the FBI database.

When my stomach grumbles, declaring its hunger, I decide it is the prime time to grab something to eat instead of glaring at my computer monitor, yearning for it to come up with something resourceful.

"I'm going to grab a bite to eat," I notify Alex on my way out of the office.

His focus doesn't shift from the surveillance footage he's scrutinizing, but he nods, acknowledging he heard me.

"Did you want anything?"

That gets his attention.

When he grins, I roll my eyes. "I'll bring you back a coffee," I grumble before snatching my satchel out of the desk drawer and rushing out of the building.

A giggle vibrates my lips when I spot a rumpled Harlow leaning against the counter at the bakery. She looks how I felt this morning, but her restlessness is worse since she would have woken with the sparrows to prepare today's baked goods to be sold.

Upon hearing my laughter, she shakes her head and groans. "This is your fault," she whispers, like her voice is too piercing for her hungover head.

"Same time next week?"

She looks set to kill until she notices my smile. "I guess that'll depend on whether you're going to ditch me again."

"Sorry," I apologize, grimacing when her return has the effect she's aiming for.

When I approach the counter, my stomach grumbles. The smell of fresh-baked goodies filtering through my nose makes me realize I am starving.

Harlow scans my face before she showcases her infamous grin. "That's okay. I would've ditched you, too, if I were going home with who you left with."

Oh no.

If she saw me leaving with Isaac, does that mean Brandon did too?

Mistaking my forlorn look, she says, "Please don't tell me he was bad in bed." She stands straighter before rolling her shoulders back. "He can't have devilishly handsome looks and an aura like his and not deliver the goods. It's a disgrace to mankind."

Glee takes care of some of my worries.

This is the reason I need a girlfriend. I need someone to help me wade through the confusion muddling my head.

After propping my elbows on the counter, I say with a sigh, "I couldn't tell you what his sexual prowess is like."

"Huh?" huffs Harlow, noticeably confused. "I saw the way he was looking at you. He was more than ready to take you to bed."

"I slept in his bed. I just didn't *sleep* with him."

A mask of shock slips over her face. "Go sit. I'll make us a strong brew, and then you can give me all the juicy deets."

Once Harlow joins me at one of the tables in the mostly empty bakery, I occupy the next twenty minutes, giving her a rundown of everything that happened with Isaac this morning.

I also extend my story to include the first time we met.

By the time I've finished relaying every lucid detail, my confusion has intensified instead of lessened.

"First, I have to say, I knew he'd be hung like a donkey." I giggle when she fans her flushed cheeks. "Second, I can understand him not sleeping with you last night. Having sex with someone who's intoxicated is too rapey in my eyes. But having sex with someone who is hungover is a different story altogether. There's no reason you shouldn't have been screaming his name at the top of your lungs this morning."

I agree with her. No self-respecting person would sleep with someone who's intoxicated since they can't give consent, but the fact Isaac didn't attempt *anything* this morning when I was capable of making rational decisions has rejection rearing its ugly head.

"Maybe he did have a meeting he had to attend, and he knew he wouldn't have enough time to thoroughly knock your socks off?" Harlow suggests, running her hand down my arm in a supportive manner.

"Yeah, maybe," I reply, although my intuition warns that isn't the case.

After talking to Harlow for another thirty minutes, drinking enough coffee to keep me awake for a week, and devouring a club sandwich without coming up for air, I return to the office with my mind slightly less messy than earlier.

Upon entering, I spot Alex at my desk.

"What are you doing?"

He nudges his head to my monitor. "You found Isaac's mysterious companion."

Once he accepts the black coffee I brought back for him, I scan the information my extended search located for Hugo. It's a Facebook profile that was opened seven years ago but has been inactive for the past two years.

I skim the information in front of me. Hugo Marshall would now be twenty-eight. When his account was opened, he was unmarried and had three siblings—Helen, Chase, and Marjorie. He lived in

Rochdale, New York, and his employment status announced he worked in security.

"It appears he is just a bodyguard," Alex exclaims, moving around my desk and freeing up my chair. "We don't need to focus our investigation on Hugo any further. It's time to return our attention to our original target."

I nod, even with my gut telling me not to drop this. The death certificate I found earlier was for a Hugo Marshall who died two years ago. At the time of his death, he was twenty-six. That's too much of a coincidence to disregard.

Now I'm not solely planning to unearth the mysterious Mr. Isaac Holt. I also plan to learn every sordid bit of information I can on the elusive Hugo Marshall.

13

—————

"Isabelle."

"You've got to be kidding me," I babble.

My heart clenches as firmly as my thighs when my eyes meet with the piercing gray irises of Mr. Isaac Holt.

This wasn't the plan when Harlow and I decided to go out and celebrate. I had no clue Isaac would be here. We chose this restaurant solely on the rave reviews it received on Yelp.

We were unaware it booked out months in advance, so when a handsome blond gent eavesdropping on our conversation offered for us to be seated with him, we readily agreed.

So to say I'm surprised his request for us to follow him to his booth would be quickly chased by my name rolling off Isaac's tongue would be an understatement.

"Hi," I greet, not wanting him to mistake my shock as rudeness.

Tonight, unlike every other time I've seen him, Isaac is minus a suit jacket and tie. He sports a dark-gray business shirt rolled up at the sleeves, and the top two buttons are undone to reveal inches of his smooth, muscular chest.

His smirk is casual as he stands from the booth to offer me his hand to shake. When I accept his gesture, he doesn't shake my hand. He kisses the edge of my palm. Air sucks from my lungs when his briefest touch scorches my skin. I yank my hand away, skittish from my body's reaction to his almost innocent touch.

Isaac smiles at my response before greeting Harlow in a similar fashion. He doesn't kiss her palm, though. He gawks at her peculiarly, seemingly dumbfounded.

Nausea churns in my stomach, panicked they may already be *familiar* with one another. I have no right to be jealous, but I am. I am terribly, horribly envious.

"I'm from the bakery," Harlow informs Isaac when she notices his confusion. "The bakery you left your card at for Izzy."

"Ah..." Isaac drawls out slowly, his expression not matching the ease of his reply. "The card that's yet to be utilized."

The unnamed blond man's Adam's apple bobs up and down before he waves his hand across the booth. "Please join us."

Harlow slides into the spot next to him, meaning I have no choice but to sit beside Isaac.

The instant I slip into the booth, Isaac wastes no time getting up and in my business. He tilts in close and takes a sizable whiff of my hair.

My thighs shudder when he growls out, "Fuck, you smell good."

His voice is ruggedly smooth, and it sends an electric zap through my body from the strands of my hair to the tips of my toes.

I try to conceal my glee about his compliment, but my lips curve upward, giving away my true feelings.

This is the first time I've seen him in person since the morning I left his apartment. He's still under investigation by the FBI, and I'm still required to scan all the tasks he gets photographed doing every day into the bureau's database, but this is our first one-on-one interaction in six weeks.

I've tried to use the time well by eradicating him from my thoughts. I read every file the FBI has on him to taint my interest, but nothing worked.

As unavoidable as the plague, everywhere I go, Isaac is right there in front of me, as tempting as ever.

Dangling Isaac in front of me is like taking a kid to a candy store and telling her she must buy a piece of fruit. Even though you know the candy will give you cavities and make your hips wider, you still want it.

Isaac isn't good for me. I should stay away from him, but my inhibitions evaporate when he is in front of me.

Isaac runs his index finger along my forearm, causing the hairs to bristle. "How do you know Cormack?"

"Who?" Not even the shortness of my reply can hide my wheeziness.

Isaac points to the blond seated across from us. "Cormack."

I twist my lips before replying, "I don't know him. He offered for us to sit with him when we couldn't get a table."

When my words continue to come out breathless, I try to place some space between us. My body's awareness of his closeness is wreaking havoc with my shrewdness. I can barely breathe, much less have cognitive thoughts.

Isaac smirks before moving closer to me, leaving even less room between us than there was.

I firm my stance before shifting my focus to Harlow and Cormack gabbing across from us.

For the most part, I play disinterested well, but try as I may, I can't help but occasionally sneak a glance at Isaac.

His focus never deviates from me.

Not once.

I'd be a liar if I said his attention didn't make my palms clammy and my panties wet.

Endeavoring to keep our interaction out of murky territory, I ask, "How do you know Cormack?"

"We met in college," Isaac answers promptly. "He was my roommate slash manager."

"Manager?" My curiosity is piqued as to why someone like Isaac would require a manager.

He smirks again before adjusting his position in a way not even a nun could keep her eyes off his crotch. "Not that type of manager. No one is the boss of me, baby."

I try not to swoon, but I sway a little since this is the first time he's referred to me by a nickname.

"I fought my way through college. Literally."

"You didn't fight. You showed up," Cormack interrupts, his tone playful. "Don't believe anything this guy tells you." He gestures his head to Isaac. "He acts all innocent, then bam, you're on your ass before you know what hit you."

"Who are you to talk? You created the ruse," Isaac jests, his aura laid back.

Cormack arches his brow. "It worked, didn't it?"

Isaac laughs a thick, vociferous chuckle that makes my pussy pulsate, but other than that, he remains quiet.

"Come on. Out with it," Harlow requests a short time later, her eyes bouncing between Cormack and Isaac. "This is more suspenseful than the *Game of Thrones* cliffhanger. You can't share tidbits of information, then leave us hanging. We need details. Very informative details."

"All right." Cormack leans over the table to build the suspense with an intense stare. "Imagine Isaac decked out in corduroy pants, leather-strapped sandals, a short-sleeved button-up shirt two sizes too small, and a pair of suspenders."

"I didn't wear suspenders," Isaac interrupts. Although his tone is stern, his eyes glimmer with mischief.

"It was a few years ago, so maybe my memory isn't as good as it was, but I swear at least once I got you in suspenders," Cormack bites back.

Even picturing Isaac in the most hideous, unsightly clothes you could find, I guarantee he'd still be the most handsome man I've ever seen. It is, after all, what's under the clothing that's the most appealing.

When Isaac notices my gaga eyes, he drags his index finger down my arm, sparking a feverish response from my body.

"Anyway..." Cormack starts again, endeavoring to return the focus to him, "once we have him decked out like a choirboy attending a church sermon on Sunday, he arrived at an underground fight ring like it was the first time he'd been to an event like that. Once an impressive purse was negotiated, he revealed his true self, but by then, it was too late for his opponents to back out. An easy five Gs for ten minutes of work."

"Wow."

Now part of Isaac's FBI file makes sense, like where he got the money he invested in stocks while still in college. His file leads us to believe it was from him distributing and manufacturing narcotics.

Although underground fighting is illegal, it doesn't hold the same repercussions as drug manufacturing and dealing.

Forever curious, I ask Isaac, "How many years did you fight?"

Don't misconstrue my interest. My interrogation is exclusively based on personal motives. I find Isaac intriguing, and the more time I spend with him, the more I want to unearth about him.

"Just under two years," he replies, his brows lowering.

"Why did you stop fighting?"

Isaac's jaw tics before his eyes flick to Cormack. When he shakes his head at Cormack's unvoiced question, Cormack's brows stitch before he bows out of the fight with a nod.

When my eyes shoot to Harlow, her high shoulders sink. She must be feeling the tension as readily as I am.

The longer the silence continues, the more the air clogs with the thick stench of awkwardness.

The uncomfortableness is only given a moment of reprieve when the restaurant hostess notifies us that our table is ready.

Happy to use her interruption to escape the awkwardness plaguing our gathering, Cormack assists Harlow from the booth before gesturing for her to follow the hostess.

Though eager to follow them, I can't. The tension centers around my interrogation, so it's only right to check that Isaac still wants me to join him for dinner before stomping over his personal space for the second time this evening.

My uncle was a big, balding Russian, but he still taught me manners.

When I wordlessly question if he still wants to share his table, Isaac's eyes roam my face as he contemplates a response.

It feels like hours pass before he hesitantly gestures for me to catch up with Harlow. I want to say I take my time fleeing the booth, but that would be a lie. I practically sprint to Harlow's side.

Cormack and Isaac shadow our stalk across the pristine marble floors. I can see their lips moving in the reflective glass adding to the restaurant's regal feel, but I can't hear a word they exchange.

Once seated, Isaac signals the waiter to bring him whiskey. "Bring the bottle."

For the next hour, he silently broods while consuming whiskey as if it's coffee. Although I try to keep my focus on Cormack and Harlow, my eyes persistently shift to Isaac.

Cormack is an absolute gentleman, and he has Harlow hanging off his every word, but with my focus fixed on what caused Isaac's sudden shift in personality, I'm worse than the third wheel tonight.

Why did such a simple question spark such an adverse reaction from Isaac? He went from flirty and friendly to cold and distant in seconds.

When the waiter removes Isaac's untouched meal, I squeeze his thigh. For the first time since we left the booth, his eyes lift from his whiskey glass to me. He assesses my features in silence, his heated gaze still potent enough to cause a shiver to run through my body, but regretfully, it's more in response to his icy glare than lusty excitement.

When Isaac's focus returns to his whiskey, Cormack tries to lessen the sting of his rejection. "Don't take his lack of interest personally, Isabelle. For as long as I've known him, he's never been interested in brunettes."

"Oh..." I wait for Isaac to deny his claim and acknowledge our confusing, flirtatious connection. To tell Cormack he couldn't be further from the truth. When that doesn't happen, I ask, "Is there a particular reason?"

Even though Isaac appears to be staring straight at me, he isn't seeing me. He's looking straight through me as he replies, "It's a personal preference. No brunette I've ever *fucked* has maintained my interest once we leave the bedroom."

I try to mask my hurt with a smile. I try to excuse his rudeness as a man who's had too much to drink, but my ruse is foiled when I reach for my wine glass. I'm shaking too much to act unaffected.

When Isaac stands from the table, prepared to excuse himself for the night, his hasty getaway is upended as quickly as my ploy to act unaffected when a group of waiters approaches our table while singing "Happy Birthday."

My cheeks enflame as my eyes snap to Harlow. She smiles and waggles her brows even with guilt flooding her eyes.

When a chocolate cake covered in candles is placed in front of me, Isaac cusses under his breath before slumping back into his seat.

Striving her hardest to ignore the tension strangling what should be a fun night, Harlow instructs, "Make a wish."

I drift my eyes between the three sets staring at me, my gaze loitering on Isaac's a touch longer than the others.

His beautiful eyes quell my anxiety enough to close my eyes and blow out the candles in one swift motion.

They even settle it enough for me to brush my lips against his soft yet stern lips.

14

———

The brush of my tongue against Isaac's lips is met with a mouth that's hard and stern. When I realize he is rejecting my birthday wish, my heart pounds so profusely it's nearly deafening.

Tears burn my eyes as my nose runs.

I've always been an ugly crier.

Tonight will be no different.

I kissed him with the hope of proving him wrong. I kissed him wanting to force him to recount the lie he just told. I kissed him because I couldn't wait any longer to feel his lips on mine.

Now, I feel like a fool.

I can't even coerce the man who has crawled so far under my skin that I'm willing to lose my job for him to give me a pitiful birthday kiss.

I am pathetic.

While slowly inching back, I pray Isaac's desires for me overwhelm him so much he refuses to relinquish my mouth from his.

With every millimeter I gain between our lips, my heart sinks further into my stomach.

Rejection has never hit so hard.

After sucking in a big breath, I open my eyes. Isaac is staring at me, but his watch doesn't give any indication of his feelings about my failed attempt to seduce him.

I turn my tear-filled eyes to Harlow and Cormack. Cormack's brows are knitted together, and he looks confused, and Harlow's mouth is ajar. She also appears on the verge of tears.

Needing to leave before more foolishness becomes exposed, I snatch my black silk clutch from the table before saying, "Thank you for a lovely evening."

Before I can dart away, Isaac's hand shoots out to seize my wrist, his brisk move causing the cutlery to clang.

I take a minute to gather my composure before lowering my eyes to him. I endeavor to show him I'm not affected by his rejection.

It is a woeful waste of time.

"I'll drive you home," Isaac offers, his tone still clipped.

When I shake my head, his eyes narrow further.

"I *will* drive you home."

Not releasing me from his hold, he throws his unused napkin onto the table, stands, and then digs his wallet out of his pocket.

No bills are removed since Cormack gestures that he will pay the bill.

After returning his wallet to his trousers, Isaac asks Cormack, "Can you take Harlow home?"

"Yeah." Cormack nods. "If Harlow is okay with that?"

With the tension still thick, Harlow wordlessly seeks my thoughts.

I nod. Isaac is a stubborn man. Just glancing at his stern eyes is all I need to know that he will drive me home whether I agree or not.

Harlow leans over the table to give me a farewell hug. "I'll call you later."

Nodding, I return her goodbye the best I can with one arm since Isaac is still clutching my other hand.

Isaac and Cormack don't utter a word before Isaac guides me toward the exit. He's so eager to leave I have to jog to keep up with him.

Halfway there, he yanks his cell out of his pocket, lifts it to his ear, and demands that his car be brought around.

By the time we make it outside, my arm feels seconds from being tugged from its socket.

I attempt to free myself, but my squirming only sees Isaac tightening his grip instead of loosening it.

"Let go of my arm," I demand, my anger growing. "You're hurting me."

He releases me before using the same hand to drag his hand through his hair.

I've never seen someone so furious over a kiss before. I wouldn't have kissed him if I knew it would get this reaction.

He's acting like... like...

Oh. My. God.

"I didn't mean to embarrass you." I hear the irritation in my tone. "It was a harmless kiss. It didn't mean anything."

"Then why do it?" Isaac's narrowed eyes turn from the blackened night to me. "If it didn't mean anything, why kiss me?"

"Because I wanted to," I reply honestly. "And I wanted you to admit you lied."

"I didn't lie!" he snaps, his tone as stern as his jaw. "I said no brunette I have *fucked* has maintained my interest outside of the bedroom." He steps closer, forcing me to take a step back. His hooded gaze is unnerving, his eyes the darkest I've seen. "If you want to prove your point, Isabelle"—even though his voice is gruff, my name still rolls off his tongue seductively—"I'll have to fuck you first."

I should be offended by his crudeness and lack of respect, but I'm not. For months I've been torturing myself over this man. He's in my thoughts day and night. He is under my skin.

He even invades my dreams.

The intriguing Isaac Holt I read about every day has nothing on the intrigue I feel when I'm with him in person. His aura makes it seem as if he's two different people.

He steps closer. And closer. And closer until there isn't enough space between us for my lungs to fully expand, and then he rests his forehead an inch from mine.

His tormented eyes filter over my face as he cradles my cheek before his thumb glides over my dry top lip. It's parched from my inability to produce saliva, my mouth a desert from his intense stare.

"Is that what you want, Isabelle?"

I'm confused by his question, so immersed in returning his stare that I've completely forgotten about his earlier comment.

"Because your body says one thing, and your eyes relay another."

His expression conveys his confusion.

He isn't the only one baffled. Our bizarre kinship is unethical. It may even be illegal, but my heart and body don't want to hear logic. All they want is Isaac. They've craved him since I collided with him at the airport.

But can I do this?

Can I sacrifice everything for a man I hardly know?

Before any words seep from my lips, a sleek sports car pulls in next to us. When the driver honks, Isaac drops his hand from my cheek and shoves it into his trouser pocket.

Faster than I can snap my fingers, his confusion is replaced with angst.

"Get in the car, Isabelle."

Not waiting for me to reply, he strides to the driver's side of the sports car Hugo is stepping out of. They talk in hushed whispers, and Hugo nods before his eyes float to me.

He offers me a wary grin before moving around the vehicle to open the passenger-side door for me.

With Isaac already behind the wheel, this is a prime opportunity to make a calculated getaway, but I can't force myself to walk away. I need to know why he responded the way he did—both after I kissed him and before we left the booth.

So, reluctantly, I head to the sleek black vehicle instead of darting down the alleyway.

"Are you okay?" Hugo asks once I'm within earshot.

I nod before accepting his assistance into the car. It's so low to the ground I'd risk a split in my skirt if I didn't have help.

"Thank you," I whisper in gratitude once seated without a single thread pop.

My pleated pencil skirt sits high on my thigh, exposing a significant portion of my bare skin, but I'm covered—mostly.

The instant Hugo closes the passenger door, Isaac pulls his car away from the curb. His engine roars to life from the heavy compression of the accelerator, his tires squealing as we whiz away from the restaurant.

He weaves his car in and out of the heavy traffic. The veins in his arms flex when he changes gears before he drifts us around a sharp corner.

If he's trying to scare me, he's miserably failing. With his assertiveness and astute business mind, I know he'd never take an uncalculated risk. He just wants to flaunt his superiority because I embarrassed him.

"I'm sorry I kissed you," I apologize, saying anything to suffocate the tension. "I shouldn't have done it."

Isaac's eyes snap to mine. Even in his angry mood, they linger on my almost bare thighs longer than what could be classed as an acceptable glance. "I won't be strong-armed, Isabelle."

I nod, accepting that a man as dominant as him would never willingly relinquish his power.

His tight jaw slackens when he notices my agreeing gesture.

After a beat, he returns his speed to an acceptable level before he mutters, "That's only happened once before. It won't happen again."

I study his profile in silence, striving to work out who was stupid enough to try to strong-arm him. It wasn't a sane man. They'd have to be a certified lunatic to go against a man as dominant and in control as Isaac.

So, I guess that means only one thing.

He wasn't referring to a man.

He was strong-armed by a woman.

Striving to ignore the stab of jealousy hitting my chest, I shift my gaze to the blackened sky to continue pondering in silence.

I've been over Isaac's FBI files with a fine-toothed comb. Nothing in them points to a past or current love interest, so his reference must have occurred before he attracted the attention of the law enforcement office—something that will only be discovered by unearthing the real Isaac Holt.

Something that will most likely remain buried, as I don't believe anyone will ever fully unravel the mystery of Mr. Isaac Holt.

When Isaac pulls into the driveway of Regina's house, I bury my thoughts for a later date, then respond to his ride home with the manners my uncle instilled in me as a child. "Thanks for everything. It was the most... *interesting* birthday I've ever had."

When I lean over to kiss his cheek goodbye, old habits hard to forget, Isaac abruptly turns his head. I freeze, panicked at what his reaction will be to me kissing him a second time without permission when my kiss lands on his mouth instead of his cheek.

"I—"

Before my apology can spill, Isaac seals his lips over mine. His mouth captures my moan when his tongue plunges between my lips before he duels it with mine.

He kisses me for several heated seconds before he fists my hair and yanks it back to deepen our kiss.

My moans urge him on.

He kisses me as I've never been kissed, a stimulating blur of nibbles, sucks, and licks.

It's a kiss so potent my thighs shudder.

A kiss every girl fantasizes about.

A kiss I will never forget.

It is intense, desperate, and needy, and will highlight my dreams for years to come.

I respond to his kiss with the same intensity, like it could be the last time I'll experience such an awe-inspiring kiss, because it very well could be.

I'm aroused and emotionally moved at the same time. I genuinely don't know whether I should burst into tears or combust into ecstasy.

There's a chance both might happen.

By the time Isaac inches back, my mind is a blurred mess of confusion, I'm sexually tense, and my eyes are brimming with wetness.

"Happy birthd—"

He stops mid-sentence, his eyes darting between mine before his thumb dabs my right eye to gather a salty droplet I didn't realize had pooled there.

When his thumb moistens from my tears, he expels a harsh breath before he locks his eyes with mine. He doesn't utter a word, but his eyes relay what he wants to say.

I'm sorry.

"Thank you," I reply, acknowledging both his silent apology and his birthday wish.

Stealing his chance to reply, I open the passenger door of his sleek ride, slide out with no concern for the dozen threads that pop under the strain, then rush into Regina's house without once glancing back at the man I no longer believe represents his FBI file.

15

———

"**Y**ou have to cancel the cake orders before my ass explodes."

Isaac's gorgeous face is puzzled until he realizes who is accosting him in the street. When I saw his town car in front of the restaurant I'd spotted him at several months ago, I decided to approach him regarding his extravagant but heartfelt gift.

When I arrived at Harlow's bakery to place my morning coffee order the day after my birthday, Harlow presented me with a giant cupcake. It was red velvet and the most delicious treat I'd ever eaten.

On the second day, I was presented with another cupcake. That time, the enticing flavor was chocolate mint.

By the third day, my curiosity intensified to a point I couldn't ignore.

After wrangling Harlow for nearly thirty minutes, she finally enlightened me as to whom my gift giver was. Because Isaac and I had left the restaurant before I sampled my birthday cake, Isaac organized for Harlow to supply me with one originally flavored cupcake per day for an entire year.

A year!

"It was sweet of you, but after only five days, the struggle to squeeze into my jeans is real."

Isaac flashes me an authentic smile, making my heart beat faster. When his eyes dart down to my jeans, I stand straighter and tilt my hips. I may not yet have a Kardashian-inspired butt, but if I keep eating the cupcakes Harlow is supplying, it won't be far off.

"That just means there will be more Isabelle to explore."

He can say that. I've seen him naked. There isn't an ounce of fat on his entire body. Well, except for the area where thickness is a necessary *and* wanted requirement. Alas, someone with my lagging metabolism must run at least three miles to ensure one cupcake doesn't make it onto her already curvy backside and squidgy belly.

Before I can derive a comeback to Isaac's remark, a lady joins us. She looks to be a similar age to me, but she has a grace that makes her appear more mature.

"Isaac, honey, are you going to introduce me to your friend?" Her tone is friendly, and her interest appears genuine, but my irritation still irks from her calling Isaac "honey."

"Isabelle, this is Clara. Clara, this is Isabelle Brahn."

My brows meet my hairline, surprised Isaac knows my last name, but considering I've slept in his bed, kissed him without permission, and am spying on him as a career, I brush off any concerns that he knows my surname.

After a beat, Clara extends her manicured hand to accept my greeting. "It's a pleasure to meet you, Isabelle."

After an awkward handshake, our gathering plummets toward uncomfortable. It seems more about social status than a lack of interest. Isaac, as always, is impeccably dressed in a tailored black suit. Clara is wearing a gorgeous pale-blue slip dress, so I stand out like a sore thumb in the jeans I squeezed into, a short-sleeved blouse, and black ballet flats.

I couldn't feel more out of place if I tried.

"I better get going." My eyes float to Isaac. "I just wanted to thank you for the gift, although it was unnecessary."

His lips tug high before he dips his chin.

"It was a pleasure meeting you, Clara," I inform her before heading toward the bakery.

"Oh, don't go. Can't you join us?" Clara requests.

I hesitate before turning back around. Isaac is watching me, but his gawk doesn't indicate if he objects or approves Clara's invitation, so I politely decline. "Thank you for the offer, but I'm underdressed."

"You look perfectly fine," Isaac responds as his eyes wander over my body before returning to my face.

I try to hide my smile, but my lips furl at his compliment, especially considering those were the words he said to me months ago outside of the business class lounge.

"Thank you," I whisper. "But I'm technically working." *What?* It's better than admitting I'm fetching coffee for agents with less experience than I have.

Isaac nods but remains quiet, and Clara clasps her hands together like she's considering a plea but follows suit with Isaac's silence.

After an awkward wave, I spin on my heels and dart for Harlow's Scrumptious Haven. I don't need to crank my neck to know Isaac is watching me. I can feel the heat of his gaze. It only cools when I enter the bakery and spot Harlow near the noticeboard.

Upon hearing the bell, she turns to face the door. Her welcoming smile has me forgetting my awkward exchange with Isaac and Clara.

Harlow yanks down a flyer from the noticeboard and asks, "Are you still looking for an apartment?"

Nodding, I bridge the gap between us. I've been seeking an apartment since I arrived in Ravenshoe. I haven't secured one yet because most apartments are either out of my price range or have hundreds of applicants, so mine is always denied.

"This place sounds ideal." Harlow thrusts the advertisement into my hand. "Two bedrooms, two bathrooms, an underground garage, and a balcony, all for twelve hundred dollars a month."

My eyes bulge. "What's the catch?"

I've always believed if something is too good to be true, it is.

This apartment seems too good to be true.

"Is it located in Ravenshoe's equivalent of the Bronx?"

Harlow laughs before slapping my forearm. "There's no Bronx area of Ravenshoe. That title belongs to Hopeton." She bumps me with her hip. "Call and make an appointment, then crumple up the ad and throw it in the bin. That will stop the masses from applying."

The advertisement is so newly printed none of the slips at the bottom have been torn off yet. Maybe if I'm quick, I could beat the other applicants.

Hopeful, I yank my cell phone out of my pocket and dial the number displayed.

"Because this apartment has recently become available, the owner wishes to keep it on a month-to-month periodic lease," the real estate agent advises, moving toward the glass double doors that open onto a beautiful balcony.

"Okay, that's fine."

A month-to-month basis suits my requirements perfectly. In my line of work, I can't commit to anything permanently, not even a relationship. *Regretfully.*

"All appliances are supplied with the apartment, and you'll have access to a laundry room downstairs."

I nod, acknowledging I've heard her as I wander around the apartment. The living area is large and would comfortably fit two double sofas. The kitchen is compact but adeptly equipped with high-end stainless-steel appliances. All the rooms have ample natural light, and the main suite has a walk-in closet.

But the one thing that sells me on this apartment is the clawfoot bathtub in the main bathroom. I could only dream of spending hours soaking in there after a long day at work or dancing.

"Will you require an application package?" the real estate agent queries, stealing me from my dreamy thoughts.

"And that's the last box." Harlow plops onto my red suede sofa while blowing her hair out of her eyes.

We've spent the majority of our morning moving into my new apartment. Because I was the sole applicant, my application was approved the next day. After paying a deposit and one month's rent, I picked up the keys the following morning, but with Alex's stringent work regime, I've only moved in now, three weeks later.

"Can you smell that?" Harlow eyes me curiously while sucking in a big breath through her nose. "That's the smell of freedom!"

I giggle at her eccentrics, even though she's accurate. I love Regina. She's like the mother I never had, but no self-respecting twenty-five-year-old likes living with their mother.

Although I rarely have the opportunity to go out on dates, it's nice to know I can invite people into my private abode if I want to. I don't need to mention whose face popped into my head first during that thought, do I?

Harlow returns my head from the clouds. "Speaking of freedom, did you get your hard-ass boss to give you the long weekend off?"

Excitement echoes in my reply. "Yes."

It was as painful as pulling teeth, but after groveling, begging, and promising to work the next four weekends in a row, Alex agreed I could have the upcoming long weekend off.

"Where are we going again?"

Harlow has nagged me the past three weeks to get the weekend off, but whenever I ask her where we're going, she only responds with, "It's a secret."

Harlow's eyes narrow a mere second before she walks into my trap. If looks could kill, I'd be dead right now.

When I stick my tongue out, she smiles before she saunters to a box of mismatched kitchen accessories.

"What are you looking for?" I question.

After pulling two coffee mugs out of the box, she twists to face me. "We need something to wash down this overpriced bottle of champagne." She raises the gift that was on my doorstep this morning.

When I saw the bottle, my heart leaped. Although it still raced when I read the card, it wasn't as erratic.

It was thoughtful of Cormack to send me a housewarming gift, but I presumed it was from Isaac, so I was left a little disappointed.

"Do you think we should drink it? I don't know much about champagne, but considering this one has Dom Perignon written on the label, I'd say it's expensive."

Harlow doesn't grace me with a reply. She pops open the bottle and pours us a generous helping into a pair of dusty mugs. "To freedom and expensive bottles of champagne," she says, handing me a chipped mug.

"To freedom." I take a mouthful of the delicious aromatic champagne to hide my mumbled comment, "And to finally being able to entertain special guests."

16

"Brandon..." My greeting is drenched with sugary sweetness.

After prancing to Brandon's desk, I prop myself on the edge near stacks of files and blacked-out documents. When his eyes lift to mine, I flutter my lashes and purse my lips before adding a little seasoning to my ruse by undoing the top button of my blouse, daringly exposing some of the cleavage scarcely contained in my white lace bra.

I fan my flushed cheeks before saying, "It's so hot today,"

I sigh, fighting the urge to cringe. I've never been good at flirting, and my pathetic attempt today proves this.

Brandon's Adam's apple bobs as his eyes rake down my body. Although he stops at my undone button for an appreciative glance, he isn't buying what I'm selling. The suspicion in his eyes announces this, not to mention his grin.

Mindful his ruse is as busted as mine, he asks, "What do you want, Izzy?"

"What gave it away?"

"The greeting was okay. It gained my attention, but you lost me on unbuttoning your shirt and saying it's hot." He lowers his eyes to my undone button before returning them to my face. "You do realize summer is over, don't you, Isabelle?"

"Ha ha."

He light-heartedly growls when I button my blouse back to respectable, soothing the sting my ego took from my botched attempt at seducing him.

Once I'm presentable, he asks, "What brought you strutting to my desk?"

"I wasn't strutting."

Air whizzes between his teeth when he laughs. "You were totally strutting. The hips were swinging, and you had an extra spring in your step. Total strut."

I smile.

Obviously, my ruse wasn't that ineffective.

"I'm glad you took such detailed bullet points of my performance."

When I punch him, he chuckles before rubbing his arm. He isn't as built as some of the other male agents, but I have no doubt he can hold his own. People are less suspicious of the smaller guys, unaware they usually pack the most brutal punch.

I check we're free of unwanted lurkers before announcing the reason for my prance. "I need a favor."

"Anything," Brandon replies without a moment of reluctance.

My reply is nowhere near as smooth. "I need access to a sealed file from the DA's office in New York."

Brandon's eyes meet mine. His brows are furrowed, and his expression is troubled. "I... I can't, Izzy."

"Please, Brandon. I wouldn't ask if it weren't important."

From the stories he's shared about his life, I understand his hesitation, but I need this file for my investigation on Hugo. Because the bureau is focusing solely on Isaac, they're missing several key elements that warrant Hugo receiving his own investigation.

The only evidence I've unearthed on any Hugo Marshall in the country is a court file for his sister, Marjorie. But it's sealed so tightly shut not even an FBI agent can access it.

"I haven't had contact with her in years, Izzy. She'll probably hang up the instant she realizes who's calling."

My eyes plead with him to at least give it a chance. Without this file, I'll have nothing on Hugo, and my investigation will become stagnant.

I can't let this go. My intuition is telling me I need to follow this lead.

Brandon scrubs his hand over his eyes. They're no longer brimming with mischievousness. They are tentative and apprehensive. "I'll try, but I can't guarantee anything."

Childishly squealing, I sling my arms around his shoulders and hug him tight. "Thank you, Brandon, thank you."

"You're welcome."

When I pull back from our embrace, which has gained us the attention of fellow officers, I notice Brandon's cheeks are pink. I don't know if he's embarrassed, but he sounds confident saying, "It will cost you, though."

I nod. I'll do anything to get my hands on that file.

"I need you to do a search on this lady."

I accept the record he's holding out for me while nodding, eager to get started.

My excitement dips when he adds, "And go on a date with me."

Confusion clusters in my head on why guilt is my first emotion felt. In the past four months, I've only seen Isaac a handful of times, but he's always in the forefront of my mind. I'm also shocked. Brandon hasn't asked me out in months. I assumed he either got the hint or another lady caught his eye.

"One date, Izzy. That's all I'm asking."

Putting aside the ridiculous notion that there's any type of relationship between Isaac Holt and me, I murmur, "Okay. But it will have to be after I return. I'm going away with Harlow this weekend."

Brandon nods and grins, easing my uncertainty. He's a nice guy and has been nothing but kind to me since I arrived, so I should be thankful he's interested, not apprehensive.

"Why don't you come to my apartment, and I'll cook for us?"

His grin turns into a full smile. "Sounds great."

Returning his smile, I open the folder of the woman he wants to conduct a search on. There are numerous surveillance photos of a lady with shoulder-length brown hair. She's of medium build, and I'd guess her age to be mid-twenties. She's attractive, but something about her puts me a little on edge.

"Who is this?"

Brandon shrugs. "We don't know. We've noticed her a few times at the nightclub over the past several weeks. We believe she may be a *companion* of Isaac's."

My stomach recoils from the way he says "companion."

No wonder I got a peculiar feeling when studying her photos.

"I haven't seen Isaac with a girlfriend the entire time he's been under surveillance, but this lady has been in the picture more regularly than his standard dates, so she may be someone significant in his life."

Ignoring the bitterness rising to my throat, I say, "All right. I'll see what I can find."

It wasn't difficult tracking down Isaac's mysterious shadow. She was photographed several times in a yellow vehicle in the parking lot of his club. Her license plate gave me access to her driver's license.

Megan Patricia Shroud is twenty-six and lives in a country town four hundred miles from Ravenshoe. She's unmarried and has no next of kin reported on her driver's license.

I expand my search on Megan, more out of curiosity than necessity, before picking up my vibrating cell phone.

I grin when I discover a text from Harlow.

HARLOW:

Champagne is chilled, wine glasses are ready, and my bag is packed. I just seem to be missing one essential element???

I grab my jacket from the back of the chair, snatch the printout of Megan's license off the printer, and then make a beeline to Alex's office, passing by Brandon's desk on the way to hand him Megan's credentials.

"Thanks, and have fun," he shouts as I bolt by.

Alex's eyes lift from the documents he's scrutinizing when I knock on his office door, but he leaves the talking to me.

"Just wanted to let you know I'm heading out for the weekend." I apprehensively step into his office. "I also wanted to thank you for letting me have this time off."

Even though I had to agree to work the next four weekends, he had a legitimate reason to refuse my request. I've only been a part of his team for under five months, but I have already requested a vacation.

"It's fine, Isabelle." His stern tone doesn't match his words.

"Bye," I murmur when he resumes perusing the documents.

As I'm about to exit his office, he calls my name.

Cautiously, I prepare my stomach before I twist to face him.

My intuition is spot on when he says, "Keep your phone on you. If we need you, you'll have to return early."

Smiling, I nod before exiting his office with a grumble. "Like filing and scanning can't wait until I return."

Although his request has put a damper on my mood, I don't let it be felt. I tug my cell phone out of my pocket and return Harlow's message.

ME:

Pop that cork. I'm on my way!

17

"I'm not taking it."

I remove a microscopic bikini from my suitcase for the third time in the past thirty minutes.

Whenever I turn my back, Harlow places the scraps of material back in against my wishes, so I don't turn around this time.

"Trust me, you'll want that bikini." She overaccentuates "trust me" while waggling her brow.

After cocking a sculptured brow, she holds my black string bikini out in front of her, pleading for me to take it.

I've packed a swimsuit, but it covers more skin than my bikini.

It's also dull and lackluster.

I'm not even sure a grandma would wear it.

Confident she's getting through to me, Harlow places the sexy swimsuit within an inch of my hands and then executes her best puppy-dog eyes.

She murmurs, "Yes," under her breath when I shove the thin scraps of material into the side pocket of my suitcase, but her eyes roll when I pack a Hawaiian print cover-up as well.

Once I've finished packing, I wheel my bag into the entryway in preparation for our departure.

A short time later, my intercom screeches.

"Hi, come on up," I greet into the intercom.

When I push the button to unlock the security door in the lobby, a massive buzz shrieks through my ears.

Dropping to my knees, I refasten the zipper that busted open when I wheeled it into the foyer. My head clusters with giddiness from my sudden movements. I probably shouldn't have mixed Xanax with champagne, but when Harlow said we were flying, I needed something to take the edge off.

"I'll get the door, shall I?" Harlow suggests when she notices me wrangling with the stubborn zipper.

I nearly choke on my spit when she swings the door open, revealing the awe-inspiring visual of Mr. Isaac Holt dressed head to toe in designer clothes.

Please tell me he's popping in for a random visit. I can barely survive being in the same room with him for ten minutes, so I stand no chance of escaping the flames being in his vicinity for an entire weekend.

My eyes rocket to Harlow, who's greeting Cormack more intimately than a friend would.

So that's where she's been vanishing to for the past several weekends?

Isaac peers down at me before smirking. If the lust detonating in his eyes is anything to go by, he likes the idea of me kneeling in front of him as much as I do.

I'm a strong and independent woman, but the idea of kneeling for a man as powerful as Isaac makes my insides clench.

"Isabelle..."

The way my name rolls off his tongue makes me wonder how it would sound in ecstasy. Would it be as deep as it sounds now or more breathless and ragged?

When Isaac stops in front of me, I raise my eyes to his, admiring his muscular physique on the way.

He's no longer smirking, but his relaxed expression quickens my pulse. He pinches his trousers before crouching next to me. Air sucks from my lungs when his handsome face comes to rest directly in front of me, so I won't mention how giddy I become when he says, "If we were alone, you wouldn't be moving from that position."

I throw my dignity out the window by pleading for him to make true on his threat with nothing but my eyes.

Regretfully, the only reply I get for my numerous begs is a wink before he stands and offers to assist me off the ground.

After inwardly whining, I accept his offer. Electricity shoots up my arm when he curls his hand around mine, and the dizziness I was experiencing earlier returns full pelt.

It isn't the Xanax/champagne combination causing my light-headedness.

It's the incredibly attractive Mr. Isaac Holt.

"Are you ready?" Cormack asks as his eyes dart down to Isaac's hand curled around mine.

Upon noticing the direction of his gaze, Isaac drops my hand quicker than a bullet leaving a gun.

When he gathers my suitcase off the ground and strides into the corridor, I stray my eyes to Harlow, who's gawking at me with a mischievous expression.

"You have no idea what you've done." I whisper to ensure Isaac doesn't hear me.

She curls her arm around my waist to drag me into the hallway while replying, "You're welcome."

* * *

I squirm the entire drive to the airport. Not solely because Isaac's intense watch hasn't faltered since I sat across from him, or the fact I'm petrified of flying, but because I'm terrified of spending the long weekend with the man seated across from me.

Terrified is a strong word, but how all rational thoughts cease to exist when he's in the same room as I am is genuinely terrifying.

No one should have that type of control over another, let alone a man I barely know. He doesn't need to touch me, and my body teeters close to ecstasy. My heart skips a beat every time he assesses my body, and just the rasp of his voice makes my clit throb.

Imagine how much harder the battle will be once we're trapped in the tight confines of a Boeing 777.

I suck in a calming breath before exiting the stretch limousine. The instant my feet hit the blacktop, my first instinct is to run—and that is precisely what I do.

My getaway is foiled when I crash into a rock-hard chest.

After ensuring our collision didn't bend my nose, Isaac points behind me. "The plane is that way."

I glance in the direction of his point, gulp, and then resume my quick exit.

Isaac chuckles. Although his laughs are as rare as hens' teeth, it doesn't lessen my desire to flee. That plane he's pointing at is not a plane. It's a sardine can. I barely survive traveling on a commercial-size aircraft, so there's no chance I'll board a plane that looks like it came from a child's toy box.

I have one foot in the limo when Isaac seizes my wrist, halting my quick exit. He doesn't speak. He just silently assures me that I have no reason to fret.

"I can't get in that plane," I say when my fear augments.

This isn't a ploy to gain his attention.

I'm genuinely terrified.

The longer I return Isaac's assuring stare, the more my panic pacifies. He runs his index finger down my cheek like his thumb is brushing the veins throbbing in my hand. It is a loving, caring gesture that quells my anxiety as well as his unique eyes do.

When his thumb brushes over my parched lips, a shallow moan rumbles from my mouth. His touch is electrifying, and my body can no longer deny that.

When he steps back, I step forward, not wanting the intangible string between us to be snapped.

He runs his thumb over my hand gripping his so tightly my nails dig into his flawless skin before he takes another step back.

Again, I step forward.

And so our blistering two-step routine continues.

Before I know it, we're at the base of the stairs leading up to the galley of the toy plane.

Isaac stands behind me. He's so close his cock braces my curvy backside as his breaths heat my neck.

"Are you coming, Isabelle?" he whispers, his words laced with a sexual undertone.

I gulp louder than I did when I saw the plane before nodding.

I can do this—even if it kills me.

With my hands clenched at my sides, I climb the stairs of the private jet. My knees knock with every step, but it isn't from fear. It's to calm the rampant tingles coursing through my body.

When I reach the galley, I plop into the first plush white leather two-seater sofa I stumble onto before searching for my seat belt.

My panic surges when my hunt comes up empty.

Where's the damn belt?

I can't fly without a belt.

Before I'm overwhelmed by a panic attack, Isaac's hands launch into the back of my chair. The fear curled around my throat loosens when they skim portions of the bare skin on my thighs.

When he produces the belt and fastens it around my waist, flashbacks of him doing the same months ago rush into my brain. They're quickly chased with the forbidden scenes of our explicit kiss in his car weeks ago.

As lust overwhelms me, my cheeks flame. Just recalling our kiss is enough to get me hot and bothered.

When a growl rumbles from above, I raise my lust-filled eyes. The situation between my legs worsens when I'm confronted with Isaac's pussy-clenching gaze. He watches me for several heated minutes before turning his focus to Cormack. They speak a handful of words, and then Isaac sits beside me.

The span of his thighs keeps my panic in a manageable range, but I still pant when the plane jerks forward.

"If you need me to carry you to the bedroom, let me know."

My eyes snap to Isaac, the offerer. "There's a bedroom on this jet?"

Smiling at my high tone, he gestures to a polished door at the back of the plane. "I'll give you a tour later."

I nearly vault out of my chair when he places his palm on my thigh. If he didn't smirk at my skittish response, I'd be none the wiser that he felt my response.

My heart rate climbs as fast as the jet soars down the runway when his index finger traces a figure-eight pattern on my bare skin. His touch ensures my mind is absent of any thought not associated with him.

Although my body screams for him to shift his finger a couple of inches higher, not once does his touch switch to disrespectful.

He doesn't need to toss his morals out the window with mine. My imagination is wondrous. Imagining his fingers running along my naked body, gripping, probing, and exploring, makes my daydream vividly graphic.

It also proves without a doubt that sexual endorphins overrule fear-inducing chemicals.

"You're getting better with flying. You didn't require nearly as much stimulation this time," Isaac says once the plane is no longer ascending.

I try to hide my smile, but forever diligent, he notices the faint curve of my lips. His heated watch doesn't falter as he releases my bottom lip from my teeth, then tilts in intimately. "Everything you just imagined I will do to your body tonight."

My thighs press together when he licks my earlobe.

I need to reel in my shrewdness. I can't sleep with Isaac. It isn't solely my reputation on the line by conversing with him. It is also my uncle's. He had an impressive reputation that took years to earn.

My name is associated with his, so I can't shroud it in controversy.

"I have a boyfriend," I lie.

Isaac's eyes missile to mine. His lips are thin, and his jaw is ticking. As he scrubs at his unshaven jaw, he scans my face, studying me in silence.

"I know you're hiding something, Isabelle," he says, stern and clipped. "But it isn't a boyfriend."

I should have known he'd see through my deceit. He has eyes that can see straight through to my soul.

That in itself is a terrifying notion.

18

---

*L*urching, I sit up, causing giddiness to cluster in my stomach. I dart my eyes around the lavish room I've awoken in while mumbling, "I really need to stop waking up in strange rooms."

I sigh when I discover I'm wearing not only a short-sleeved shirt but also my bra and panties.

When a toilet flushes, my eyes rocket to the side of the room. My heart stops beating when the hinges on the white panel door creak open, and Harlow prances into the room.

"Sleeping beauty finally wakes."

I flop onto my pillow and throw an arm over my eyes to shelter them from the sun streaming through the thick, pleated curtains.

The mattress dips when Harlow sits on the edge. "Here, take these. They'll help with your head."

Her voice makes me wince when it screeches through my ears before clustering in my thumping head.

Peering out of my left eye only, I spot her holding pain medication in one hand and a bottle of water in the other.

I scoot up the bed until I'm leaning on the black leather button-pressed headboard, then down half the bottle with three headache tablets.

"Are you sure it was champagne in that bottle? My head is telling me a different story."

I feel more hungover now than I did when I downed cocktails like soda months ago.

"Yes, it was only champagne." Harlow giggles. "But if you had mentioned you took Xanax, I would have limited the number of glasses you consumed."

"Oh." *Now my pounding headache makes sense.*

"Yeah, oh... That's the best blackout concoction I know." She grins and shakes her head. "But oh... my... god, girl, you should've seen Isaac. He was all frantic and possessive when you wouldn't wake up. He wouldn't let anyone near you, let alone touch you. It was h-o-t HOT. He only settled down when Cormack discovered Xanax in your purse, and I explained we were drinking champagne before we left."

"Cormack went through my purse?" My mind frantically strives to remember if I placed my FBI identification there.

"Yeah..."

When her sentence seems unfinished, I say, "Harlow..." My tone alone demands further explanation.

She waits a beat before saying, "They also found your strip of condoms."

"I don't have condoms in my..."

Oh shit. Yes, I do.

"They're an old stash. I packed them when I went on vacation. They were an emergency stash. Everyone has an emergency stash. Just in case... in case—"

"You need to have sex in a washroom thirty thousand feet in the air?" Harlow interrupts.

When I rib her, her giggles erupt into muscle-clenching, cheek-tightening laughter.

Once her laughter calms down, her eyes glistening with tears, I ask, "What was Isaac's reaction to the condoms?"

She clutches my hand in hers, and her eyes bore into mine. It's the most serious I've seen her. "He growled. Not a dainty pussycat roar. He full-on growled a sexy-as-sin rumble." She sighs like she's watching *The Bachelor*. "Then he scooped you into his arms, and that's where you stayed until he laid you on this bed."

Disappointment twists in my chest. I'm upset I missed Isaac's sexy-as-sin growl. If it was anything like the little one he did on the plane, it could have lit a fire in my stomach for years.

I shut down my disappointment when Harlow says, "He only left thirty minutes ago because he had some business calls to attend to. He made me promise I wouldn't leave your side until he returned."

"What time is it?" I ask, curious to discover if a long sleep is why I feel the most rested I've ever felt.

Or is it compliments to sleeping in Isaac's arms?

I'd say it is the latter.

Harlow paces to a floor-to-ceiling window boarding the headboard. She dramatically opens the burgundy-and-gold drapes to reveal a blinding stream of sunlight that makes me wince in pain from its brightness.

"I slept all afternoon and night?" I ask, my mind a jumbled mess of confusion.

The plane was scheduled to land at three o'clock in the afternoon, but there's no doubt it's morning sunlight streaming through the window.

"Yep." The "p" pops from her mouth. She joins me back by the bed, her face morphing from playful to taut. "Please don't leave me alone with them for that long again."

I giggle until I realize she's serious.

Tilting my head, I arch my brow, requesting further information.

She gives up the goods two seconds later. "Cormack and I have been on a couple of dates."

"I figured that out when you rammed your tongue down his throat yesterday," I interrupt, my tone cheeky.

Harlow grins before continuing. "He's great. I really like him, but I didn't realize he was... *this*." She gestures to our elegant surroundings.

The room I've awoken in is massive, easily the size of a studio apartment. It's decorated with antique furniture and abstract paintings, giving it a distinct aura of wealth and superiority.

"First a stretch limousine, then a private jet, and now..." She stops mid-sentence, her brows scrunching. "I don't think calling this residence a mansion would be a justified response. I've already gotten lost three times this morning."

This time, when I laugh, she joins me.

"You won't be laughing when you get lost and no one finds you for days."

"I don't understand the problem, Harlow. If you like Cormack, and he likes you, why does it matter if he's rich?"

"He isn't just rich, Izzy. He's filthy, never-needs-to-work-a-day-in-his-life rich, and I own a bakery with books that spend more time in the red than in the black," she responds forlornly. "I don't belong here."

"Harlow." I seek her gaze. "I saw you with Cormack yesterday before the limo and the private jet. You like him, so don't judge him on his wealth. Judge him on the man he is, the same man you greeted with jubilation yesterday."

"I do like him."

"Then that's all that matters. Ignore everything else because it doesn't matter. It's just static noise in the background," I encourage her. "If you like someone, throw everything else aside and worry about it later."

She nods as her lips tug high. I return her smile, happy I eased her uncertainty, but am left a little lost when she thrusts out her hand in offering.

Curious, I accept her offer of a handshake, albeit hesitantly.

"Hi, Pot, I'm Kettle. It's a pleasure to meet you," she introduces while shaking my hand so firmly my arm almost pops out of its socket.

Her giggles boom around the room when I dive for her. I knock her onto the mattress and tickle her ribs until she commences begging me to stop.

My tortuous hands stop tickling Harlow when the main entrance door of the room opens with a creak. The pulse in my neck thrums when Isaac enters looking ravishing in two parts of a three-piece suit.

His eyes study my sweaty face for several seconds before they wander over the parts of my body that are exposed since my shirt rose to my stomach while I was tickling Harlow into submission.

After fixing my shirt to a more respectable level, I scoot up the bed to lean against the headboard. I'm so entranced by Isaac's presence I don't notice Harlow sneaking out until Isaac takes her place on the bed.

He sounds genuinely concerned when asking, "How are you feeling?"

I smile. "I'm good."

"Did you take the tablets I left on the bedside table?" He smirks when I nod. "Good."

We sit across from each other in silence for several minutes. It isn't awkward. It feels right.

Isaac runs a hand over his hair before locking his concerned eyes with mine. "Do I need to be concerned that you have a problem with drinking?"

I smile. It isn't the right time, but it can't be helped. I'm pleased he cares enough about me to be worried about my well-being.

"No, I don't have a problem with drinking. That champagne was the first alcoholic drink I've had since the last time you took me home." Grimacing, I quickly add, "I knew we were flying, and I accidentally mixed medication with alcohol. My thumping head alone will ensure it won't happen again." Needing the focus off me, I ask, "Do I need to be concerned that you have a problem with taking inebriated women into your room and undressing them?"

His scrumptious laugh rumbles through to my clit.

"At least this time you let me keep my panties," I quip, needing to do something to stop me from responding to his laughter with my lips.

Isaac stops laughing before his tongue darts out to moisten his lips. Our kiss was weeks ago, but I can still recall how delectably sinful his mouth tastes. "I didn't take your panties last time, Isabelle."

Just my name rolling off his tongue has me eager to chase my climax. "You gave them to me."

That confession secures my fall into orgasmic bliss and places it back onto the ledge.

"No, I didn't."

"Yes, you did," he interrupts. "When you found my... *trophies* other women have left behind, you removed your panties before shoving them into the drawer with the explicit remark that it would be the only way I'd add your panties to my collection."

"Oh..." That sounds like something I'd do in a moment of drunken angriness.

Hold on. Does that mean my panties have been in that drawer all along? Yuck!

"No, Isabelle. Your panties aren't in that drawer."

I really need to stop mumbling out loud.

After a brief stint of silence, I ask, "Where are they, then?"

Mortified by my boldness, I seek anything but Isaac's amused face.

Sheets ruffling fill the awkward silence when he adjusts his position so his breaths flutter against my neck when he answers, "They're in my *very exclusive* collection." I smile, pleased my panties are valuable enough to be added to his private collection. "And unless you want to add another set to my collection, I suggest you shower, get dressed, and then join the rest of us for breakfast."

Before my lusty head can contemplate his request, its smarter counterpart, the one my uncle forever encouraged me to use before anything else, forces me out of bed and into the bathroom Harlow exited earlier.

Isaac's groan of frustration warrants an icy-cold shower, not to mention the angry stomps of the naughty devil on my shoulder.

19

___

I break the world record for the quickest shower. Not solely because I fail to put any heat in the water, but because I'm interested to find out what had Harlow so rattled earlier.

Once I throw on a pair of denim shorts and a short-sleeved shirt, I exit the guest bedroom.

Holy hell!

If the hallway is this elegant, what's the rest of the house like?

I appraise a range of oil paintings adorning the wall outside my room.

One painting captures my attention a little longer than the rest. It's a beautiful self-portrait of Frida Kahlo. If it's an original—and I have no doubt it is—its estimated worth is in the millions.

"She isn't my type," says a husky voice in the distance. "The one-eyebrow thing does *nothing* for me."

Turning to the voice, I'm met with light-blue eyes brimming with mischief that offset a handsome preppy-boy face. The stranger's blond hair is long enough for the tips to curl upward. He's wearing black board shorts and a light-blue T-shirt that matches his eyes. He's also barefoot.

Once he finishes studying me as eagerly as I eyed him, he

winks. "You, on the other hand, are very much my type." He struts my way. "Colby McGregor." He offers me his hand to shake. "If I'd known you were waiting for me, I would have woken earlier."

I grin, loving his playful banter. "Isabelle Brahn." I accept his handshake before nudging my head to the painting. "Is it an original?"

"Uh-huh," he answers, not the slightest bit impressed he has a painting worth millions hanging on the wall outside his room. "When my mom found out Madonna bought some of Frida's self-portraits, she had to get one, too." He shrugs. "If you think this one is impressive, wait until you see my favorite painting."

He guides me further down the impressively long hallway.

When we reach the end, he swivels me to face an oil painting displayed in an ebony frame.

I can't help but laugh when my eyes drink in all the hideous details.

"Is that you?" I ask when my squint exposes a hint of a face outline.

Colby nods. "Yep. I figured if Frida could make millions selling self-portraits, I may as well give it a go."

"I hope you didn't quit your day job."

The portrait is beyond revolting. It looks like someone painted an extremely basic picture and then threw a glass of water over it. But I can admit, it's endearing his family framed it for display as proudly as masterpieces worth millions.

"Maybe self-portraits aren't my thing. Maybe I need something more inspirational to paint." Colby's focus shifts from the painting to me. "Maybe nudes are more my thing?"

"Jeez, Colby, could you lay it on any thicker?" asks a perky female voice. "Did you check if she was here with someone, or are you going to whip it out and pee on her leg before any other guy sniffs her?"

"I'm going to whip it—" Our interrupter slaps Colby's chest so hard it winds him, which ends his playful taunt mid-sentence.

Then she shifts on her feet to face me. "Hello, I'm Cate McGregor. Cate with a C. This douchebag's little sister."

Cate is so short she'd be lucky to be five feet tall. She appears several years younger than I am. If I had to guess her age, I'd say mid-to-late teens, possibly early twenties. Her platinum-blonde hair is cut in a daring pixie design, and her petite frame wears fringed denim shorts and a pink bikini top.

She has an aura that makes me want to befriend her, even with her fashion sense exposing we're on different sides of the wealth scale.

"Hi, I'm Isabelle."

"Oh snap..." Cate darts her eyes between Colby and me for several long seconds. "Don't go there, Colby. She's off-limits."

Colby doesn't grace her with a reply. He merely chuckles a laugh that bellows down the hallway.

Cate narrows her eyes at him before curling her hand around mine and guiding me through a maze of hallways, doors, and over-sized sitting rooms.

Harlow wasn't joking. This place is massive. I'm pretty sure I'll get lost trying to find my way back to my room.

The smell of freshly baked bread and bacon becomes more prominent the farther we walk. When we enter a massive kitchen that looks like it belongs in a fancy restaurant, Cate relinquishes my hand and approaches a Spanish lady placing muffins into a woven basket on the island bench.

The muffins aren't the only scrumptious treats on display. Croissants, Danish pastries, donuts, bacon, eggs, fresh-cut fruit, and everything you could imagine is laid out.

My stomach rumbles, my hunger rampant since I failed to eat dinner last night.

"Help yourself to anything you want," offers Cate, handing me a porcelain plate. "Once you're done, come join us outside."

She nudges me with her hip before leaving the kitchen via a pair of French doors.

I cram my plate with a range of goodies before walking out the same doors. I sense Isaac's watch before I see him. He's seated at a table alongside an impressive grotto pool. He smirks at me in greeting before gesturing for me to join him.

Smiling, I walk toward him, my pulse quickening with every step. His gaze is powerful and solely focused on me. As much as I shouldn't admit this, I love that he has trouble taking his eyes off me as much as I do him.

My grin enlarges to a full smile when he pulls a chair out for me to sit.

"Thank you," I whisper graciously.

He eyes my plate with a roguish sparkle in his eyes. "Hungry?"

My cheeks heat with embarrassment at my lack of dignity when I answer, "Starving."

When he raises his mug to his mouth, my hunger is no longer associated with food. I can't stop staring at the handsome features of his face, not to mention how his Adam's apple bobs when he swallows his beverage.

"Eat, Isabelle," Isaac demands when my stomach grumbles.

When I turn my gaze away from him so I can focus on anything but his captivating eyes, I'm surprised to notice Clara sauntering our way.

What is she doing here? Is she here with Isaac?

She's elegantly dressed compared to how I've seen everyone else this morning—everyone but Isaac.

"Isabelle, what a pleasure to see you again," Clara greets me before greeting Isaac with a kiss on his cheek.

"Hi, Clara."

I pull off a chunk of the croissant and pop it into my mouth. My mouth salivates when graced with its presence, but trying to swallow it is like eating cardboard.

Clara has all but crawled into Isaac's lap. Her arm is draped around his shoulders, and her backside is perched on his suit-covered thigh.

When her red-painted lips press against the mug where Isaac's lips were mere moments ago, jealousy rips through me.

It's the smallest gesture but has the biggest impact on my faltering ego.

What are they like behind closed doors if they're this intimate in public?

Clara is beautiful, and her grace means she'd be an ideal partner for Isaac, but not even admitting that stops waves of jealousy from crashing through me.

I have no right to be jealous. I have no claim to Isaac, but I can't control the unruly connection I feel when he's near.

It is too intense to ignore.

No longer hungry, I leap up from my chair. "Please excuse me. I—"

Isaac tugs me back onto the wrought iron chair with a thud. "Eat."

"I—"

"Now, Isabelle."

His narrowed eyes remain on me, hot and heavy, until my teeth shred through a bagel slathered with cream cheese.

Once it settles like a rock in my stomach, Isaac abruptly stands, sending Clara tumbling to the ground. She regains her footing and runs her hand down her black skirt to smooth the crinkles before cozying up to Isaac's side. Her glare is no longer friendly and is solely focused on me.

I drift my eyes to Isaac when he says, "I'll be back in a minute."

When I nod, he grips Clara's hand in a white-knuckle hold, then drags her to the French doors I walked through only moments ago.

I try to keep my focus off them, but like you can't tear your eyes away from a train wreck, mine continually shift to them.

Isaac's arms are folded over his well-defined chest, but his composure remains calm. Clara is on the other end of the spectrum. She waves her arms frantically and motions to me several times during her tirade. Her face is also constricted with tautness, and her eyes are welling with tears.

I don't know how I missed it, but her wintry-blue eyes are as evident as the sun in the sky. Clara has the same blonde hair, light-blue eyes, and flawless beige skin as the other McGregors I've met this weekend.

Mr. and Mrs. McGregor must be fascinated with the letter C. All their children were given names beginning with it. I'm certain.

When Clara's huff echoes in the silence of the morning before she disappears through the patio doors, I turn my attention back to my overflowing plate, pretending I wasn't spying on their discussion.

Isaac returns to our table a second later but remains quiet, his mind elsewhere.

I try to ignore the massive elephant sitting in the room, but my quintessential need to know everything gnaws at my insides until I blurt out, "Have you slept with Clara?"

Isaac freezes with his mug halfway between the table and his lips, his eyes drifting to me. His gaze is unyielding, and it would make most people quake in fear, but my stupid thighs tremor in excitement.

"Are you jealous, Isabelle?"

"No," I reply with a brisk headshake.

His smirk turns into a genuine smile as his eyes study the deceit on my face. "You have absolutely nothing to be jealous about."

I appreciate his assurance, but the best federal agent in the country raised me. I couldn't stop this interrogation even if I wanted to. "Stop skirting and answer the question."

Isaac shakes his head to hide his smirk before he answers, "No, Isabelle. I have not slept with Clara."

I strive to conceal my relief, but my inner vixen hollers too loudly to conceal it. "So what was that about?" I pop a chunk of bagel into my mouth since my hunger has returned full force. "Because she was acting very much like a scorned woman."

"Do I need to call a lawyer?" Isaac's brow arches high as he returns my stare. "Because this sounds like an interrogation."

Recalling one of my uncle's favorite lines, I say, "Only people with something to hide need to call a lawyer."

"I have nothing to hide"—he cockily shrugs—"because I always ensure my hands are thoroughly clean."

"Just because your hands are clean now doesn't mean they weren't stained previously."

"Just because your hands are clean now doesn't mean they won't become stained," Isaac counterbids. "You don't know what the future holds, Isabelle. Nobody does. So until the day your body is laid in its final resting place, you can't guarantee your hands will remain clean."

I completely miss the angst in his tone. "Yes, I can. Morally and ethically—"

"What about for someone you love? You wouldn't get your hands a little bit dirty for someone you love?"

My brows scrunch as my eyes bounce between his. Just being here abundantly proves what he's saying is true. I've only associated with him a handful of times, and I'm already willing to risk my career just to be near him, so I can only imagine the depths I'd go to for someone I love.

Sensing I'm on his side of the fence more than against it, Isaac says, "Not everything is black and white. There's a whole heap of gray no one pays any attention to."

He gives me a second to absorb his statement before he tosses a napkin onto his half-eaten plate of food and returns to the house, not once glancing back at me.

20

I sense Isaac's presence before I see him. An aura like his permeates the air, and you can't help but be drawn to him like a moth to a flame.

My eyes lift from my Kindle when he sits on the smidgen of the daybed I'm not sprawled across. I've been lazing in the mid-morning sun, reading.

After dropping my Kindle on my face numerous times, I flipped onto my stomach and have been kicking my legs wildly in the air.

I've been reading nonstop for the past two hours. Harlow and Cormack invited me to lunch with them, but I'd never volunteer to be the third wheel, no matter how much I don't want to be alone.

Isaac leans over my shoulder to peruse the book I'm reading. His hand balancing on the lower half of my back could be classified as friendly, but my body reacts as if it's sexual.

I haven't seen him since breakfast. I assumed he was agitated from our conversation and was avoiding me, but with how close he's sitting, I'd say my assumption was wrong.

"Phew, I was getting worried it was another Mills and Boon book."

Smiling, I roll over to face him. Because he doesn't move his hand, it brushes my hip and lands on my stomach when I roll onto my back.

The veins in my neck thrum when his change in outfit shows off his god-gifted body. He's more casually dressed than earlier, his muscular physique well-displayed in a fitted white shirt and black running shorts.

When a trail of sweat runs down his cheek, and I detect an increase in his manly aroma, I determine he must have recently returned from a run.

"What are you reading?"

His raspy purr makes my insides hotter than the sun. "*Thoughtless* by S.C. Stephens." I'm breathless from his closeness. "It's a story about two people who shouldn't be together but are destined to be together. I've read the entire series three times already."

His brow arches high as his lips crimp.

"Don't laugh. You don't understand the entrapment you experience when you're introduced to a character like Kellan Kyle," I reply. "He's my number-one book boyfriend."

His lips twist into a smile. "Guys like him make it hopeless for a man to date. All girls are expecting a Kell—"

"Kellan Kyle."

"Yeah, and instead, they get a man who comes home reeking of BO after working ten-plus hours. He drinks beer that smells like it was fermented in used college socks and snores louder than the freight trains running through Philly."

I laugh. It can't be helped. A man like Isaac should never worry about being compared to a book boyfriend. A real-life man would have a hard time competing against him, let alone a fictional character.

Air snares in my throat from the intense look Isaac is giving me. When I tilt my head and cock my brow in silent questioning, he says, "That's the first time I've heard you laugh."

My cheeks inflame as a grin inches my lips high.

His confession plummets our exchange into silence. It isn't awkward. It's more electrifying than anything. The intimacy crackling between us is so diverse it feels as if we're being invisibly bound.

I sigh when Isaac ends the silence by standing. My disappointment doesn't linger long when he plucks me up from the daybed while asking, "Did you pack a swimsuit?"

Unable to reply for the fear I'll whine, I nod.

"Good." Isaac nudges his head to Cormack's family's mega-mansion. "Go get changed."

"Okay."

I should ask more.

Say more.

Do more.

Instead, I hesitantly walk away from him to don a bikini that will throw my morals out the window even faster than Isaac's panty-wetting smirks.

Clenching my fists at my sides, I spin to face the full-length mirror in my room. I've spent the last ten minutes debating whether I should wear the highly indecent string bikini Harlow convinced me to pack or the one-piece suit I packed for someone's long-lost grandma.

Stupidly, I listened to my lust-fueled heart and put on the tiny bikini.

"It's not too bad," I mumble to my reflection.

My areoles aren't showing, and tiny material triangles almost cover the meaty part of my breasts.

When I spin again, I frown. More of my backside is exposed than I would have liked. Another inch and I'd be kicked off a family beach for indecent exposure.

I dart my eyes to the hideous Hawaiian print cover-up and my more conservative suit. I consider putting them on, but before my head can overrule the naughty devil on my shoulder, a knock sounds at my door.

Panicked, I yank the shorts I wore earlier up my legs, then advise my caller they can enter.

Time slows to a snail's pace when Isaac enters wearing nothing but swim trunks and a sexy smirk.

Holy. Shit. Cakes.

I've died and gone to heaven.

His body is better than I'd remembered. Every spectacular dip, plane, and bump is on display for the world to see, and I drink them in like I'm in the middle of the Sahara and my mouth hasn't been offered a drop of liquid in months.

Not a word is exchanged between us when Isaac curls his hand around mine and walks us to a beach stretching each way for miles.

Although it's fall, the weather is so nice my shoulders happily absorb the warm rays.

Once we reach a wooden shed attached to a jetty, Isaac releases my hand to gather a short-sleeved wetsuit and a life jacket from inside.

When he returns, he secures my hand again, like hand-holding is second nature, before guiding us to the end of the jetty. Excitement heats my veins when I notice two Wave Runners tied to the end of the pier.

I've always wanted to ride a jet ski.

He dumps the life jacket onto a wooden bench before twisting to face me. "Strip."

I eye him curiously, unsure of what he means.

I'm barely clothed as it is.

With his smirk hitting every one of my hot buttons, he drops his eyes to my tiny denim shorts.

Cringing, I slide them down my thighs, which are shuddering from his intense gaze, before I kick them to the side.

Like the situation between my legs could get any worse, Isaac crouches down in front of me to assist me into the wetsuit.

Images of me kneeling in front of him yesterday morning come racing back into my mind. It was less than twenty-four hours, but it seemed like a lifetime ago.

I shake my head to clear it of wicked thoughts before placing my feet into the openings of the wetsuit.

It takes several rough yanks to get the rigid material up my thighs and over my stomach. It isn't a tortuous project. During the process,

Isaac's hands continually brush my inner thighs and stomach. Occasionally, they even scrape past the erogenous zone above my panty line.

You'd have no idea he's dressing me with how wet I am. One more brush of his fingers to the right area, and I'll crumble into ecstasy.

When Isaac bobs down to hunt for the zipper in the lower half of the wet suit, he suddenly freezes before he sucks in a big breath through his nose.

His plan deviates for barely a second before he tugs on the zipper until it's tucked in a flap two inches under my chin.

"Do you want to wear a lifejacket?" he asks, his voice throaty like it too is burning through the fiery effects of ecstasy.

Unable to form words, I shake my head.

He nods before moving to one of the Wave Runners. When he straddles it, the muscles in his arms flex, and I have to fight like hell not to release the moan rumbling up my throat.

Is this why romance readers are thirsty for new MC books?

I grow worried Isaac heard my shameful response to something as mundane as a man straddling a jet ski when he smirks before he offers me his hand.

The muscles in his stomach clench when I band my arms around his waist, but it has nothing on the squeal I let out when our Wave Runner darts away from the jetty at the speed of a rocket.

The next forty-five minutes are pure torture.

My bikini is so thin it feels like I'm naked under my wetsuit, so my vivid imagination is getting carried away.

Every jolt the jet ski does adds to the pulse in my pussy. My barely covered chest is squashed against Isaac's back, and my nipples scrape his silky-smooth skin as they bounce along with the Wave Runner.

A snippet of reprieve washes over me when the jetty approaches the horizon. I've loved our ride and have never smiled so broadly, but having Isaac so close and fighting not to touch him is the worst form of cruelty.

He's right there.

Not even an inch in front of me.

But I can't touch him.

It's forbidden.

Desperate to lessen the tingling sensation running rampant through my body, I scoot back half an inch.

It turns into an unmanageable inferno when Isaac curls his hand around my thigh and tugs me back in.

We sit even closer now. My breasts are flattened against his back, and my deviant head is convinced I could use the waistband of his board shorts to get off.

Not even air exists between us, and it has my morals slipping at a rate too fast to contain.

I'm not the only one feeding off the tension. Every feeble movement I make sparks a response from Isaac. His ab muscles contract when my fingertips float over them, and his nape prickles with goosebumps when my lips get so close to his skin that I can taste the salt spray that's graced them.

The air shifts when I stop fighting the Wave Runner's jolts. I use its rocks as a cover to count the ripples in Isaac's stomach before tracing my fingers over the formidable V muscle every woman fantasizes about.

My lengthened breaths indicate I'm treading in dangerous waters, but I can't stop myself. My body's needs, desires, and cravings are outweighing my shrewdness.

I'm caught in the trance of lust.

Isaac groans when the exploration of my fingers tiptoes over the fine hairs near the tip of his perfect V muscle. His response spurs on my pursuit. I scoot even closer before the lash of my tongue cools his salty, sun-scorched skin.

His grip on the handlebars tightens when my hand dips under the waistband of his shorts. His cock is swollen and struggling to be contained in his swimming shorts.

When I curl my hand around his thick shaft, my needs too perverse to ignore for a second longer, the Wave Runner stops surging forward.

It stills as quickly as my massive surge of brazenness unravels.

I want Isaac more than my lungs crave air, but should I be doing this?

Seemingly sensing my hesitation, Isaac curls his hand over mine before guiding it up and down his impressively large cock. His rhythm is fast enough to be pleasurable but slow enough that he won't come anytime soon.

"Just like that, baby," he breathes out, his words husky with lust.

When he releases my hand, I slide it up and down his veined cock in the rhythm he demonstrated, but when I reach the head, I run my thumb over his knob to gather a bead of pre-cum formed there. I use it as lubrication to quicken my strokes.

My seamless pumps have him racing toward release at a record-setting pace, and I'm right there with him, enjoying every second of the thrilling ride.

Isaac's moans quicken when I cup his balls with my spare hand. I squeeze and knead them until pre-cum dribbles over my hand and is absorbed by his shorts.

When his breath catches in his throat, I know he's close to climax.

I am too. The thought of his imminent release is enough to encourage my own.

"Fuck, Isabelle."

The sexy roughness of his voice pushes my climax to the very edge. It usually takes a lot of stimulation to make me come, but hearing his gruff moans has it teetering.

I pump his cock hard and fast, almost desperately, then just as the vein feeding it swells in preparation for release, Isaac curls his hand over mine, stopping my strokes.

Disappointment slams into me when I discover the reason for his rejection. Colby is on a Wave Runner heading toward us, his speed unchecked.

Not wanting to be caught with my hands down someone's pants —literally—I attempt to pull them out of Isaac's shorts.

He seizes the wrist of the hand coated in pre-cum before he holds it in place. Although the devil on my shoulder is tap dancing in glee, I squeeze his cock hard, trying to force him to relinquish my hand.

My pussy gets wetter when his cock only twitches in response to my painful squeeze.

After Colby pulls his Wave Runner close to ours, he asks, "Are you guys okay? Are you out of fuel?"

Isaac's tone doesn't match the cheekiness of Colby's. "We're a little busy."

With a cocked brow, Colby scans my flushed face and dilated eyes. I'm sure they expose why we're busy, but instead of being mortified about the situation he's stumbled upon, he grins and winks before throwing Isaac a rope.

"Let me tow you back."

"We don't need a fucking tow." When Isaac returns the rope to Colby, I yank my hands from his shorts.

It doubles the anger radiating out of Isaac, but Colby acts oblivious. "Come on, Isaac, everyone needs a *hand* now and again."

Overcome with embarrassment, I bury my head between Isaac's back muscles.

Colby chuckles, but it does little to ease Isaac's stiffness.

And no, I'm not referencing the massive bulge between his legs.

"I'm joking, Isaac. Don't be so riled up all the time," Colby quips. "I came out to tell you Henry Gottle is here to see you."

Isaac cusses at the same time my stupidity smacks into me. "I forgot I had a meeting with him." He waits a beat before bossing Colby around like his family isn't uber-rich. "Tell Henry I'll be with him in a few minutes."

With a chuckle more telling than any grin, Colby revs his Wave Runner. Its engine's purrs trickle through my ears until they match the buzz of a mosquito.

Once I'm confident he's out of eyesight, I stop hiding my flaming cheeks and endeavor to eradicate them by sucking in some big breaths.

I shouldn't have bothered. After taking a minute to slacken the tightness of his jaw, Isaac twists to face me. He appraises my face long enough for the color in my cheeks to return more robust than ever before he increases the wetness between my legs with a promise. "We'll finish this later."

Our ride back to the jetty is done in silence, my orgasm that was racing for the finish line securely locked away.

My excitement vanished when Colby mentioned Henry Gottle was here to meet with Isaac. I was tempted to ask if Isaac's guest is Henry Gottle III, or his father, the suspected mob boss of New York City.

Fortunately, my levelheadedness resurfaced before the question seeped from my lips.

Even knowing he has a guest waiting, Isaac assists me out of my wetsuit and back into my shorts. Once the wetsuit is dumped onto the wooden jetty, along with the life vest we didn't use, he gathers my hand before striding toward the main house.

When we round the corner of the vast veranda, we're greeted by a man in his early thirties with inky-black hair.

I won't lie. I'm somewhat surprised at how attractive he is. Anytime I think of the mob, my thoughts stray to wrinkled, overweight men with moles on their faces.

"Henry, sorry I forgot about our meeting." Isaac's tone exudes authority and reveals he is the alpha in the room.

"That's fine." Henry's eyes drift to me. "I can comprehend your forgetfulness."

Isaac's gaze narrows when he notices who has caught Henry's wandering eye, but he still offers an introduction. "Isabelle, this is Henry Gottle, a *business* associate of mine."

It dawns on me that Isaac's greeting was more of a jab than a formal introduction when Henry replies, "I would have said longtime friend, but I guess business associate will do."

While I accept Henry's handshake, my eyes bounce between Isaac and him. It's hard to tell if they're friends or business associates. Isaac is more reserved around Henry than with Cormack, but he seems more laid back than he appeared in surveillance photos with real business associates.

I learn more about Isaac's personal life than any surveillance team ever could when he mutters, "I may have said friend if I wasn't left handling the repercussions of your wretched wife."

"Try living with her," Henry grumbles, his tone serious. "Three years I had to put up with that."

They shudder in sync before they chuckle full-heartedly.

I take it that neither of them is fans of Henry's ex-wife, Delilah Winterbottom.

"I got her out of your hair, but now I'm calling in those chips," Isaac says, getting down to business like a federal agent isn't in the room with them.

He is the only person not concerned. Henry's eyes shoot to mine. Suspicion is all over his face. He's worried about me being present during their conversation, and I can't blame him for that.

"I'll go grab some lunch."

I smile when Isaac says, "If you want to stay, Isabelle, you can stay."

His trust means the world to me, but I don't deserve it.

"It's fine. I'm famished anyway."

I am hungry, but I'm not leaving to find something to eat. I don't want to risk unearthing anything I may be forced to disclose to the bureau.

I'd never intentionally spy on Isaac while interacting with him on a personal level, but I swore an oath to uphold the law, so if I stumbled onto something significantly illegal, it would be my moral obligation to inform the authorities, wouldn't it?

My worry settles when I overhear a part of Isaac's meeting as I exit the room.

"I need you to find a loophole in the UFC so my fighter, Jacob, can fight a current UFC contender."

ormack, Harlow, and I have been seated at an elegant Italian steak restaurant for half an hour. It is a hive of activity, but with the hum of conversations, laughing, and cutlery scraping against plates, it's difficult to participate in any discussions being held across the table.

The conversation between Harlow and Cormack is engaging but inappropriate for three... unless you're into that type of thing.

"Thank you," I praise when the waiter hands me a black-and-gold-embossed menu, grateful for the distraction.

When I scan the prices on the menu, I nearly fall off my chair. Every entrée listed costs more than I make in a day.

Ignoring the hungry rumbles of my stomach, I order the most inexpensive item on the menu—a side serving of salad.

"*E per il vostro corso principale?*" the waitress questions.

"I'm sorry, I don't speak Italian," I reply, praying she understands English.

"She's asking what you'd like for your main course," advises a ruggedly handsome voice I immediately recognize.

My breath hitches when Isaac slides onto the seat beside me

before kissing my cheek. "Sorry I'm late. I had some business to take care of."

This is the first time I've seen him since our ride earlier today. I'm unsure if his meeting with Henry was for the entire afternoon or if he had other matters to attend to.

I tried to keep myself immersed in the world of Kellan Kyle so I wouldn't snoop, but my mind continually drifted to Isaac.

My views on him have significantly swayed toward the positive the past twenty-four hours—more so since I've yet to stumble on a shred of evidence that matches him to the person his FBI file shows him to be—but I'm wary as to why he was meeting with a well-known mafia family member.

"Do you know what you want?" Isaac asks, interrupting me from my thoughts.

"A side salad is fine." My voice trembles from his closeness. "I'm not hungry."

Air whizzes out of Isaac's nose before he twists his torso to face the waitress. "She'll have the sixteen-ounce steak with a baked potato and a side salad." He hands her back my menu while saying, "I'll have the same."

"I'm still full from lunch. That's why I ordered a salad."

He arches a perfect brow before announcing he is watching me as closely as the bureau is watching him. "The half-a-club sandwich and few slices of pear you ate at lunch weren't enough to skip dinner."

Shame pummels me, but it won't stop me from saying, "I can't afford two hundred dollars for a piece of steak."

His breath flutters my neck, and my thighs shake when he asks, "How fast can you run in those heels?" He winks when he spots my confusion. "We either run before the bill arrives or wash dishes with Roberto for the next week."

He gestures his head to a man entering the restaurant from the alleyway. Roberto's white apron barely covers his vast waistline, and it is covered with food and red wine.

When it dawns on me what Isaac is saying, I say, "I'll be sure to kick off these bad boys before dessert arrives." I click my black pumps together before confusion overrides my wittiness. "How do you know his name is Roberto?"

Isaac drapes his arm over the back of my chair. "This is pretty. Did you do something different?" He tugs on the strands of hair cascading down my back, sidestepping my question like a professional interrogation evader.

I could continue to interrogate him, but I don't since his presence is saving me from the dreaded third wheel act I signed on for when I accepted Harlow and Cormack's dinner invite.

"Harlow curled the ends."

He rakes his eyes over my fitted wrap dress before lifting them to my face. His gaze is hungry. This could be my ego talking, but I'm reasonably sure it isn't a hunger for food.

"You look beautiful, Isabelle."

"Thank you," I reply breathlessly.

For the next two hours, I enjoy splendid food, wine, and even better company.

Isaac has been the frankest I've ever seen him. From the stories he shared, I can easily perceive his fondness for his baby brother, Nick, and his excitement about becoming an uncle for the first time is also paramount.

I feel privileged to have experienced a side of him not many people witness and have quickly become trapped by his allure.

Isaac chuckles when I pretend to unbuckle my heels when the waiter hands us the dessert menu. He orders our dessert in Italian and impresses me with his impeccable pronunciation

"My nonna was Italian. She taught me to speak it fluently by the time I was eight," Isaac announces when he notices my curious glance.

"Are you close to your nonna?"

"No. She passed away five years ago." I eye him curiously when he removes my wine glass from my hand and places it back on the table.

"I'm sorry." I sympathize, even when puzzled as to why he removed my glass of red. It was recently refilled. I don't want it to go to waste.

"You've already had three glasses."

"Yes... and I told you I don't have a problem with drinking."

"You may not have a problem, but I do."

I cock my brow, requesting further information.

He gives up the goods two seconds later. "I don't converse with drunk women." A fire erupts in my womb when he leans close to ensure his following words are only for my ears. "I don't converse *sexually* with drunk women."

Oh.

My.

God.

My pupils widen as desire scorches through my veins. It doubles the sexual charge between us, making it so strong it crackles and hisses in the air.

My hand trembles when I accept a plate of tiramisu from the waitress, shamelessly exposing my excitement to Isaac's tease.

Either sensing my excitement or wanting to triple it, Isaac places his hand high on my bare thigh. His touch sends a jolt of pleasure to my throbbing clit, making tiramisu the last thing on my mind.

"Are you not hungry?" Isaac questions a short time later, eyeing my untouched dessert.

"I am... just not for food."

In a two-minute lusty haze, I go from being seated in the restaurant to sitting in the passenger seat of Isaac's car.

I think I murmured goodbye to Cormack and Harlow, but my body is coiled so tight, dying to release months of pent-up frustrations, I've lost the ability to focus on anything but the man beside me.

It's been over a year since I've had sexual contact with a man. It's been so long because my last bed partner pretty much squashed the fantasy of a night beneath the sheets.

His ruggedly handsome face didn't match the rest of his body— his body hair was vast and thick and stunk like a wet dog. Our two-minute tumble in his bed didn't create half of the spark I get from one sneaky glance into Isaac's entrancing eyes.

I'd only just finished unlatching my bra when the event was over.

He murmured that it was the greatest sex he'd ever had, rolled onto his side, and then spent the five minutes it took for me to gather my clothing and dart out of his house snoring.

Since that day, I've been apprehensive about dating.

Well, until I met Isaac.

Isaac cusses when a cell phone shrills through the speakers of his car. The monitor on the dashboard announces he has an incoming call from Hugo.

"What?" Isaac greets, expressing his annoyance.

"Sorry for the intrusion, boss, but we have a problem with 57." Hugo sounds regretful for the interruption, but his voice still has a hint of playfulness to it.

"Send Patrick," Isaac demands.

"Can't. He's away with his kids this weekend."

Isaac's eyes drift from the road to me. He watches me long enough there's no way he could miss the needy press of my thighs before he asks Hugo, "What kind of problem?"

"The manager was vague, but he said he has issues with a staff member issuing free drinks to his friends."

"Why the fuck can't the manager handle this type of situation?" Isaac interrupts, his thoughts parroting mine.

Hugo remains quiet, his ragged breaths the only indicator that he hasn't hung up.

"It's okay," I assure Isaac when I see the indecisiveness in his hooded gaze.

"Oh, hey, Isabelle," Hugo greets, his tone playful.

I smile, loving that he recognizes my voice from only hearing me speak two words.

"Hi." I bite my bottom lip, loathing that my greeting came out shy. I'm not shy. I'm just swimming in waters so far out of my depth that I face imminent drowning.

"I'll take care of it," Isaac informs Hugo before he disconnects the call without giving Hugo a chance to reply.

After freeing my lip from my teeth, he says, "Five minutes, tops, Then I'll be biting that lip."

22

———————

Isaac's nightclub is a few blocks from the Italian restaurant where we had dinner. It's a stylish club that screams sex and sensuality.

That saying is true—sex sells, and Isaac is using it to his full advantage in his nightclubs.

The club is packed with patrons, and the line to get in goes down the block and around the corner.

Upon entering the manager's office of 57, Isaac assesses the room. Four people are seated in the impressively large space. Two men appear petrified. One is smirking broadly, while the only female in the room is glaring at Isaac's hand wrapped around mine.

"You're both fired," Isaac informs them, pointing to the man with shoulder-length hair whose name tag says "manager" and to a twenty-something-year-old male staff member.

The manager attempts a remark, but the instant Isaac's livid eyes land on him, his mouth clamps shut. "If you can't handle a situation like this in-house, then you're *not* management material for my clubs. You"—he glares at the employee caught stealing—"will pay for any drinks you gave your friends before you leave."

The employee's throat works hard to swallow as he nods.

"And if you *ever* step foot in any of my clubs again—"

"I won't," he promises, his short reply incapable of hiding his fear.

Isaac turns to face a brute with a shaved head at the side of the room. He is massive. His bicep is bigger than my head. "Make sure he pays his bill before he leaves, and add a generous tip for the bar staff."

The bouncer smiles while nodding before he yanks the employee out of the chair by the scruff of his collar.

When they leave, he relinquishes my hand and heads for the mahogany desk. His strides are effortless yet commanding, and they make my pussy pulse with desire.

Watching him in his element is a riveting experience. He's bossy and demanding but still as sexy as sin.

When he reaches the desk, he removes a checkbook from the top drawer. "This will cover your severance."

He thrusts a torn-out check toward the manager. Just as he's about to accept it, Isaac yanks it back. "Or perhaps the fact you're leaving unscathed should be reward enough."

He scrunches the check into a ball before dumping it on the desk.

"Y-y-yes, thank you, boss." The manager's head wobbles like a bobblehead toy before he scampers out of the office, leaving the check where it fell.

The veins in my neck twang when Isaac shifts his focus to me. Most people would mistake his gaze as infuriating. I only see unbridled lust.

"Come here, Isabelle," he instructs, his voice tempered.

He snarls when I shake my head, denying his request, but it isn't directed at me when I announce the cause of my rejection. We're not alone. A female staff member remains in the corner, watching our exchange with her mouth ajar.

"Get out." My excitement intensifies when Isaac's dedication remains steadfast on me even while ordering her out of the room.

"Boss, while you're here, I wanted to ask—"

"Get out!" Isaac shouts again.

She nods before scurrying out of the room even faster than the manager.

Once we're alone, Isaac repeats his earlier demand. "Come here, Isabelle."

His tone is clipped, but it doesn't stop a tremor coursing through my body when my name rolls off his tongue.

Although his dominance instigates wetness to pool between my legs, it also pins me in place and makes me unable to move.

Isaac mutters something under his breath before he rounds the desk. He glides instead of walking as a mere man would.

That's not surprising.

Nothing about him could ever be seen as mere.

He crosses the room in under a second and crowds me against the heavy wooden door of the manager's office even quicker than that.

The first lash of his tongue to my gaping mouth causes my knees to buckle, and then his kiss makes me completely legless.

His kisses convey his personality perfectly—powerful, alluring, sexy, and knee-buckling hot.

He steadies my sways with one hand while the other holds my mouth hostage to his. His kiss is delicious and toe-curling good. It goes above and beyond my greatest expectations.

When I snake my fingers over the ridges of his back before raking them through his hair, he groans into my mouth.

The sound alone almost causes me to combust, so we won't mention my body's response when he keeps his promise by sinking his teeth into my bottom lip.

He bites on the fleshy skin with enough force to mark but not maim. It is an erotic, hot exchange that has me wishing I hadn't denied his advances for so long.

After Isaac's tongue soothes the sting of his bite, he glides it along mine, stroking and absorbing my taste.

He kisses me for several long minutes, stealing every last snippet of worry left lingering in my mind.

When he inches back, a whimper escapes my mouth. "Please," I beg, my dignity lost.

Just his fingers probing the pressure points at the back of my neck and the skills displayed in his kiss have me close to orgasmic bliss.

If he stops this now, I may never recover.

No longer capable of restraining myself, I thrust my hips upward. I moan when my oversensitive clit connects with the rim of Isaac's cock, and then all sense of control is lost.

Isaac bites, nibbles, and kisses my neck as he rocks his hips, grinding his erection against my damp panties.

One expert roll has me throwing my head back and my eyes snapping shut. It brings my orgasm to an inch of the finish line, but I still need more.

After marking my neck in a way that can't deny what event we're undertaking, he lowers his focus to my chest. He untethers the cord holding my dress together, hissing when my barely covered breasts are exposed.

When his eyes lift to mine, they no longer show torment and indecisiveness. They reflect nothing but unbridled horniness.

Isaac smirks while gliding his index finger along my bra's thin lacy material. His finger feels rough and smooth at the same time. It matches the throaty moan I release when he traps my nipple in his warm and inviting mouth.

After lavishing my breasts with his skilled tongue, he diverts his attention to the skin underneath my breasts and across my stomach.

His name rumbles up my throat when the tip of his nose grazes over my clit, but that's as far as the stimulation goes. He chuckles at my wail when he veers away from the one part of my body screaming for his attention.

I rake my fingers through his hair that's damp at the roots from the stifling heat in the office, before endeavoring to guide his head back to my pussy.

"Patience, Isabelle," Isaac breathes heavily against my thigh.

I want to protest, but watching him bite and suck on my inner thighs is a riveting experience. The sting of his teeth and the roughness of his five o'clock shadow assure me it won't be long until I'm screaming his name in ecstasy.

Usually, it takes dedicated attention to bring me to climax, but I'm so close to the brink that the slight brush of his fingertip on my clit will have me free-falling.

My breathing turns ragged when Isaac guides my left leg onto his shoulder. My body is so lax my movements are sluggish and slow. When he runs his nose down the seam of my panties, my toes curl.

He inhales an undignified whiff, not the slightest bit ashamed, before releasing it with a throaty growl. "You smell so fucking good."

When he sucks my clit into his mouth through my lace panties, an orgasm rips through my body so hard and fast stars form in front of my eyes.

Although we're in public, so there's a possibility we could be caught at any moment, I can't help but scream when Isaac slips my panties to the side and devours my pussy with powerful licks and greedy sucks.

The controls of my body have been relinquished to the man who caused it to implode with one heart-stopping suck.

Quiet ramblings spill from my mouth on repeat as Isaac slowly guides me down from the most intense orgasm I've ever experienced.

He consumes my pussy with dedicated licks and playful bites, not the least bit confronted I combusted within minutes of our exchange commencing.

Just as I rein in the shudders racking through my body, Isaac shreds my panties off me—their feeble material no match for his strength—before he continues devouring me without pause.

His eagerness to bring me to climax again adds to the giddiness hazing my mind.

"*Oh...*" I moan, stunned at how rapidly my second orgasm is building.

It is intense.

Blinding.

Perhaps even scary.

I lose the ability to hold up my weight when another toe-curling climax rockets through my body without warning. The only reason I don't tumble to the floor is because Isaac has my thighs pinned to the door, stopping my concern. The ease of his hold makes me seem as light as a feather.

After every climatic shake has been exhausted, Isaac stands and kisses me hard on the mouth. I can taste myself on his tongue when he slides it along my lips before delving it inside my mouth.

He kisses me until I'm close to combusting for the third time in under ten minutes.

When he drags his mouth away, I throw my head back and call out. This time, it isn't in euphoria.

It is from spotting a blinking red contraption in the corner of the room. Our every move is being monitored—possibly recorded.

Forever diligent, Isaac senses my hesitance. After pulling away from my nipples that are hard enough to cut diamonds, his confused eyes dance between mine.

"I want this," I assure him without hesitation when I notice his odd expression. "I just don't want to be recorded."

He's confused until I nudge my head to the camera, and then his hardened expression relaxes.

Did he think I was rejecting him? If he did, he has no reason to fret. He's the most riveting man I've ever met. I'd never reject him. My body is incapable of saying no to him. But the thought of someone watching us during an intimate act makes my stomach swirl.

"Can you get Hugo to turn the camera off?"

My body is thrumming from the two star-producing orgasms, but I'm not ready for our night to end just yet.

Isaac's tongue darts out to lick his lips. When his pupils dilate, I know he tastes me on his mouth. "I could." His voice is as rough as mine from the screams I released during climax. "But I want to fuck you in bed." He tilts my head so I'm looking at him, then says, "Because once I'm done with you, you'll no longer have the ability to walk straight."

I gulp, knowing what he says is fact, not fiction. He's barely touching me now, and my orgasm is once again teetering on the brink, dying to be freed.

After winking at the lust creeping across my cheeks, Isaac yanks his cell phone out of his pocket and squashes it to his ear. "I need you to wipe the images off the camera in the manager's office at 57 for the last hour." His mouth crimps before he nods. "Thanks, Hugo."

He disconnects his call and then places his cell phone into his pocket, along with my shredded panties.

Not speaking, he disappears into a bathroom, only to return five seconds later with a washcloth. My clit throbs when he cleans me in a nurturing manner. The rough and abrupt Isaac from when we first arrived at the club no longer exists, replaced with an attentive and gentle lover.

With a grin I've not seen him wear before, he ties my dress back into place. I eye him curiously, confident I missed something.

I make a promise to listen to my intuition more often when Isaac says, "Hugo turned the cameras off the instant he knew you were coming to the club with me." His smirk enlarges to a full-toothed smile. "At times, I swear he knows me better than I know myself."

Once I'm dressed, sans underwear, Isaac guides me out of the manager's office. Blaring music booms into my ears the instant we enter the hallway. Sweat clinging to heated skin steams in my nose from the mass of bodies dancing under warm, strobing lights.

Either oblivious or ignorant to the shocked stares of the patrons in his club, Isaac weaves us through the densely populated dance floor. It isn't a hard task. When the crowd sees Isaac coming, they part, giving us an unobstructed path to the club's exit doors.

The cool night air is refreshing to my sweat-slicked face and neck when we merge onto the sidewalk. I'm exhausted, but my excitement for what's about to come keeps my legs moving.

Isaac's grip on my hand tightens so much I wince when a heavily accented voice snarls, "The prodigal son returns."

"Get in the car, Isabelle."

Isaac shoves me toward his sleek sports car before he spins on his heels to face his greeter head-on.

Too curious for my own good, I also turn around. My pulse thuds in my ears for a completely different reason when my eyes lock on the non-stoic face of Col Petretti, suspected mob boss and the twelfth most wanted man on the FBI wish list.

To Col's right is the man the bureau believes is his top henchman. He's been with Col for longer than I've been born, yet he remains nameless. The FBI simply calls him Col's right-hand man.

To Col's left is his youngest son, Dimitri. I've yet to peruse his file, but I believe it is as thick as his father's since he's being groomed to take over the family business.

Isaac glares at Col furiously. The twitching of his jaw is so profound I can almost hear its ticks.

"What's it been... six years? And I don't even get a greeting from you." Col's words drip with sarcasm. However, Isaac doesn't take a nibble from the bait he's dangling in front of him.

He remains quiet, his fists clenched and his jaw spasming... until Col's focus shifts to me.

When he rakes his eyes down my body, my skin crawls. It is a demoralizing gawk that has me regretting the food I scarfed down during dinner.

Upon noticing the direction of Col's gaze, Isaac pulls me into his side.

Col mocks Isaac's protectiveness. He inhales a giant, undignified whiff through his nostrils, pretending he can smell his fear.

Isaac doesn't take his taunt sitting down. He shifts his narrowed eyes to Dimitri, who is more focused on his phone than the bone-rattling showdown between two men I'm confident have battled more than once.

When Dimitri's focus lowers to his polished black shoes, Isaac sniffs back. Col appears lost until he follows the direction of Isaac's gaze. When he spots Dimitri's lowered head, his jaw spasms and his nostrils flare before he shouts, "Go!"

Dimitri's eyes snap up from his phone and shoot to his father. He appears a little lost or perhaps considering a response.

I wait with bated breath. From what I've read on Col, if Dimitri denies his direct order, his punishment will be severe—favorite son or not.

I expel the breath caught in my throat when Dimitri does as ordered. He walks away from our group.

With one battle lost, Col takes another shot. He steps so close I can smell the herbs that garnished his meal tonight.

His eyes scan my flustered, post-orgasmic face before whispering, "You're exquisite. You have the face of an angel." His volume drops even lower. "*E voi diventerete uno.*"

When he attempts to touch me, Isaac snatches his wrist and yanks it back before he can. His grip is firm enough even Col's wrinkles can't hide his grimace.

"Don't fucking touch her," Isaac snarls, his tone clipped and unnerving.

My heart skips a beat when Col's right-hand man adjusts his suit jacket to expose he's carrying two semi-automatic Glocks on his waist.

"Isaac, let's go."

I scramble backward, pulling Isaac with me, but his stance is so strong that he doesn't budge an inch.

His angry gaze remains focused on Col. His jaw is spasming, and his his back molars are grinding together.

"Please, Isaac, he has a gun," I beg, motioning my head to Col's henchman.

If he doesn't agree to come with me, I'll blow my cover and announce I'm an agent. Col has always been paranoid about being infiltrated by an undercover agent, so my confession may scare him enough to force him to end our exchange immediately.

Isaac's eyes flick to Col's henchman for the briefest second. He sniffs, goading him before he says, "A real man doesn't need a gun. His body is his weapon." He relinquishes Col's wrist from his grip before taking a step back. "It'll be in your best interest to remember that."

I sigh in gratitude when he recommences directing me to his vehicle, not once glancing back on Col or his henchman left speechless on the sidewalk.

23

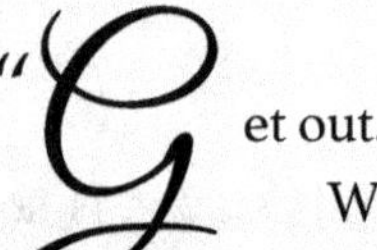

"**G**et out."

While shaking my head, I relatch the seat belt Isaac recently unlatched.

"For once, do as you're told. Get. Out!"

Again, I shake my head. "No."

Isaac growls. This time, it isn't a sexy-as-sin growl. It's a rumble that shows his unrelenting anger.

He throws open the driver's side door so hard I'm surprised he doesn't break the hinges, stomps to the passenger door, and then yanks it open so violently I cannot hold it closed.

Once I'm cradled in his arms like a bride on her wedding night, he angrily strides to the veranda of Cormack's family's mansion, only stopping once he dumps me onto a wicker chair.

His slit-eyed gaze snaps to me the instant I spring out of the chair. "Stay here."

I freeze, scared by his infuriating glare.

I'm not stupid. I know where he's going and what he plans to do when he gets there. That's why I'm trying to stop him from leaving. You can't insult a man with a reputation like Isaac's and not create a devastating ripple.

Isaac didn't utter a word the entire drive home. He clutched the steering wheel tightly and kept his focus on the road.

I tried to soothe his anger, but nothing I said altered the furious mask marring his handsome face. He was in the car with me, but his mind was elsewhere.

Tires screech as Isaac's car rockets out of the driveway, gaining the attention of Harlow and Cormack, who are sitting in the den.

Cormack rushes onto the patio before asking, "What's going on?"

"We ran into Col Petretti on the way home," I stutter, my mind too blurred with confusion to acknowledge I'm exposing a proficiency with mafia entities.

"What happened?" Panic echoes in Cormack's tone. "Did Col say anything? Do anything? Izzy?"

He shakes me, lifting my fogged haze. "He didn't say anything. Well, he did. He said I have the face of an angel." I'm confused as to why that would cause a negative response from Isaac, and the bewilderment colors my tone.

Cormack is clearly not in the dark as much as I am. "Fuck." He scrubs his hand over his head. "Where did you see Col?"

"At 57." My eyes lock with his as hope forms. "Can you stop him?"

He *pffts* me. "No one can stop Isaac, but that doesn't mean I won't try."

He places a peck on Harlow's gaping mouth before he darts to a garage housing his extensive collection of pricy cars.

———

By the time Isaac and Cormack return, two hours have ticked by. Harlow encouraged me to take a shower and change out of my dress, but I've spent the last hour and a half wearing a hole in the expensive Persian rug in the den.

Isaac drifts his eyes to me as he enters the room. His anger is still visible in his narrowed gaze, not to mention his balled hands.

I scan his body and sigh in relief when I notice he is without injury.

My steps toward him halt when he exits the room as quickly as he arrived. I'm tempted to go after him but lose the nerve when Cormack warns against it.

"You won't get anything out of him, Izzy." His tone is as low as my heart now sits. "He locks up his emotions tighter than Fort Knox."

"Then you either tell me what's going on, or I'll force him to tell me."

I want answers, and I want them now.

"If you force him, you'll lose him forever."

Tears well in my eyes so fast they burn from the sudden rush of moisture.

"I haven't seen him look at anyone the way he looks at you in years," Cormack says, lessening my fret. "Not since Ophelia, but if you force his hand, you will lose him."

I dance my eyes between Cormack's repentant pair, silently pleading for more information.

Who is Ophelia?

What did he mean when he said Isaac looks at me differently?

Did Ophelia force Isaac's hand previously?

And last but not at all least, is Isaac as captivated with me as I am him?

Cormack responds to my wordless interrogation, but it is not close to what I need. "If he wants you to know, he will tell you himself."

I've been tossing and turning for the past several hours. I'm exhausted from my earlier orgasms, but the gnawing pit in my chest is keeping me awake.

The tension between Col and Isaac was palpable, but it seemed much more than solely rivalry at play. Their hate for each other is personal and delves deeper than a mob turf war. I'm certain of it.

When hinges creak, I crank my neck to the door of my room. My pupils widen when Isaac enters under the cloak of darkness. He's wearing the same three-piece suit he wore at dinner, though more crumpled.

I remain quiet when he undresses at the foot of the bed. He removes his shoes first, closely followed by his jacket and business shirt. His strip tease ends when he's down to nothing but black boxer shorts.

My heart squeezes when he slides between the sheets and flips me over until my opposite hip is indenting the mattress. When he splays his hand across my stomach and tugs me back, my curvy backside flattens against his erect cock.

I'm almost sure his anger is forgotten until he murmurs, "No questions. Just sleep, Isabelle."

I don't know how he expects me to sleep. Not only are hundreds of questions running through my head, but his monstrous package is also grinding against my ass.

Sleep is the last thing on my mind.

Isaac must sense my reluctance. He glides his hand up and down my arm in a soothing motion, lengthening my blinks.

Over time, my breathing shallows, and I fall into a blissful yet lusty sleep.

I don't need to open my eyes to know Isaac is no longer in my room. His aura permeates the air. His power, stature, and importance are something you feel, not visualize. That's how I know he left hours ago.

After sluggishly opening my eyes, I quickly stretch, adoring the stiffness two toe-curling orgasms caused my body. Isaac's confrontation with Col filtered through my mind all night, but I slept restfully. Consecutive climaxes shatter me, so when you add that to being spooned by a man with a seemingly impenetrable shell, I slept like a baby.

I climb out of bed and head to the guest bathroom. My toes grip the carpet pile as I increase the length of my strides, the shower beckoning me to it.

Images of Isaac nipping, lashing, and tasting my mouth rush to the forefront of my mind when spurts of warm water cling to my top lip.

My leisurely shower becomes hurried when my tongue darts out to wet my top lip. I can still taste Isaac on my mouth.

I dry myself before securing my recently shampooed hair into a messy bun. With the temperature already hot enough to announce I'll either spend the day catching a cool sea breeze or swimming in the grotto pool, I turn my eyes to the bikini hanging on the railing in the bathroom.

Confident it will aid in releasing Isaac's tension from last night, I pop them on with a pair of tiny cotton shorts and a crushed natural linen blouse I leave open at the front.

When I exit my room, I balk. Compared to the bustle of the main house yesterday, today it's eerily quiet.

I move through the vast rooms of the McGregor residence at the speed of a rocket, seeking any signs of life.

I veer left when a hive of activity sounds through the French doors attached to a rec room. Upon exiting, I notice a buffet set up on the covered patio next to the pool. Harlow, Cormack, Cate, and Colby are gathered around a wrought iron table, enjoying the splendor of croissants, fresh fruit, pastries, and coffee.

When Harlow motions for me to join them, I signal that I'll be right over once I have my required morning caffeine fix in my hot little hands.

I nearly drop my mug of coffee when "Isabelle" rolls off a tongue that had me quivering last night.

Isaac steps closer, trapping me between his fit body and the buffet table. I don't think he's hard, but he doesn't need to be for my deviant head to acknowledge the thickness braced against my thin cotton shorts. And don't get me started on his delicious scent lingering in my nostrils, or I'll never leave this buffet table with my dignity intact.

Air catches in my throat when Isaac takes advantage of my frozen state to raid the buffet. He snags a croissant off the table, his arm skimming my side boob on the way.

When my nipples bud, loving his meekest touch, he smirks, winks, and then leaves, his cockiness uncontained.

Once the shred of dignity I barely hold is collected, I mosey to the table where everyone is gathered.

"Holy fuck." Colby stares at me with his mouth gaping for several long seconds before he stumbles out of his chair. "Ta-take my seat."

I try to hide my smile at the clumsy delivery of his offer, but I find it endearing that the sight of me has him tripping over himself. My lips tug higher before I can stop them.

When Colby notices my smile, he shakes his head and chuckles. "You have me acting like a teenage boy." He doesn't stutter this time around. "But seriously, Izzy, you need to issue a warning before you bring out *that* ammunition." His lusty eyes lock onto my chest at the end of his statement. "Where the hell were you hiding *them* yesterday?"

Since I assume his question is rhetorical, I remain quiet.

My assumption is proven wrong when he cocks his brow, impatiently awaiting a response.

My answer is daft but the only one I can give. "Under my shirt."

Colby chuckles before waggling his brows. "You should bring those puppies out to play more often. I—"

He's interrupted by a stern cough across the table. While shooting daggers at his little brother, Cormack says, "You were warned yesterday."

Colby isn't fazed by his brother's glare or statement. He smiles and winks before whipping off his shirt.

In case you're wondering, I'm not the only one hiding desirable assets with clothing. Colby's pecs are impressive, his stomach is ridged, and his guns are banging. But even with his drool-worthy body on display, he still can't compete with Isaac.

Isaac's body isn't just perfect. It's pussy-clenching delicious.

No one could ever steal my admiration for that man.

My bare feet pad along the ebony hardwood floor as I go to the room Cormack assigned to me this weekend. I desperately need a shower to rid my body of the sand and salt embedded on my skin. I'm still wearing my bikini, but I placed a blue cotton dress over the damp material hours ago.

Tonight's setting for dinner was casual, but I still don't think it's suitable to wear only swimwear at any dinner table, though no one informed Colby of that.

He sat barefoot and in only board shorts. His hair was tousled loosely on top of his head, and his pasty-white skin had colored from spending hours at the beach.

Colby is such a charmer. He could woo the panties off any girl he sets his sights on, but he chose the wrong lady to pursue. My attention remains fixed on Isaac, even though he's giving clear signs he wants to be left alone.

I felt his eyes on me throughout the day, but we haven't exchanged a single word. His gloomy mood should make me hesitate to interact with him, but for some reason, it doesn't. I don't believe his sulky attitude should be rewarded, but I can't help but feel I'm missing out on a prime opportunity to unearth the real Isaac Holt— the one no one else gets to see.

My mind is such a jumbled mess I'm beginning to wonder if our exchange in his nightclub office happened or if my overactive imagination is more phenomenal than I comprehended.

One might assume my focus is consumed with unearthing every detail about Col and Isaac's relationship, considering unraveling that secret would be critical for the bureau's investigation, but it isn't.

I can't stop thinking about what Cormack said.

Who is Ophelia, and what does she mean to Isaac?

Why would I lose Isaac if I tried to coerce him to share information?

And why did a dark pit form in my chest the instant I thought I might lose him?

These are the questions I desperately want answered, but no one seems willing to tackle them.

As I enter the hallway of my room, the flash of a smirk halts my long strides. Isaac is leaning against the doorjamb of my room a few doors down from where I've stopped. His arms are crossed in front of his chest, and the edge of danger beaming out of him would have most men shuddering in their boots. Instead of feeling fear, my body quivers with anticipation, and stupid butterflies form in my stomach.

I offer him a friendly smile before bridging the gap between us. The grooves between his brows would have you convinced I'm not trying to hide my nerves with a megawatt smile.

He's angry—still.

As I skirt past him to enter my room, he seizes my wrist, halting both my wish to flee and my heart.

Air traps in my throat when he tilts in close and says, "Stay away from Colby."

Shocked at the direction of his anger, I grit my teeth before yanking open my room door with enough force for it to slam into Isaac's hip.

The hit doesn't keep him down for even a second. "You shouldn't have a problem with my request unless you're interested in him," he snarls out, following me into my room. "Are you interested in him, Isabelle?"

His question doesn't warrant a reply, so I glare at him instead.

He isn't the slightest bit intimidated by my anger. If anything, he finds it amusing. His eyes shimmer with mischief, and his lips curve high.

Needing to do something before I kiss his smirk off his face, I say, "I'll answer your question if you answer one of mine."

"Not going to happen," he instantly replies, not even considering my suggestion.

Anger boils up from my stomach to my face, but since I don't want to give him the satisfaction of knowing he's made me upset, I demand he leave my room before I march into the bathroom and slam the door behind me.

While striving to get my anger under control, I have the longest shower I've ever had. I take my time pampering my exhausted body.

The past forty-eight hours have felt like the longest days of my life. I'm not solely exhausted. I am also emotionally drained.

My interactions with Isaac have given me the worst case of whiplash. He goes from lavishing me with his attention to cold and distant quicker than I can snap my fingers. But no matter how hard I fight to force him to the back of my mind, he always pushes to the front, demanding every ounce of my attention.

And I give it to him because even hardly knowing him doesn't stop my heart from yearning for him when he isn't around.

I freeze when a disturbing thought enters my head.

Even covered in body wash, I exit the shower, dazed and confused.

When I catch my wide-eyed expression in the vanity mirror, the truth can't be hidden for a second longer.

No, I can't be.

I'm not allowed to fall in love with Isaac.

He's a target.

A mobster.

He's the very definition of the men I agreed to take down when I joined the academy.

I can't fall in love with a man I'm investigating. I hardly know him. He is a stranger. So what if he makes every hair on my body bristle to attention with the simplest touch? That doesn't mean anything. Right?

With my head screaming "no" on repeat, I remove the bubbles with a thick towel and throw on a pair of panties and a short-sleeved cotton shirt I find discarded on the floor.

When I exit the bathroom, I freeze for the second time.

"What are you doing in my bed?"

Isaac's shirtless torso is leaning against the leather headboard of my bed.

"This is *my* bed," he responds, "and that's *my* shirt." He points to the shirt I've just put on.

"What?" Confusion clusters in my head so fast that I feel giddy. "This is the room Cormack assigned to me."

Isaac shakes his head. "This is my room. I brought you in here the first night when you blacked out on the plane, and last night—"

"You didn't sleep with me because you wanted to. You slept with me because I was sleeping in your bed," I interrupt. "I'm so sorry." I shove my clothes into my suitcase with the urgency of a wife who walked in on her husband cheating. "I didn't realize."

I'm almost packed when Isaac yanks my suitcase out of my grasp, places it back onto the luggage stand, and then says, "Get in bed, Isabelle."

I shake my head. "There are at least a dozen rooms in this mansion. I'm sure I'll have no trouble finding a warm bed for the night."

"Now!" Isaac barks, startling me.

His eyes never leave mine as he glides back under the sheets. He's not goading me to make a break for it. He is displaying his confidence that I'm not going anywhere because he already knows what my head doesn't want to acknowledge.

I love him.

I suck in numerous breaths to settle my nerves before stepping toward the bed.

"Good choice," Isaac murmurs when I slide in next to him.

Over the next two hours, I count every rose petal adorning the ceiling medallion. It was tedious because I had to wait for the moon to adjust its position to finish the lower half.

Even in the darkness of the night, my heart still skips a beat when I spot Isaac's profile. He has such alluring features I can't help but stare. Plump lips, a straight nose, and his dimpled chin couldn't look bad even if covered with days of growth. He's so attractive my heated stare is busted only seconds into my gawk.

"You should take a picture. It'll last longer."

I smile before rolling onto my hip to face him head-on. "Are you awake?"

He mimics my position while answering, "Yep. You need to learn to count in your head."

"I'm so sorry," I respond, grimacing. "I have a terrible habit of mumbling out loud."

"I've come to realize that," he jibes, his tone playful.

We lay across from each other in silence for several minutes, each appraising the other's moonlit face in great detail. I have so many questions I want to ask him, but shockingly, not one of them has to do with the investigation the bureau is running on him.

I'm about to assess his face for the hundredth time when Isaac veers our exchange in a direction I never saw coming. "One question."

After drawing in a shaky breath, I ask the one thing I've wanted to know since last night. "Did you love Ophelia?"

A jab hits me square in the chest when he answers without hesitation. "Yes."

"Do you still love her?"

I realize I have a lot to learn about interrogation and tact when he answers, "I said one question," before he rolls onto his opposite hip and pretends to sleep.

24

As I stumble into the private jet, my knees knock with every step. Isaac is seated on the only single reclining chair. This is the first time I've seen him today. When I woke this morning, he had already vacated our room.

He jerks up his chin in greeting before devoting his attention to the plane's window, revealing his dreary mood from yesterday has returned full force.

I plop into the closest chair before fumbling with my belt. I'm all thumbs, meaning I can't get the buckle to latch together.

Seeing my struggle, Isaac cusses under his breath before he releases his belt to aid in securing mine.

Once my belt is tight around my waist, he returns to the reclining chair.

With everyone seated, the jet taxis toward the runway, and I grip the armrest for dear life. I'd give anything to wipe away the stupid tear sitting high on my left cheek, but I'm too terrified to loosen my grip on the armrest.

The closer we get to the end of the runway, the more my panicked pants fill the silence of the cab. I feel like I'm drowning even without being near a drop of water. My fear is asphyxiating me.

"Breathe," Isaac demands upon hearing my loud wheezes.

My body snaps to his command, but my panic is too intense to fully surrender. I can't get enough oxygen, and my lungs are burning in protest. I genuinely feel like I'm suffocating.

When I shake my head, wordlessly relaying that I can't fill my lungs, Isaac kneels in front of me. I want to scream at him to return to his seat and put his belt on this instant, but my fear has rendered me speechless.

He clasps my hands in his before aligning our eyes. "Breathe, Isabelle."

This time, my body obeys. The crippling pain spread across my chest lessens when I inhale a sharp, greedy breath.

"Good girl."

He brushes away a handful of tears marking my cheeks, his touch almost loving. Once he's taken care of the moisture on my face, he traces the cupid's bow on my top lip. Not even tasting the saltiness of my tears can stop tingles from dancing across my face.

New tears form in my eyes. It isn't just my fear of flying that has me wanting to sob. It is from glancing into the eyes of the man I've fallen in love with and knowing I can't have both him and my career.

Without warning, Isaac unlatches my belt and pulls me into his arms.

"What are you doing?"

He doesn't grace me with a reply. He continues toward the back of the plane, his strides effortless and graceful.

When we enter the bedroom at the end, Isaac secures the lock and then places me on the bed. My insides tighten when he stoops down to unclasp my shoes.

Once they're removed, he dumps them next to the springy mattress before toeing off his polished dress shoes.

My pulse rings in my ears when he undoes his cufflinks so he can remove his jacket. His striptease this time around is as tempting as late night's brief show—perhaps even a little more since his eyes aren't holding their earlier anguish.

Electricity bolts up my arm when he plucks me up from the bed.

My breasts press against his chest, budding my nipples as he asks, "Do you want this?"

I nod.

"No, Isabelle. Say it," he demands, apparently unimpressed with my non-verbal reply.

My thighs shake as I say, "I want this."

He smirks before stepping back. When he hears my shameful groan about the loss of his contact, his sultry grin makes my thighs shudder more.

He rakes his eyes down my body before returning them to my face. My furious pulse drops from my ears to my clit when he says, "Strip."

Embarrassment swamps me, but the desire in his eyes has me feeling more daring than usual, so I strip as instructed.

Isaac stares at me like I'm his salvation as I undo each button of my shirt. His eyes remain fixated on my face until the last button on my blouse is undone.

When I shimmy my shoulders, sending my shirt plummeting to the floor, he draws in a sharp breath. My lingerie is a steel-gray Victoria's Secret Dream Angel padded-bra-and-lace-panties combination. I purchased it when I realized its dark-gray coloring perfectly matches Isaac's eyes—especially when they're primal and hungry.

I stop slithering my arms around my back to unlatch my bra when Isaac says, "Leave the bra."

His wicked smile when I jump to his command for the umpteenth time this weekend makes me wet.

While chewing on my bottom lip, I undo the button of my jeans and then lower the fly.

As I tug them down my thighs, Isaac loosens the knot on his tie, his eyes never leaving me. His smile grows when he notices my color-coordinated panties.

"Please don't shred these. They cost *way* more than you think."

He doesn't grace me with a reply. He smirks while twisting his tie around his right hand and pacing closer to me. "Are you a screamer, Isabelle?"

"No."

That may be because no guy has made my body ignite the way Isaac can, but it is the truth nonetheless.

My clit thuds when a salacious smirk stretches across his face before he growls, "You're about to become one."

I roll my eyes at his pigheadedness, but the lash of his tongue on my mouth has them freezing halfway.

Our kiss is as violent as the pent-up frustration we've faced over the past two days.

I yank the hem of his business shirt out of his pants before fumbling with its finicky pearl buttons. When they refuse to cooperate with my desperate hands, I clasp his shirt in my hands and rip it open.

Isaac groans into my mouth when the buttons sprawl onto the polished wooden floor and tinkle around us. "That shirt cost way more than you think."

I tug on his black leather belt before lifting my eyes to his. "I'm sure you can afford another one."

My blood thickens with lust when his chuckle rumbles through my pussy.

Through a stimulating blur of bites, sucks, and kisses, I become trapped between the wall and Isaac. When he curls my legs around his waist, I grind myself along the ridges of his cock, my patience to feel him inside me stretched thin.

"Do you have a condom?" I ask, praying to the Lord he has some form of protection.

I'll never forgive myself if I have to stop this now.

Isaac wets his lips before slipping his hand into his pocket. I smile when he produces a Trojan condom. The tingles wreaking havoc with my pussy grow when he rolls the condom down his gorgeously thick cock.

Once it's in place, he returns his eyes to mine. Air leaves my lungs in a rush when he shreds my panties off my body in one quick tug, their frail material no match for his strength.

"You're buying me another pair."

Because I pull his lips to mine by the back of his sweat-drenched head, he has to talk over my mouth. "It will be my pleasure."

Cupping my ass, he guides me backward until my torso braces on a wood-paneled wall. When the crown of his cock brushes the entrance of my pussy, my eyes drift to the bed.

My mind was hazy from two earth-shuddering orgasms, but I'm reasonably sure he said he wanted to fuck me in a bed. Something about me no longer having the ability to walk once he was done with me?

When he notices the direction of my gaze, Isaac says, "Next time."

I smile, pleased he's already planning a second round.

My body instinctively tenses when Isaac says, "Hold on, baby, this is going to hurt."

My nails dig into his shoulders when he impales me in one ardent thrust. Tears spring to my eyes as I struggle to acclimate to taking a man of his size without preparation.

It hurts—even more than it did when I lost my virginity.

With his eyes locked on my face, Isaac remains motionless, giving me time to adjust to his sheer girth. Although my body is stinging with pain, it's also relishing the pleasure of being the fullest it's ever been.

My cheeks heat when Isaac murmurs, "Fuck, you're tight."

Suddenly, he stiffens before his eyes search mine. No words escape his lips, but his freaked expression is questioning enough.

"Thank fuck," he mutters when I shake my head at his unspoken interrogation.

It's been a while since I've participated in anything remotely sexual, but I'm not a virgin.

Isaac adjusts me until I'm positioned in a way designed for pleasure more than pain before asking, "Ready?"

Instead of gracing him with a reply, I squeeze his cock with the walls of my vagina. His raspy moan nearly makes me combust on the spot, much less the pulses of his cock as he slowly inches out of me.

The first few pumps are painful, but the pleasure far outweighs the discomfort, so I encourage him to continue.

"More. Please."

Over the next several minutes, he thrusts into me on repeat before adding a flick to his hips. His prowess is outstanding. Most men would have bowed out after the first squeeze of my pussy, but Isaac powers on, and soon, my orgasm builds with the same level of intensity he's showcasing to fuck me senseless.

When Isaac pulls down my bra and traps my nipple in his mouth, I throw back my head and moan. While maintaining the tempo that's driving me into a quivering, blubbering mess, his skillful tongue and mouth tease my nipples into hardened peaks.

I'm moments away from free-falling into orgasmic bliss. My body is heightened beyond belief.

"Eyes on me, Isabelle," Isaac demands when the power of our exchange overwhelms me so much my eyelids flutter shut.

After forcing my eyes back open, I tighten my grip around his shoulders, afraid I may fall during ecstasy. I'm spiraling so fast I'm certain my limbs will surrender as quickly as my morals do when I'm in the presence of this alluring man.

"I've got you," Isaac assures me, sensing my concern.

He's got me.

It feels so good.

He is so deep, and I'm stretched so wide.

So full.

So...

Oh.

His name thunders from my lips when I implode into the most body-shattering orgasm I've ever experienced.

I moan on repeat while relishing the spark adoring every inch of my body. I can't stop shaking. Moaning. The strength of my climax is blindsiding.

I'm so overwhelmed by the sensation heating my veins that I snap my eyes shut.

"Eyes, Isabelle," Isaac barks out, never once easing his unrelenting thrusts that have reduced me to a tremoring mess.

When my eyes pop back open, my climax intensifies. His watch is primal, and it enhances the ferocity of the electricity crackling in the air.

I moan again when his hooded watch stretches my orgasm from the length of one to two.

Once every pleasurable shudder has been exhausted, Isaac moves us to the bed. A disappointed moan spills from my lips when his throbbing cock slides out of my pussy before he places me on my feet at the end of the mattress.

"Bend over the bed, palms flat on the sheets." Isaac's voice is hoarse with lust. "Legs open wide."

Blinded by excitement, I do as requested without protest.

When I hear the hiss of a man who likes what he sees, I tilt my head to the side and peer behind me. My mouth salivates when my eyes lock in on Isaac's magnificent body. Just watching a bead of sweat roll down the bumps in his stomach before being absorbed by the dark patch of hairs above his mouthwatering cock has me on the verge of toppling into ecstasy all over again.

My heart rate kicks into overdrive when Isaac spots my gawk. He hits me with a frisky wink before he places his dark-blue tie over my eyes and then secures it behind my head.

"It will heighten your senses."

I nod instead of telling him I don't need any assistance in enlightening my senses when he's in my vicinity.

Isaac adjusts my position so my ass is thrust high into the air before his hand slips between my legs. My knees scrape across the crisp sheets when his index finger finds my clit not even two seconds later.

My breaths come out in ripples when he says, "Open wider, Isabelle. I want to see all of you."

Either too impatient to wait or as eager as I am to move our exchange forward, Isaac pries open my thighs to his desired width before he takes a step back.

When ruffling sounds behind me, I prick my ears, straining to unearth every move he makes.

Thankfully, I'm not left in suspense for long.

Time stands still when the head of Isaac's cock braces the opening of my pussy.

"This will be hard and fast."

He waits for me to nod before slamming back into me with one quick thrust. I purr a grunted moan of satisfaction, relishing being filled by him again.

He fucks like a well-oiled machine, ramping my screams up from breathless to ear-piercing in no time.

My moans lengthen when one of his hands grips my hip and the other fists my hair. His hold is dominant and strong and has my second orgasm rapidly gaining in intensity.

He takes charge of my body.

Commands every inch of it.

He fucks me how I've never been fucked.

The wave in my stomach crests when he tilts my head back so he can cover his mouth over mine. His tongue invades my mouth as roughly as his cock assaults my pussy. The stimulating kiss hits every one of my hot buttons, and it pushes my third climax to within an inch of the finish line.

I grip the satin sheets in a white-knuckled hold when an orgasm rockets through my body like fireworks exploding in a dark sky.

Isaac's husky grunts become more prominent when I muffle my screams with a pillow. I never thought I was a screamer, but Isaac has proven me wrong. My throat is as raw as my heart.

I knew he would be fantastic in bed, but I'm still astounded by his stamina.

"One more," Isaac grunts once I've returned from oblivion.

I shake my head. My body is slack, unresponsive, and covered head to toe in sweat. The only reason I'm still upright is because of his grip on my hip. The sting of his fingers is partly responsible for the wetness caking my skin.

A squeal rips from my mouth when Isaac flips me onto my back. I blink in quick succession to adjust to the brightness illuminating the room when he removes my blindfold.

Any further protests are disregarded when I catch his expression as he stuffs his cock back inside me. He looks as content as my body feels.

He swallows my moan when his mouth seals over mine. This time, his kiss is passionate and slow, expanding my heart with every caress, nibble, and lick.

Even his relentless pumps ease. He still has control of every inch of my body, but he's more making love to me now instead of fucking me into oblivion.

When he tilts my hips higher, giving him unrestricted access to my throbbing pussy, I'm surprised by the familiar tightening in my lower stomach.

My next release gains intensity so quickly that Isaac has no choice but to demand my eyes back to his.

"Eyes," Isaac grunts between thrusts.

My orgasm sprints over the finish line, excited he can already intuit my body so well he knows when I'm moments away from climax.

His groan vibrates through my pussy when I hook my leg higher on his waist so our hips can grind in sync.

I want him to lose control.

To surrender to the madness.

I want him as spent and exhausted as I am.

He pumps into me on repeat, stealing the air from my lungs with every perfect stroke until I'm overcome by tingles for the umpteenth time tonight.

"Oh god…" I pant.

The desire to snap my eyes shut is overwhelming when I surrender to the madness of an all-encompassing orgasm, but I keep them open, fighting through the sensation eating me whole. I quiver and shake as my pussy tightens around Isaac's cock, silently begging for him to spiral out of control with me.

When my nails dig into his ass with enough force to mark, spurts of cum erupt from his cock.

"Fuck, Isabelle," he groans before trapping my bottom lip

between his teeth. His bite is painful, but his tongue soon soothes the pain.

Once every drop of cum has been released, he frees my lip from his menacing teeth before rolling off me. I can't help but smile when he needs a minute to recover before he stands from the bed to remove his condom.

Once he's disposed of the condom into a trash can, he rejoins me in bed. Even exhausted beyond comprehension, my cheeks burn from their high incline when he spoons his sweaty torso around my equally sticky back.

With multiple star-inspiring orgasms rendering me immobile, I soon fall into a blissful post-orgasmic sleep.

"Isabelle..."

I shoo away something brushing over my lips. When they chuckle in response to my grunted request to be left alone, and it dawns on me that I'm not waking up alone in my apartment, I jolt upright and crash into a hard surface.

"Shit," I mumble while rubbing the sting on my forehead.

The sting switches to a throb when I spot the cause for my early morning head knock.

The incredibly attractive and fully dressed Mr. Isaac Holt is standing at the side of the private jet's bed, pinching the bridge of his nose.

Oh shit!

I scamper across rumpled bedding and yank his hand away from his nose to inspect it. "Is it bleeding?"

"It's fine."

I continue with my perusal of his nose while he appraises my naked body. I'm too mortified that I headbutted him twice in less than six months to relish in the delight of his eagerness to pursue my nakedness for the second time today.

"I'm fine," Isaac growls when I continue to fuss over him.

He must have been close when I lurched up, as his nose already has a red bump forming. A reason for his closeness is unearthed when I lick my lips. I can taste him on my mouth.

"Were you kissing—"

"We're back in Ravenshoe."

"What?" I stammer, utterly confused.

When I dart my eyes to the window, I gasp. The plane is in an airport hangar instead of in the sky.

"Why didn't you wake me?"

"You looked tired. I wanted you to sleep."

I smile before clambering out of bed and yanking on my shirt and jeans sans underwear.

My happiness takes a massive step back when what he said dawns on me.

"We did the entire landing *without a seat belt*?" My last four words are shouted. "Are you insane?"

He scoffs at me. "Do you truly believe a scrap of material will save you when a plane is plummeting to the ground?"

I freeze as my brows furrow. "I'm never flying again."

Isaac chuckles before clasping my hand in his and guiding me out of a room that smells like raunchy sex. I scrunch my brows when I discover the plane is deserted. My bewilderment intensifies when I spot Hugo leaning on Isaac's town car when we exit the aircraft's galley.

"We landed over two hours ago," Isaac confesses.

My eyes bulge. "You let me sleep that long?"

"You looked tired."

My smile remains planted on my face while Hugo stows our luggage in the back of Isaac's car and during the entire trip back to my apartment. It only falters when I catch the quickest glimmer of remorse in Isaac's eyes when he follows me into the elevator of my building.

"Did you want to come inside?" I ask once we reach the front door of my apartment.

My heart plummets to my stomach when Isaac shakes his head. "I have some business to take care of."

He's lying. He always maintains eye contact when he's being truthful, but his eyes strayed to the floor when I asked if he wanted to come in.

"Okay." Ignoring the pit in my chest, I thrust my hand toward him. "Thank you for a lovely weekend."

My cordial gesture puts him off, but he still accepts my hand. He doesn't shake it, however. He raises it to his mouth and kisses my palm.

"The pleasure was all mine, Isabelle," he croons before spinning on his heels and striding down the hall.

I stand mute, utterly confused as to why his departure appears fueled by reluctance instead of relief.

25

"*If* you sign a contract, you're required to fulfill your contract for set amount of time on said contract."

"But—"

"No buts, Isabelle. You're not getting out of your contract. I don't care if your cat gets run over by a truck or your grandma dies. You signed a contract, so you will fulfill your obligation," Alex snarls. "Now go do the job you're paid to do." His angry roar reverberates through the office building.

After gathering the scraps of dignity I have left, I scamper out of his office. I've just experienced the worst shredding of my life. He tore me apart.

After tossing and turning all night, I concluded that my relationship with Isaac is unethical, no matter how confusing it may be.

So, not wanting to shroud Alex's team and my uncle's name in controversy, I decided it would be best to relocate my position to another unit.

There are hundreds. No, scrap that. Thousands of people are targeted by the FBI every week, so it wouldn't be difficult to be transferred to another unit, but the instant I suggested a transfer to Alex, he shot it down.

He refused my request, scrunched my transfer application into a ball, and threw it into the trash. He then went on a half-hour-long tirade about my integrity and due diligence to his team and how I'd let everyone down by transferring to another unit.

Who would have thought a coffee girl was such an integral part of a team?

Brandon's eyes lift as I hurry past his desk.

"What crawled up his ass and died?" I ask.

He grins before shaking his head. After dumping my satchel into the bottom drawer of my desk, I plop onto my chair and fire up my computer.

The first thing that pops up on my monitor is the results of the extended search I'd started for Megan Shroud before I went away. I had completely forgotten about her.

I'm so immersed in reading Megan's extensive medical history report that I don't notice Brandon until he waves a manila folder in my face.

"Hey," I greet, my mind hazy. "Did you look any further into Megan Shroud over the weekend?"

"No. I showed Alex her credentials you gave me. He said to drop it. It looks like she's an acquaintance who has formed an attachment after a one-night stand. Every guy's worst nightmare." He misses the pained expression crossing my face since he screws his face up with a chuckle. "Why, what did you find?"

I swivel my monitor to face him. "Your worst nightmare."

The longer he scans the screen, the more his brows furrow. "Jeez, that's what you call a certified lunatic."

Too curious for my own good, I ask, "When was she last photographed at the nightclub?"

"Umm..." Brandon flicks through a selection of images in the folder he's holding. "She was at the club this weekend." He hands me two pictures of Megan in the line to enter Isaac's nightclub.

"According to her medical records, she's supposed to be an inpatient at a psychiatric hospital in Hopeton."

Brandon watches me apprehensively but doesn't utter a sound as I print out Megan's medical records and bolt toward Alex's office.

"Come in," Alex instructs, his mood still surly.

When he notices my approach, he rolls his eyes. I ignore his imprudent response and hand him Megan's medical information.

His eyes narrow before he snatches them out of my hand.

"Who is Megan Shroud?" he asks a short time later.

My brows join as my gaze seeks Brandon, who's sitting on my desk, eyeballing the exchange between Alex and me.

He just informed me that he advised Alex of Megan this weekend, so why is Alex acting clueless?

I shrug off my confusion for a more appropriate time before returning my focus to Alex. "She's been photographed at Isaac's club numerous times over the past several months."

His eyes meet mine. "Hundreds of women are photographed at his clubs every day."

"But she was there every day and night for the past several weeks." I try not to let my concern for Isaac be heard in my reply. "She's also been in and out of psychiatric hospitals her entire life."

"Then he should be more cautious about who he takes to bed."

"Who said he's slept with her?" I ask through gritted teeth.

Alex glares at me, his expression announcing he I am an imbecile.

"Would you like me to supply you with the extensive list of women Isaac Holt has slept with?"

They have a list?

With my stomach twisting so much I feel ill, I keep my reply to the point. "No."

"Then drop it," Alex instructs. "We're here to investigate Isaac, not every floozy he's slept with."

It's a fight, but I nod, though my gut won't let me drop this even if my heart sided with my head.

When I return to my desk, Brandon doesn't ask how my impromptu meeting with Alex went. My distressed look tells the whole story.

"Maybe try again in a few days when his brooding mood improves," Brandon suggests.

I flop onto my chair. "He's never in a good mood."

He chuckles before shifting our conversation from business to personal. "How was your weekend?"

A smile tugs my lips higher. "It was good." Even with the whole Col Petretti and whiplash issues that plagued my weekend, I still thoroughly enjoyed my time away.

"How was your weekend?" I ask, not wanting our friendship to be one-sided.

"Quiet."

I arch my brow. Even though my day is full of the most boring, tedious tasks you could imagine, Alex's team is always a bustling hive of activity, so I find it surprising Brandon had a quiet weekend.

My heart beats double time when Brandon says, "The surveillance team lost track of Isaac for three days. No one knew where he was." He waits for our eyes to align before continuing. "That's why Alex is in such a pissy mood. Isaac only resurfaced again last night."

He hands me the manila folder he's been hogging for the past twenty minutes. A lump lodges in my throat when I scan the surveillance photos inside. Isaac looks impeccable in a black three-piece tailored suit, and his vibrant red tie matches the dress of the slender blonde intimately attached to his side.

"I don't know how the surveillance team keeps losing him, but—"
He knows we're tailing him.

I realize I said my last statement out loud when Brandon asks, "How do you know that?"

Air snags in my throat as I scan the images, trying to unearth a legitimate excuse as to how I'd know that.

"Look." I lift the picture of Isaac helping his companion out of his car at the back entrance of his nightclub. "He's looking at the camera and smiling. He knows we're watching."

Brandon removes the photo to appraise it more thoroughly. "He does. Good call, Izzy."

I smile at the praise in his tone but can't tear my gaze away from the final surveillance photo at the back of the stack. It's time-stamped three hours after the picture Brandon is holding. It shows Isaac and his female companion next to the open back door of his Mercedes-Benz.

They're kissing.

26

A whistle sounds from Brandon as he enters my apartment. "Wow, Isabelle, swanky residence."

I kiss his cheek before gesturing for him to enter. A grin curls my lips when he hands me a bouquet of irises and baby's breath.

"Thank you," I say before I offer to take his coat.

Once I have his black woolen jacket on a hanger in the coatroom, I enter my compact but well-designed kitchen to search for a vase for the flowers.

As Brandon shadows me, his eyes dart around my apartment. I've lived here for nine weeks, but this is the first time I've invited him inside. I've always valued privacy, but I've appreciated it more since I commenced working with the bureau. It's an undervalued commodity in the eyes of the FBI.

I giggle when Brandon sucks in a prolonged breath through his nose. "Something smells delicious. It reminds me of how my grandma's kitchen smelled when she cooked." While rubbing circles on his stomach, he drags in another big whiff. "Marinara meatballs?"

Grinning, I nod.

"Hold on." He holds up his index finger, requesting a minute before taking another sample of the scents lingering in the kitchen.

His moan should only come out when he's in ecstasy. "Oh, for the love of god, please tell me that's homemade peanut butter and chocolate chip cookies?"

"They're due out of the oven any minute," I answer just as the oven dings.

Brandon doesn't respond. He growls, and his mouth salivates.

After removing two trays of cookies from the oven, I slap Brandon's hands away. "They need to cool and harden. And you'll spoil your dinner if you eat them now."

I grin at his puppy dog eyes before handing him the still-warm tray. I swear he demolishes the first cookie so fast his taste buds don't get a chance to sample their scrumptious flavors.

"Would you like a glass of milk with your cookies?" I question since he's acting like a boy who's never eaten homemade cookies.

He sprays crumbs over the counter when he answers, "Yes, please."

I smile, glad he's enjoying the treats Harlow made for him. I lack domestic skills. I can cook a mean batch of marinara meatballs and spaghetti Bolognese, but that's the limit of my culinary creativity.

Brandon told Harlow months ago how much he missed his grandma's peanut butter and chocolate chip cookies, so she made me a double batch and brought them over this afternoon. All I had to do was bake them for twelve minutes, and presto, freshly baked goodies.

Brandon's happiness over something so minor makes me feel bad about how I dodged his numerous requests over the past two weeks to schedule our date. I want to say I came to my decision on my own, but that would be a lie.

After a week of Isaac being photographed exiting his clubs with a range of blonde beauties on his arm, not an ounce of guilt was felt upholding the offer I made to Brandon before I went away.

I can't believe I was so stupid to think I could fall in love with a man like Isaac Holt. He couldn't even go a night without a female companion warming his bed. I guess that's why he shared his bed with me. He's probably one of those guys who can't sleep unless they're next to a warm body.

"Brandon, can I ask you something?" I ask while moving to the fridge to fetch the glass of milk I offered.

"Anything," he replies without hesitation.

I try to think of a polite way to ask my question, but it shoots out of my mouth before I can stop it. "Do you think Isaac Holt is a criminal?"

Brandon stops gorging on the cookies like it's his final meal before saying, "His file—"

"Don't tell me what his file says. Tell me what *you* think."

He contemplates for several moments before he shrugs. "I don't know what to think."

He isn't the only one.

"But I will say one thing. I've been part of this investigation for nearly a year, and I've not yet stumbled on one shred of information that corroborates Alex's presumptions of Isaac."

That piques my interest. "Do you think he's hiding something?"

Brandon chuckles. "Are we still talking about Isaac, or have we switched to Alex?"

"Both."

"Everyone is hiding something, Isabelle," he replies, his chuckles weakening. "Even you."

I don't refute his accusation. Even if I wanted to, he'd see through any ruse I'd dangle in front of him. Brandon appears laid back, but when you watch him closely, you soon realize he's a genius wrapped up in a humble boy-next-door disguise.

"Speaking of secrets." His mouth is once again stuffed to the brim with cookies. "That file you requested has arrived."

While smiling at my gaping mouth, he nudges his head to his leather satchel on my dining table.

"Can I?"

When he nods, I smack a sloppy kiss on his cheek. I probably shouldn't be so bold, but I've been waiting to get this file in my hot little hands for weeks.

"You have to promise Alex will never find—"

"Alex will never know," I interrupt. "I promise, Brandon."

He went through hell to secure this file for me, so I'd never allow him to be reprimanded for it.

"Come on, I'm dying." He ribs me with his elbow.

After releasing the butterflies in my tummy with a quick exhale, I open the thin manila folder and scan the police report displayed on top of the documents and photographs.

Brandon watches me with caution when an unexpected tear rolls down my cheek.

The file on Hugo's sister is worse than anyone could have ever comprehended.

Marjorie Anne Hawke, a twenty-four-year-old native of Rochdale, was struck by a vehicle on May 12, five years ago. She was thirty-four weeks pregnant at the time of the accident. She initially survived the impact, but her son was delivered stillborn by cesarean the same day.

Marjorie's husband, Carey Hawke, returned from active duty in Iraq, and on his request, Marjorie's life support machine was switched off.

She passed away three hours later.

"That's incredibly sad, but it doesn't warrant the shroud of secrecy shadowing her family."

"No, but this does."

Brandon hands me a heavily blacked-out court document. One name stands out when I scan the file—Mr. Roberto Petretti, son of Col Petretti.

"Roberto didn't do *any* time, even with being arrested at the scene and recording a blood-alcohol level three times over the legal limit." Brandon's eyes dart up from the document and lock with mine. "And his name was never reported in any news or press articles. He would have had to give the DA something *substantial* to get a plea that lenient."

"Or someone," I add.

There's no doubt Marjorie is Hugo's sister. He's in nearly every family picture in her file.

My heart breaks when I see the photo of Marjorie and her husband, Carey. It looks like it was taken not long before her accident. They're smiling at each other, and his hand hovers over her protruding stomach. It's a beautiful photo that shows their unbridled happiness before their lives were brutally ripped apart.

Although I am devastated for Hugo and his family, I'm also relieved. Isaac's reaction two weeks ago now makes sense. His hatred of Col is personal. It has nothing to do with the mob.

27

"Thanks for a great night, Izzy. But next time, I'll cook."

I playfully slap Brandon's arm. "It wasn't that bad." My bottom lip drops into a pout. "It was your fault the Marinara sauce burned. You shouldn't have told me about the file until *after* I'd finished cooking."

His chuckles bellow down the corridor. Although we spent most of our night discussing work-related matters, I enjoyed the past two hours in his company. Brandon is a great guy. He is witty and kind, and our conversation flowed as freely as the wine.

I'm feeling a little bit tipsy.

"I appreciate you getting me that file, Brandon."

It would have taken him a lot of wheeling and dealing to get it, and I'm incredibly grateful he came through for me.

"No worries, Izzy. I was happy to help."

A thick cloud of awkwardness plagues the air when the elevator dings, announcing its arrival on my floor. With Brandon apprehensive, I lean in to peck his cheek in farewell.

As my lips brush his cheek, he tilts his head, and my kiss lands on his mouth instead.

I freeze when his tongue glides across my lips.

After placing one hand on my neck and the other on my back, he tugs me closer. I should be pulling away and throwing down the friendship card. Instead, I stupidly moan, my body choosing its own response to Brandon's teasingly slow embrace since my heart is too decimated to react accordingly.

When Brandon inches back, I open my eyes. His cheeks are pink, and his eyes are glossed with more than the sheen of alcohol.

"I've wanted to do that for months."

I smile apprehensively. His kiss was touching, and he is a skilled kisser, but our embrace didn't create the knee-wobbling reaction I get when I kiss Isaac. It felt more like a friend kissing a friend.

"You don't have to say anything," Brandon says, noticing the worried look on my face. "I shouldn't have been so stupid to think someone like you would be interested in someone like me."

My heart slithers into my stomach. He's a wonderful guy. Any girl would be lucky to have him. I'm the only stupid person standing in this corridor, pining for someone they can't have.

I hug him fiercely. "If my heart weren't foolishly seeking an unattainable man, I'd have forgone my three-date rule and dragged you back into my apartment."

He laughs before his eyes seek mine. Although they still show their confusion, their hurt has lessened from the honesty in my tone.

"So, I was too late?"

I nod. "That's the only reason. Any girl would be privileged to date you."

He eases the heaviness in my chest when he asks, "Can you get me their numbers?" When I giggle, he adds, "I'm not joking. Have you tried dating these days? It's a battlefield."

I grimace. Battlefield is too kind of a word for dating in this new age.

When the elevator dings again, Brandon and I end our night back in friendly territory. After a kiss on the cheek, we briefly hug and then part.

Once he enters the elevator, he spins to face me. "If it doesn't work out with Mr. Unattainable, let me know."

I smile and nod. "Without a doubt."

He flashes me the quickest grin just before the elevator doors shut.

My long strides into my apartment halt mid-stride. Isaac is in my dining room. His fists are balled at his sides, and his narrowed eyes roam over the empty dishes and wine bottles on the wooden tabletop.

"What are you doing in my apartment?" My voice quivers, not in fear but because of how quickly my pulse races from seeing Isaac again.

This is the first time I've seen him in person in over two weeks.

"How did you get in?" I interrogate, stepping toward him.

I'm sure I locked the door on my way out, but even if I didn't, you don't just enter someone's apartment without permission.

I freeze again when Isaac's eyes lift to mine. They display his undeniable anger.

His jaw tics when his narrowed gaze travels over my long-sleeved jersey dress. I chose this outfit to ensure Brandon knew our date was a casual get-together between friends and not a romantic date.

From Isaac's snarl, I'd say my clothing choice was a mistake.

"Who was the man in your apartment, Isabelle?"

"How do you know it was a man?" My anger rises as the images of him with a bevy of blondes rush back to the forefront of my mind.

"Lipstick, no lipstick." He hooks his thumb to the two wine glasses.

My glass has an outline of my light-pink lipstick, whereas Brandon's has no lipstick smears.

"He's a *friend*." I overemphasize my last word.

Isaac's low and menacing groan surges through my pussy, but before my traitorous body can react to the extra pulse surging through me, his cell phone starts ringing.

He keeps his focus on me as he removes his phone from his pocket. His greeting is short and clipped.

"Yes."

I don't know who he's talking to, but the tic in his jaw grows as their conversation continues.

My heart stops beating when he disconnects his call and places his phone back into his pocket. His gaze is furious and solely focused on me.

I back away when he steps toward me, intimidated by his unnerving composure.

He smirks at my skittish response before continuing his original endeavor.

Before I can protest, he traps me between his impressive body and the wall in my entryway.

After yanking my head to the side, he bites, sucks, and nips on my exposed neck. He has me coming undone in mere seconds and willing to give up everything just to be beneath him again.

When he hears my moans, he grips my ass and pulls me forward until his cock braces against my throbbing clit and halfway up my stomach.

I whimper, devastated when he withdraws from our embrace as quickly as he came.

He absorbs my kiss-swollen lips and flushed cheeks before settling his attention on my eyes. "No more men in your apartment."

Since my legs can no longer hold their own weight, when he places me back on my feet, I slide down the wall and sit on the floor. Through lusty eyes, I watch Isaac exit my apartment without glancing back in my direction.

I've barely regained the ability to stand, let alone comprehend what happened, when someone knocks on my front door.

Begrudgingly, I scamper off the floor and pace to the door. I inhale deeply to relieve my flushed cheeks before opening the glossy door. I'm shocked and, if I'm being honest, a little disappointed when I discover Brandon on the other side.

Both my heart and my body were hoping it was Isaac.

The longer Brandon appraises me, the more his brows scrunch. "I... umm... forgot my coat." He spins on his heels and heads back to the elevator. "But you look busy, so I'll come back later."

"It's fine," I say, ending his wish to flee. "I'm not busy."

My flushed cheeks and wide eyes are awkwardly exposing my arousal, but I'm not so busy I can't gather his coat for him.

When he remains frozen partway down the hallway, I drag him back into my apartment. His eyes bounce around the interior more eagerly than when he arrived hours ago, and when he doesn't find what he's looking for, he returns them to me.

I smile before moving to the coatroom to collect his jacket.

When I catch a glimpse of my reflection in the entryway mirror, I realize the cause of Brandon's odd response. Clear as day for all to see on my neck is an unmistakably large love bite.

I'm going to kill him!

After ushering Brandon out of my apartment, hailing a taxi, wrangling with a colossal bouncer to cut a long line, and weaving through a mass of sweaty bodies, I find Isaac in his office at the back of his nightclub.

Two walls are lined with mahogany bookshelves that reach the ceiling. Every shelf is filled with a range of books. Isaac's back is turned, and he is peering out a window that faces the alleyway I often jog down.

With my anger getting the better of me, I grab one of the hardcover books and send it hurtling across the room.

"You son of a bitch!"

Isaac slowly turns to face me, his glare stern and unnerving. The roughness of his five o'clock shadow can't hide the tightness of his jaw, and his lips have thinned.

His eyes dart to the book that missed his back by mere inches before shooting back to mine. "I'll call you back."

He snaps shut the cell phone I didn't realize he was holding until now, then houses it in his pocket, but he doesn't remove his hand.

His smug expression is all the indication I need to know he marked me on purpose.

"This wasn't an accident. You branded me like some sort of animal." I stop talking and grit my teeth, fighting the urge not to scream.

The tightness of his jaw is more noticeable when he steps closer.

Not trusting myself around him, I flee for the door.

Isaac slaps the door closed, blocking my exit, before he crowds me against it and hisses in my ear, "Did you enjoy his kiss, Isabelle?" When he curls his hand around my throat, I feel the surge of his pulse through his fingertips. "Did it make the veins in your neck throb faster like they do when I kiss you?" My disloyal nipples harden when his hand glides over my breasts. "Did your breasts become heavier and your nipples erect?"

Unable to speak through the lust clamped around my throat as firmly as his hand, I shake my head.

Butterflies flutter in my stomach when he cups my pussy. The sting of his grope forces a pleasurable whimper to escape my lips.

"Did you get wet?" he asks, his tone unapologetic.

Blinded by rage, I buck against him. He has no right to question me after how many women have entered and exited his nightclub on his arm over the past two weeks.

"He needs to learn not to touch what isn't his."

Through gritted teeth, I sneer. "I'm not yours either."

Isaac balks as his hand holding the door shut balls into a fist.

I use the distraction of his anger to my advantage. I grip the handle and yank on the door.

It wouldn't have budged an inch if Isaac hadn't pulled away from me so fast that air blasts my neck.

Although part of me wants to stay and fight, I scurry out of his office, denying him the opportunity to see the first tear splash down my cheek.

28

"Hey, Isabelle," Hugo greets me when I stumble onto the sidewalk outside Isaac's nightclub.

He's leaning on the back quarter panel of Isaac's town car. His grin falters the instant he sees the wetness welling in my eyes.

Ashamed at my immaturity, I scrub my eyes before twisting away from him.

Hugo gets back up in my business before nudging his head to Isaac's car. "Get in. I'll take you home."

"Thanks, but I'd rather hail a cab."

In reality, I just want to get as far away from anything or anyone associated with Isaac.

I grimace when Hugo says, "It'll be at least a two-hour wait."

My eyes rake the street, taking in the long line at the taxi stand.

Confident he has me over the fence, Hugo smiles before opening the back door of Isaac's car. His grin turns blistering when I veer past him and hop into the front passenger seat.

I latch my belt while he slides behind the wheel.

Focusing on the star-filled black sky, I try to unravel my confusion. Hugo also takes the quiet route, though I occasionally feel his eyes shifting from the road to me during our travels.

"Did Isaac do that?" he asks a short time later.

"Yep."

He wrings the steering wheel and works his jaw side to side. "Don't take this the wrong way—"

My huff interrupts him. "Anytime someone says 'Don't take this the wrong way,' it gets taken the wrong way."

Hugo's lips furl. "I know you're not happy about it, but would you rather him not care that you were kissing someone in the hallway of your apartment?"

"Are you saying I should be happy he branded me?"

"I'm not saying that, but he cares enough about you that the instant he knew you had a man in your apartment, he left an *important* meeting to go to you."

My brows squeeze as my confusion intensifies. "How did he know I had a man in my apartment?"

I've seen Isaac's town car parked outside my apartment and Harlow's bakery numerous times over the past two weeks. To begin with, I thought it was endearing. Now I realize it's more about Isaac not wanting another man mowing his turf.

When it dawns on me who was sitting behind the steering wheel, I ask, "Are you protecting me, Hugo, or spying on me?"

He swallows raggedly before returning his attention to the road.

Not a word seeps from his lips for the remainder of the trip, revealing where his loyalty lies.

When he pulls into the front of my building, I unlatch my belt and climb out of the car, mumbling a quick thanks for the ride. I'm halfway down the sidewalk when Hugo calls out my name. His face is marred with apprehension, his eyes full of remorse.

"Give Isaac the benefit of the doubt," he requests. "Not everything is black and white. There's a whole heap of gray—"

"No one pays any attention to," I interrupt, repeating the saying Isaac quoted weeks ago.

Hugo grins so broadly that the corners of his eyes crinkle. It is one of the smiles he wore while pictured with his family and reminds me I've yet to offer him my condolences for his loss.

His smile drops when I say, "I'm sorry for what happened to your sister, Marjorie."

For the quickest second, his face scrunches up before a mask of composure slips in its place. "Thank you."

I want to offer him my sympathies in a more heartfelt way, but he doesn't seem like the hugging type, so instead, I awkwardly wave and enter my building.

My top lip crimps into a snarl. "Stop smiling, Harlow. It isn't funny."

When I yank the collar of my shirt up, trying to hide the gigantic hickey Isaac gave me, she boisterously laughs.

Her chuckles are so loud she startles the lady sitting at a window seat. Her scared yelp echoes around the nearly empty bakery.

"I'm not laughing at you, Izzy. I think it's hot."

She moves to the table next to mine to gather used dinnerware before she can spot my disgust. "You think branding is hot? What's wrong with you?" My tone is quickly changing from angry to playful. I can't stay mad for long, let alone at someone with Harlow's personality.

"I don't think branding is hot, but it's sexy he wants other guys to stay away from you. That warning..."— she nudges her head to the red welt on my neck—"is a clear stay-the-hell-away message for *any* guy. It's more efficient than putting a ring on a girl's finger."

"A love bite doesn't discourage men. It encourages them."

Harlow's manicured brow shoots up into her hairline. Clearly she hasn't come across as many horrid men as I have.

"Because they think I'll put out," I inform her. "I once went on a date with a guy who told me he only pursues single mothers. When I asked him why, he said it was because he knew she wasn't a virgin, so she'd be more likely to put out."

Harlow gags. "That's disgusting." Her tone doesn't match her words. Her cheekbones rise as her mouth curves.

The instant I spot her teeth, a smile sneaks onto my face.

"At least he was honest," she says between giggles.

I roll my eyes before returning my attention to the gossip magazine I was reading before Harlow interrupted me.

My eyes bug when they land on an article in the back pages of a well-respected magazine.

Three eligible bachelors were taken off the market in one devastating weekend.

It isn't the headline that has my heart palpitating faster. It's the photo of Isaac, Cormack, and Colby standing side by side.

I speed read the printed article under their picture.

Millions of women around the world are sighing in sync this weekend. Latest reports circling the gossip mill say billionaire McGregor brothers Cormack (28) and Colby (24) are no longer on the market.

The two eligible bachelors were sighted at their elaborate family beachside estate, enjoying a lavish long weekend with their respective partners. It has been reported things are seriously heating up with each respective couple and that this weekend was a way of formally introducing their new loves to their extended family.

In related matters, philanthropist Isaac Holt was also spotted riding a jet ski the same weekend with a brunette female companion.

Later that night, he was sighted exiting his award-winning multi-million-dollar nightclub, 57. Several patrons were surprised when he was spotted holding the hand of an attractive brunette.

Sources believe it was the same brunette he was spotted with earlier that day. Isaac is well known for his playboy lifestyle, and it's the first time the public has witnessed a significant partner in his life in the past six years.

Many single females are waking up to this sad news.

"Did you see this article?" I ask Harlow, who has finished gathering the crockery from the table next to mine.

"Yeah," she replies apprehensively. "Thankfully, they didn't get any photos of the actual weekend. Cormack said that's an old picture from the Fourth of July weekend."

My heart stops beating. I didn't consider the fact the paparazzi would follow Isaac and Cormack. I only scanned the area for surveillance vans.

I sigh, glad no incriminating evidence was captured that weekend.

"You should be sighing," Harlow jests. "You're the brunette in *both* reports. Colby didn't bring a girlfriend that weekend. They're quoting from people who witnessed you guys at the beach on Saturday morning."

She smiles at my wide-eyed expression before sauntering to the bakery counter, leaving me free to return my attention to the article.

The image they picked is a good photo. It shows the trio's best qualities and has me mentally picturing the devastated faces of millions of women when they drink it in after reading this article.

It's just a pity the article is only accurate for one of the three men photographed.

Cormack is the only one taken.

"Oh, before I forget, can I borrow your black pumps Friday night?" Harlow asks, spinning to face me.

"Sure, no worries." I waggle my brows. "Do you have a hot date with Cormack?"

She only freezes for the quickest second, but it's enough for me to notice.

"Harlow?"

When she bolts, I take off after her. Since no customers are waiting to be served, I shadow her to the kitchen at the back of the bakery. She's washing dishes, her anger so paramount she chips two plates.

I've never seen Harlow pissed, but I'll admit, she's scary as hell when mad.

When she spots me at the side of the kitchen, her glossed-over eyes apprehensively lock with mine before she says, "I'm going on a double date with Cormack Friday night."

I eye her curiously, startled by the hurt in her tone. From the stories she's told me over the past two weeks, things are going great with Cormack and her, so I don't understand her devastation until she says, "We're going with Isaac. I assumed his date was you. Obviously my assumption was wrong. You don't have any clue about Friday."

I grit my teeth hard, fighting off the urge to scream. Isaac marked me as a warning for other men to stay away, and then not only does he continue to date, but he throws it in my face by ensuring my friend witnesses his philandering firsthand.

Harlow snatches up her handbag from a wooden shelf under the sink. "I'll cancel the date."

I snatch her phone out of her grasp. "Don't cancel." I pause for a beat to give my scheme time to formulate. "Add another two people to the reservation."

She eyes me curiously before the most mischievous grin etches on her mouth.

Confident she understands my objective, I remove my phone from my pocket and dial a frequently called number.

"Hey, Regina, remember that detective you wanted to hook me up with?" Her agreeing murmur is as shocking as my next request. "Can you see if he's free Friday night?"

29

*D*amn! I underestimated Regina's hotness radar. Glacier-blue eyes, a straight and prominent nose, and a razor-sharp jaw hidden under day-old stubble, all combined on a face that looks like it belongs on the cover of *GQ* magazine.

Although his blue suit doesn't look as expensive as the suits Isaac wears, it showcases his muscular physique well.

When he smiles, my heart freezes. Straight, pearly white teeth and small dimples in the creases of his mouth add even more allure to his already gold-standard appeal.

"I might need to start paying more attention to Regina's recommendations." His voice is gruff, as if he smokes a pack of cigarettes per day.

I know he doesn't because I got his life history from Regina this morning. Ryan is twenty-eight. He's been working at the Ravenshoe Police Station since he graduated from the police academy at the tender age of nineteen. He was promoted to detective three years ago, is unmarried, has no kids, and although he has no trouble attracting the ladies, Regina assures me he's not a ladies' man.

The reminder sees me extending an invitation I usually reserve for friends. "Did you want to come in for a drink?"

I originally planned to use Ryan to exact revenge on Isaac, but his boyish charm and friendly demeanor have me reconsidering my initial approach.

No one deserves to be used.

Ryan smiles before glancing down at his watch. "With how thick traffic is tonight, I don't think we'll have enough time for a drink." He returns his eyes to me. "But I won't say no to a nightcap later."

"I'm sorry, but I have a *stringent* three-date rule."

While smiling at his grimace, I grab my coat off the entryway table, exit my apartment, and close the door behind me.

The drive to the restaurant is pleasant. Our conversation flows freely, preventing any awkward silence.

Although Ryan doesn't know I work for the bureau, he has heard of my uncle. He even shares a few stories that I haven't heard before.

By the time we walk into the restaurant, I'm so giddy about unearthing memories about my uncle that I've forgotten we're meeting people here until the hostess walks us to the table Isaac and his date are already seated at.

Isaac's date is beautiful in an edgy, pretentious way. Unsurprisingly, she's blonde—that seems to be Isaac's preferred choice of late —and wearing a dress I'm confident costs more than I earn in a week. It's just a pity she ordered it two sizes too small. Her breasts are threatening to spill at any moment.

When Isaac looks up, our gazes collide with palpable tension. He lowers his eyes down my body, his focus loitering on my bare thighs longer than what could be classed as an acceptable glance.

My ego awakens. I chose this dress with four-inch-high stilettos because I knew they'd make my legs look like they went on for miles. My outfit is the perfect cock-teasing ensemble.

Isaac's gaze turns icy-cold when he notices Ryan's hand interlocked with mine. While working his jaw side to side, he returns his eyes to my face. His stare quickens my pulse, but I don't attempt to pull away from Ryan. I let Isaac stew, grateful the shoe is finally on the other foot.

"Isaac, I haven't seen you in months. Where have you been?" Ryan releases my hand to offer it in greeting to Isaac. "How is Nick? How many months left until we have another Holt player running around?" His knowledge of Isaac's personal life exposes him as more than a casual acquaintance.

When Isaac stands, his demeanor demands the attention of everyone around him. Numerous women—and even a handful of men—watch him as if he's performing an act instead of doing something as simple as greeting someone with a handshake.

"I've been around. I have just been busy." Isaac's slit-eyed gaze shifts to me before he says in a friendlier tone, "Jenni is due in a couple of months." Even his bad mood can't hide his excitement when he talks about his nephew.

"Isabelle, this is Isaac Holt," Ryan introduces, unaware we've already met. "I've not yet had the pleasure of arresting him, but I'm sure my day will come soon." He grins and winks. "Isaac, this is my date, Isabelle."

Isaac isn't the slightest bit fazed by Ryan's wish to cuff him. His focus remains steadfast on me as he offers me his hand to shake. Not wanting Ryan to feel out of place, I accept his offer.

My heart thumps in an unnatural rhythm when Isaac kisses my palm instead of shaking my hand.

Although my heart is flipping, my outward appearance doesn't give any indication that his simplest touch has affected me.

I keep a cool, calm head—for the most part.

"Are you going to introduce us to your date?" I arch a brow at Isaac before dropping my eyes to his date, who's more interested in the polish on her nails than participating in a conversation.

"Isabelle, Ryan, this is..." Isaac's brows draw together as confusion slides over his face.

"Tatiana," she informs us. Her nasally whine screeches through my eardrums. If I'd only heard her speak, I would've assumed she's a twelve-year-old boy going through puberty.

"Tatiana." Isaac shakes his head, hopeful it will hide his smirk.

It doesn't.

I huff in disgust that he doesn't know his date's name before plopping onto a spare chair across from Tatiana.

Thankfully, not long later, Harlow saunters toward our group. When I drink in her outfit, my mouth gapes. It isn't solely her beautiful canary-yellow dress that has my eyes bugging. It's the pair of gold-and-black Jimmy Choo Lana stilettos encasing her feet capturing my attention.

When we were fantasy shopping online a few weeks ago, she told me they were her dream pair of shoes, but at nearly twelve hundred dollars a pair, they were to remain a fantasy.

"Cormack's two-month anniversary present," she explains to my questioning expression before sitting beside me. "I got him a present, but it's only suitable for him to open in private."

Her frisky ribbing improves my mood. I'm glad things are going well for Cormack and her.

After sitting next to me, Ryan places his hand on my thigh. When I balk, he grins. He seems pleased by my reaction to his touch. He shouldn't. Although I did respond, it was more because I wasn't expecting his hand on my thigh than the zing of intimacy.

Ryan is gorgeous, but no man can ignite my senses like Isaac, especially when he's within sniffing distance.

"How do you know Isaac?" Ryan asks, gesturing his head to Isaac, who has returned to his date's side.

Isaac must have supersonic hearing. Ryan's question only just left his mouth when he angles his head and arches his brow, not attempting to conceal he's eavesdropping on our conversation.

Still angry, I answer, "I don't know him. He's practically a stranger."

A ravenous smile morphs onto Isaac's face before his tongue slides across his top lip in a slow, teasing lick. It reminds me of his tortuously slow pace in his nightclub office weeks ago.

When his nostrils flare, I know he too is recalling our time together.

I dart my eyes away, needing to look at anything but his sinfully hot face. Isaac laughs. It makes the situation between my legs ten times worse, but I am determined to give him a taste of his own medicine.

I'm not leaving this restaurant until he is reeling in as much jealousy as I am.

For the next hour and a half, I focus solely on Ryan. It isn't hard. He is a perfect gentleman who throws in the occasional flirty line, so I don't feel like a complete dud when it comes to dating.

He asks me what I'd like to eat instead of assuming, and not once does he bat an eyelid when the waiter fills my wine glass—unlike Isaac.

Every time the server returns with a bottle of red, Isaac's eyes connect with mine. His lips thin into a sharp line, and his brow arches when I nod at the waiter's silent question of a refill.

Although sitting across from Isaac has been awkward, the night has gone surprisingly well. But I swear if I hear, "It feels so big," come out of Tatiana's mouth again, I will snap.

I was under the impression restaurants made sure patrons had their own chairs to sit on, but apparently no one informed Tatiana of that. She's been sitting in Isaac's lap since the first course was served.

Isaac doesn't seem concerned about her closeness, but I've heard several other diners' gasps of disdain when Tatiana's immature giggles bounce around the restaurant.

Tatiana is beautiful, but she's a dimwit. I'm surprised someone as entrancing as Isaac is interested in dating someone like her.

This time, when Ryan places his hand on my thigh, I don't balk. I peer up at him like he is the dessert menu in front of me.

If he's shocked by the sudden attention I'm giving him, he hides it well. "What would you like for dessert?"

"Umm." I return my eyes to the menu, stumped when none of the items displayed create a single iota of interest. "There are too many choices. Why don't you pick something for me?"

Ryan sneakily orders from the waitress, piquing my interest.

What is he up to?

My mood deflates like a balloon when a screechy voice says, "It feels so big."

I knot my napkin around my fingers, fighting like hell not to scream out the obscenities running through my head.

It is a hard feat.

One Harlow doesn't win. "Okay. We get it. It feels so big. It's so big. Isaac has a ginormous cock." She glares at Tatiana across the table. "But can you please shut your mouth for the next thirty minutes so I can enjoy my dessert without your nasally, whiny voice piercing my ears? Thirty minutes of peace! That's all I ask."

I snap my eyes to Cormack, eager to gauge his response to Harlow's outburst.

He's staring at her in awe, and it melts my heart that he's so supportive of her—unlike Isaac with me.

When Harlow gives me her I've-got-your-back look, I bestow my thanks with a smile before returning my eyes to Tatiana.

Her mouth is hanging ajar, and she's shooting daggers at Harlow. "You're just jealous."

"Oh, honey, please. I have *absolutely* nothing to be jealous of."

She doesn't. Harlow wins hands down in the looks department, and don't even get me started on personality.

Karma bites my ass hard when Tatiana informs Isaac he can show her *exactly* how big he is tonight.

Isaac doesn't respond.

How can he when he's too busy glaring at me?

I discover the cause of his balled hands when Ryan says, "Open up."

He dangles a cream-dipped cherry in front of my mouth. Since I was distracted by Harlow and Tatiana's showdown, I didn't notice the waitress serving Ryan one of the biggest banana splits I've ever seen.

Feeling playful and perhaps a little tipsy from the number of wines I've had, I accept Ryan's offer.

A groan tickles my throat when a burst of cherry goodness engulfs my taste buds. That one cherry alone could top the world's most expensive steak.

Ignoring Isaac's menacing growl vibrating across the table and

Harlow's boisterous giggle egging on my defiance, I dig my fingers into the ice cream and fish out a cherry for Ryan.

"Your turn."

My cheeks heat when his teeth graze my fingertips before his tongue collects the cherry wedged between them.

Ryan winks before tilting into my side. He's so close we could be perceived as intimate.

My eyes snap to his when he questions, "How far do you want to take this?" His grin exposes he isn't angry that I'm using him to rile Isaac, but I still feel bad when he says, "You're striving to make Isaac jealous, aren't you?"

"What gave it away?"

"I'm a detective." His mouth curves into a huge grin. "And I'm not just good at my job. I'm the best they've ever fucking seen." He stills my nervous fidgeting before continuing, "That... and the fact Isaac hasn't taken his eyes off you all night."

My eyes shift to Isaac, who's glaring at Ryan and me. His freshly shaven jaw is spasming, and his hand resting on the white tablecloth is clenched in a fist. He looks seconds from charging.

As I return my eyes to Ryan, I say, "He will kill you."

"Please, you don't think I can handle Isaac Holt?" He smugly smiles before asking, "The bigger question is, can you?"

My pulse quickens, but I continue my ruse since the alcohol running through my veins is making me more brazen than usual. "I can handle Isaac better than you think."

"All right, if you're su—"

Before all his reply spills from his lips, I kiss him.

Our lips barely brush when an arm curls around my waist and I'm yanked away from Ryan. It could be anyone, but Isaac's scent gives him away. It is more potent when he is teeming mad.

"Put me down," I request when I notice several diners are watching our exchange with amusement.

I had hoped Isaac would react, but I would never have thought he'd drag me out of a restaurant while hundreds of patrons watched in hilarity.

"Put me down!" I demand more sternly.

I try to get him to release his hold by jerking out my arms and legs. He grunts when my heels collide with his thighs, but other than that, he doesn't utter a word.

Frigid air bristles my arms with goosebumps when he walks us outside. I expect him to put me back on my feet now that we're outside, but he doesn't.

Instead, he shoves me into the back seat of one of his town cars before hitting me with a stern finger point. "Stay here."

Not waiting for me to reply, he slams the door shut and reenters the restaurant.

After ruefully tugging on the door handle, I flop into the dark-gray seat with a huff. The door is locked, and there's no locking mechanism in sight.

I stop banging my fists on the window when a gruff chuckle echoes throughout the cab.

Turning my infuriated eyes, I'm greeted with Hugo's mischievous grin. He's watching me through the rearview mirror.

"Hey, Izzy," he greets, his tone brimming with amusement.

I'm not angry at him, but you wouldn't know that with how low my tone is when I demand, "Unlock the doors, Hugo."

He shakes his head. "No can do. I like my job."

I glare at him, unappreciative of the humor in his tone.

He isn't the least bit fazed by my irate scowl. His grin enlarges the longer I stare at him.

I'm about to crawl over the privacy divider to unlock the doors myself, when the back passenger door pops open, and Isaac tosses my coat and purse inside.

A victorious smile curls my lips. I am pleased that he collected my belongings even while angry.

My smile is wiped off my face when Tatiana slides in beside me. Her floral scent makes my wine-sloshed stomach churn, not to mention the lusty look in her eyes.

When Isaac fills the vacant spot next to her, my anger returns full pelt. "Open the door, Hugo!"

Blood surges through my veins so fast I'm afraid I may soon have a coronary.

Hugo snubs my request. He locks his eyes with Isaac in the rearview mirror and asks, "Where to, boss?"

Isaac's eyes flick to mine for the quickest second before he answers, "Isabelle's apartment."

He watches me but has Tatiana snuggled in the crook of his arm.

I nearly heave when he runs his index finger over my clenched fist, and the hairs on my arms bristle.

Disgusted with my body's reaction to his meekest touch, I grunt, "Move!"

When I dive over Tatiana's stick-thin thighs, I kick my leg out, ensuring my four-inch heel digs into Isaac's thigh as I throw myself over the privacy partition.

"Close your eyes, Hugo, or you'll get an eyeful," I warn before scissoring my legs into the front seat as he speeds down the street.

My maneuver is extremely unladylike, with my backside being thrust into Hugo's face, but effective when I plop into the seat beside him.

Hugo remains quiet, but his teeth glow in the moonlight when I lean across him to raise the blacked-out partition, blocking my view of Isaac and his date.

By the time we arrive at my apartment, my anger has augmented from a slow simmer to a full boil. I thought Tatiana's annoying voice was torture, but not hearing it was ten times worse.

Once I raised the privacy partition, I couldn't hear or see what Isaac and his date were doing the entire trip.

I chewed off two French-manicured tips just to force myself not to lower the partition.

"Thanks for the lift," I grunt when Hugo finally releases the lock mechanism.

While mumbling incoherently about him not deserving my

praise, I flee to the safety of my building. My angry strides slow when a car door opens in the distance. Turning my head, I spot Isaac gliding out of the back of his vehicle.

I huff before quickening my pace.

After darting through the spinning glass doors of my building, I rush toward the elevator, my heart rate increasing with every step I take.

"Thank you," I praise the gentleman holding the elevator open for me.

I repeatedly stab the close door button, praying the doors will close before Isaac can board the elevator.

A triumphant melody plays in my head when the doors slam shut as Isaac enters the foyer.

As I mosey to the back of the elevator, I suck in numerous big breaths. My overheated skin relishes the coolness of the mirrored walls when I lean against them.

Hearing my sigh, my elevator companion asks, "Exciting night?" His tone is friendly, but it still has an edge of cheekiness.

"You could say—"

I'm interrupted by the elevator jolting before it plunges into terrifying blackness. It's darker than usual since even its dashboard isn't illuminated.

The wine I consumed tonight threatens to resurface as my panic about being trapped in a small dark box surges.

Claustrophobia and I have never been close friends.

"It's okay. It should only be a few minutes before it begins working again," assures my companion when he hears my ragged breaths filling the cab.

My death grip on the railing lessens when the elevator lights flicker back on a second before it jerks back into action.

Since I am too busy calming the insane beat of my heart, I don't realize the elevator is descending instead of ascending until we're almost back at the lobby.

I retighten my grip while watching my co-rider step toward the dashboard.

"Push any button." I'd rather take the stairs than be stuck in this death trap as it plummets to the basement.

His swallow is audible when he illuminates every button on the dashboard, but the elevator continues descending, not once stopping on any of the floors we've requested.

I comprehend what is happening when the doors ding open on the ground floor. There, in all his six-foot-plus glory, is the incredibly alluring Mr. Holt, who is smirking condescendingly.

"You're an asshole."

He grins at my comment like it had no malice before he shifts on his feet to face a security officer who works in the lobby of my building.

After slipping the attendant folded-up bills, they shake hands before Isaac enters the elevator and demands the departure of my co-rider. "Get out."

He doesn't argue with Isaac. He hurries out of the elevator as fast as his legs will take him.

I try to follow him out, but Isaac stops me before I get two steps away from him. Even fuming with anger, I can't deny the electric zap bolting up my arm.

I yank out of his grip and return to the back of the elevator to lean on the mirrored wall. I need something to take the heat from my cheeks. Isaac's presence is so strong it suffocates the air surrounding him, overwhelming anyone within a five-mile radius.

Once the elevator starts ascending, Isaac twists to face me. His narrowed eyes study my body before they lift to my face. His gaze is unnerving and primal, and it has my pulse quickening.

When he drinks in my flushed cheeks, he cockily winks.

It makes my anger stronger than ever.

"You're a pig." I cross my arms in front of my chest, still annoyed at spending the last two hours in the presence of him and his dim-witted date.

There isn't an ounce of dishonesty in his tone when he replies, "And yet, you still want to fuck me."

He stares at me, daring me to deny his statement.

I do, albeit hesitantly.

"You wish."

He inhales an unashamed whiff through his nostrils before releasing it with a growl. "Deny it all you want, Isabelle, but I can smell how aroused you are."

My knees pull together as the moan I fight to hold back vibrates my lips.

When he approaches me, I hold my hand out in front of myself, stopping him mid-stride. My resolve is already slipping, so the closer he gets, the more my levelheadedness will falter.

Ignoring my silent warning, he nods, smiles a devilish grin, then steps closer.

In a blur of bites, tongue lashes, and mini climaxes, I somehow end up pinned against the wall of my entryway. My dress is bunched around my stomach, and two of Isaac's gifted fingers have my orgasm teetering on the brink.

Our movements are frantic, fueled by a lust-filled frenzy that has no end in sight. Stars form, I scream his name, and my legs buckle when fireworks erupt through my body so hard and fast I nearly tumble to the floor.

My climax is long and brutal, and it zaps the last of my energy.

Once my pussy stops clenching around Isaac's fingers, he removes them from my soaked pussy before using them to slide down the zipper of his trousers.

When they gather in a heap around his ankles, I suck in a breath from witnessing his perfect cock springing free from his black trunks.

Just the pre-cum beading at the tip has a fiery warmth rebuilding in my lower stomach.

When plastic ripping sounds through my ears, my insides tighten... but not in a good way.

Any guy who tells you he's carrying a condom in case of an emergency is full of shit. We only put a condom in our wallet with the full intention of using it the night we put it in there.

I slap my hand over my mouth as my stomach heaves. Isaac didn't know I would be at the restaurant tonight, so he was planning on using that condom with Tatiana.

I place my palms on Isaac's sweat-drenched chest and push with all my might, but he doesn't budge an inch, so I use words instead.

"Get out!" I clench my fists so firmly my nails dig into my palms. And although my breathing returns, instead of panting in ecstasy, I'm gasping in pure, unbridled rage.

Isaac's brows join as he glares at me in confusion.

He shouldn't be confused.

He knows the game he's been playing.

He's been participating in it since the day we met!

I've watched him emerge from his nightclub with various women on his arm for weeks. I stupidly told myself that not everything is as it seems. I remembered what he said about there being a heap of gray no one pays any attention to. I gave him the benefit of the doubt, as Hugo requested.

How could I have been so stupid?

"Get out!" I shout again as tears spring down my face.

When Isaac remains frozen, both baffled and angry, I slip under his arm and bolt to the bathroom, locking the door behind me.

He doesn't chase after me, proving what I've always known.

I'm just a game to him.

A game I won't let him win.

30

"Hey, it's nearly ten o'clock, and we have the weekend off." I butt my shoulder on the entryway of a dimly lit conference room no one ever uses. "So, why are you still hiding in there?"

My enthusiasm for the weekend off gets sliced in half when I scan the various moldy boxes surrounding Brandon.

For the past two weeks, I've thrown myself into work. I've only been cooped up in my apartment when I need to shower and sleep. But no matter how occupied I am, my thoughts always drift to Isaac.

"I no longer have the weekend off." Brandon's tone relays his disappointment, not to mention his gag.

Smiling at his playfulness, I enter the room and lift the lid on the first storage box.

It's filled to the brim with documents and reports.

My lips twist. "What are all these files?"

"They're your uncle's records Alex had shipped here." Brandon heads for a more extensive selection of boxes on the right-hand side of the room. "These are your uncle's files from when he worked undercover in the Petretti family." He points to the smaller pile I'm standing next to. "And those are his records on the Gottle family."

My brows scrunch. I didn't know my uncle worked undercover in either of those families.

Guilt plagues me when I blurt out, "Isaac Holt has no association with either the Petretti or the Gottle family."

My statement isn't solely fabricated. From what I've perceived outside the B=bureau's umbrella, Isaac's connection with those families is personal, not business-related.

"We already know Isaac is acquainted with Henry Gottle from the surveillance image you got of Delilah Winterbottom months ago, but I agree, no known association between Col Petretti and Isaac would warrant me investigating them." Brandon huffs. "Other than being rivals, I can't find any connection between them, but Alex is adamant I have to spend my weekend rifling through these documents until I unearth Isaac's dark secrets."

"Do you believe Isaac's secrets are held within these boxes?"

He cusses under his breath and runs his hand through his hair. "Maybe ask me again next month?"

I smile before saying, "Where do you want me to start?"

He brushes off my offer with a wave of his hand. "It's fine, Izzy. Go enjoy your weekend."

I don't grace him with a reply. I remove my coat and hang it over his jacket flung over a spare chair.

He grins at my silent offer before he rolls up the sleeves of his crisp blue business shirt, pulls a handful of manila folders out of the closest box, and then gestures for me to sit opposite him.

His grin morphs into a full smile when I murmur, "You're paying for pizza."

Brandon snags the last slice of pizza out of the grease-lined box while saying through a mouthful of cheese and pepperoni, "So we've worked out Delilah is a cradle snatcher, dating a man six years her junior, and her husband, Henry Gottle III, went to the same university as Isaac Holt, and Cormack McGregor."

"Yep." I swallow a greasy clump of pizza. "Cormack and Isaac were roommates, and Henry was their resident advisor."

"Henry now works as a promoter for the UFC in New York City, and he hasn't had any known contact with his father in over five years."

"Nearly six," I interrupt, checking the information my uncle noted in his file on Henry Gottle III. "Isaac's fighter, Jacob Walters, was a UFC fighter before he was issued a two-year probation for assault on a man named Callum Parker. Jacob retaliated when Callum brutalized his on-and-off-again girlfriend, Lola. Isaac funded Jacob's extensive legal battle."

"But why would Isaac be interested in organizing a fight for Jacob in the UFC? Wouldn't he make more money by keeping him in his private fight circuit? The rumor is those fights can range from five thousand to over one hundred thousand a fight."

"This is why." I hand him an arrest warrant for domestic abuse filed three years ago for Curtis Parker. "That's Callum's brother, Curtis. Curtis is a contracted UFC fighter. His contract is locked up so tight he can't fight anyone not in the UFC for at least the next three years. Jacob and Curtis fought early in Jacob's UFC career. That's the only match Jacob was defeated in. After that match, the referee was cited for bias. Maybe if Isaac can organize this fight for Jacob, Jacob will continue fighting for Isaac?"

"So Jacob is the reason behind Isaac's association with Henry. It has nothing to do with the mob? Jacob just wants a rematch?"

Smiling, I nod. "Henry's ex-wife, Delilah Winterbottom, started working at Destiny Records one month before her husband filed for divorce. Destiny Records is owned by Isaac's best friend, Cormack. Some may say it's a coincidence, but I think Isaac did Henry a favor by getting Delilah out of his hair, hoping Henry would help him find a way for Jacob to fight Curtis."

Brandon's brow arches as his lips curl into a grin. "It's plausible." He seems genuinely surprised. "I'll put it in a report and see what Alex says in the morning."

I smile, glad that his views on Isaac are swaying toward the positive. Even being hurt by Isaac, I'll continue to defend him until I find a credible reason to believe he's the man his FBI file portrays. My uncle may not have taught me to cook or clean, but he did teach me how to make informed opinions.

Oh, and how to shoot a pistol like a real gunslinger, but that's a story for another day.

"That's one mystery solved. Now, on to a much bigger one." Brandon strays his eyes to the tallest stack of boxes.

Following his gaze, I catch the time on my watch. My eyes bug when I realize how late it is. "It's almost two!"

"Sorry, Izzy. I didn't realize it was so late," Brandon apologizes. "I hope I'm not keeping you from anything."

He's fishing for information on the bombshell I dropped on him weeks ago about chasing an unattainable man, and although I don't gnaw at the bait he's tossing my way, I give it a little nibble. "Watching re-runs of *Sex and the City* or unearthing the secrets of an enigma. I'll take what's behind Curtain B, please, Roger."

Since I am deliriously fatigued, I giggle at my joke with more gusto than it deserves. It was pretty pathetic.

My laughter halts when I catch Brandon's admiring watch.

"What?"

The room becomes stiflingly muggy when he says, "You have a beautiful laugh."

"Thank you." My response is as bad as my comedy skits, but it was the only reply that popped into my head, so I ran with it.

Furthermore, after the severe beating my ego took two weeks ago, I'll accept any compliment I can get.

Not wanting our exchange to slip into uncomfortable territory, I grab a handful of the folders from the vast Col Petretti section.

When I slump back into my chair and pull it close to the desk, Brandon smiles before holding out his hand for his share of the pile.

Mumbling, I move away from the pointy object digging into my cheek. A groan rumbles up my throat before I reluctantly open my eyes. The sun is barely contained by vertical blinds on the conference room windows, and my head is thumping from the minimal amount of sleep I got, so I'd say it is barely past dawn.

Peering down, I discover what was piercing my face the past few hours—my open ballpoint pen. I scrub my hand across my face to check that no red smears are on my cheek.

A ghost of a smile forms on my face when I spot Brandon. He's slumped on a hard chair across from me. My smile enlarges when I learn the cause of the warm curled around me. His jacket is draped over my shoulders. He must have placed it there after I'd fallen asleep.

Brandon is an absolute sweetheart, but for some reason, I'm drawn to an alpha male who infuriates me more than he nurtures me.

My bones creak when I stretch my weary body. After spending three hours reading Col Petretti's file, we're no closer to finding any connection between him and Isaac.

Other than me personally knowing they've met, there's not one shred of information in Col's file that alludes to him knowing Isaac either privately or in business.

"Shit," I croak out when my cell phone beeps in my pocket.

I yank it out and silence it before it wakes Brandon. After sneaking out, I glance down at my phone screen. Confusion smashes into me when I read Harlow's message.

HARLOW:

Get your coffee at Starbucks this morning.

My heart thrashes against my ribcage as I dial the number for Harlow's bakery and press my phone to my ear.

"Harlow's Scrumptious Haven, how can I help you?"

"Hey, Harlow, it's Izzy. Is everything okay?"

"Oh, hi, Mom, how are you?" she replies quickly.

I remain quiet, completely dumbfounded.

"I heard you and the ladies from bowling got into a little mischief last night. *Dad* isn't happy with you this morning. How many times have you been told if you're going to spend all night out with your *friends*, you should inform someone?"

My confusion grows tenfold. Her father passed away years ago. "What the hell are you talking about, Harlow—"

"Hey, give the phone back. I'm talking to my mom."

I can barely control my breaths when the deliriously seductive voice of Isaac sounds down the line two seconds later. "Where are you, Isabelle? And don't you dare say your apartment, as I know you haven't been back there all night."

One, how the hell does he know that? And two, he has no right to question me. His *dates* haven't stopped since we returned from our weekend away. The long line of women didn't falter even after I kicked him out of my apartment two weeks ago.

Before I can respond, Alex walks through the glass door of our office. When he notices my wide-eyed expression, he quickly closes the distance between us. He appears surprised to see me in the office so early but keeps his tone professional when he greets me. "Good morning, Isabelle."

"Morning," I babble, trying my hardest to ignore the angry growl of Isaac rumbling down the line.

"If he touched you, I'll break every fucking bone in his body," Isaac snarls viciously, quickening my pulse further.

Although I can't see him, I can imagine how fast his jaw is spasming right now.

Unleashing my inner bitch, I reply, "I'm sorry, I am indisposed right now, but be sure to say hello to Tatiana for me," before disconnecting the call.

There must be something wrong with me because not only is blood flooding my body so fast my veins are bulging, but my pussy is soaking wet.

An angry Isaac is sexy as hell, so imagine what an angry *and* jealous Isaac would look like.

When I fan my cheeks, I catch Alex's confused gaze raking over my face. "Are you okay?" he questions, noticing my flushed expression.

I smile and nod, not trusting my tired head to deliver the goods. I may be treading in shark-infested waters, but I'm fine nevertheless.

I freeze partway to the conference room when part of Isaac's threat runs through my mind. *I'll break every fucking bone in his body.*

I sprint back to the conference room and rustle through the folders I skimmed earlier this morning. My hurried movements wake Brandon. He rubs his eyes before joining me next to the huge stack.

Desperate for answers, I ask, "How many years ago was Col Petretti's son admitted to the hospital?"

Brandon takes his time considering a response. His head is obviously still fried from only two hours of sleep. "Umm... around six, seven years ago."

After I find Col Junior's (CJ's) hospitalization records, I gather Isaac's bank records, which date back to when he was a freshman in college.

My eyes dart between the hospital files and Isaac's bank statements for barely thirty seconds before I find what I'm seeking.

"Look." I thrust the papers toward Brandon. "Isaac's hefty Monday morning cash deposits during his first two years at college ceased the weekend Col's son was admitted to the hospital. CJ's medical report indicates he was covered in bruises, and he sustained multiple broken bones and fractures."

While Brandon examines the extensive medical report, I continue. "Isaac was a fighter in the underground fight ring, just like his fighter, Jacob, is now. I'd put money on it that Isaac and CJ fought that weekend..." I suddenly stop talking, realizing I'm spilling information I gained in confidence.

Alex's question as he enters the conference room, not to mention the guilt it hits my chest with, announces that the light bulb switching on in my head occurred too late. "How do you know Isaac was a fighter?"

"Ah... I'm just assuming." My heart rate increases as I strive to cover my lie. "It doesn't seem like an industry you get into unless you have prior knowledge."

"Your investigating skills are really starting to flourish, Isabelle. I'm pleased with your dedication of late," Alex commends me.

I remain quiet, riddled with guilt that I unknowingly snitched on Isaac. Even angry at him, I never meant to intentionally break his trust.

"We recently discovered Isaac was a fighter in an underground fighting circuit during college. That fighting ring's organizer was Col Petretti."

"Ah... hold on," Brandon interrupts Alex, his eyes meeting mine. "CJ's injuries weren't from a fight. That weekend, he was involved in a traffic accident with his sister, Ophelia."

My eyes burn from a sudden rush of moisture in them. "What?"

"CJ and his younger sister ,Ophelia, were involved in a fatal car accident six years ago." Brandon hands me back the medical records and a police record of the crash.

As I scan the reports, my mind flicks back to the night Isaac ran into Col outside his nightclub.

"he prodigal son returns. What's it been... six years? And I don't even get a greeting from you.

He hasn't looked at anyone the way he looks at you in years. Not since Ophelia.

My stomach gurgles as a shocking fact after shocking fact smacks into me.

"Was anyone else in the car with them?"

When Brandon shakes his head, I ask the question my heart doesn't want the answer to. "Did Ophelia survive the accident?"

My vision blurs with tears when Brandon once again shakes his head.

31

"Where is he?"

Hugo's eyes lift to mine. He smiles before releasing the lock mechanism of Isaac's town car. When I slide into the passenger seat, he pulls into the midday traffic and heads outside the city. He remains quiet but occasionally glances my way.

As soon as I could, without drawing attention to myself, I left the office and went straight to Harlow's bakery. I knew either Isaac or Hugo would be there waiting for me. In the past few weeks, I've noticed that Isaac's town car is parked somewhere along that street whenever I exit the bakery.

I used to think it was because Isaac is a dominant alpha male, and he couldn't stand the idea of another man moving in on his turf. Although part of his stalker behavior is because of that, I now have a better understanding of why his behavior can be so erratic.

After experiencing a loss, most people are reluctant to form an attachment again. They fear if they do, they may also lose that attachment. Although finding out Isaac has suffered a significant loss doesn't excuse his poor behavior of late, my heart still yearns to comfort him.

I dart my eyes to Hugo when he pulls into a rundown building an hour from Ravenshoe. He ignores the silent questions beaming out of me as he parks next to Isaac's sleek black sports car.

Once he turns off the ignition, he nudges his head to a roller door slightly ajar at the side of the warehouse.

I unlatch my belt, open the door, and slip out of the Mercedes. My steps toward the warehouse freeze when Hugo backs away from the rundown industrial building.

"Isaac will give you a lift home," he says to my panicked expression before skidding out of the gravel driveway, leaving nothing but a cloud of dust in his wake.

I hate that he's left me defenseless to Isaac's charm, but since my determination is higher than my worry, I clench my fists and then stride toward the metal-and-glass building.

Air traps in my throat when I walk into the desolate space. Isaac is wearing nothing but black gym shorts and dark running shoes. He's covered head to toe in sweat and is undertaking a grueling routine on a cracked boxing bag hanging from the ceiling by a rusted chain.

Seemingly sensing my presence, his onslaught on the bag stops. When he cranks his head my way, I'm pinned in place by his ruthless glare.

He rakes his eyes down my body before he turns his attention back to the bag. This time, his fury is unleashed with so much force that sand trickles from the bag like blood seeping out of an open wound.

My panties moisten from watching him work the bag so expertly. The way his muscles contract as he moves around the bag is an incredibly arousing visual, but even with it being a sexually inspiring sight, anger projects off him in invisible waves.

That anger is only there because of me.

Aware there's only one sentence a man like Isaac wants to hear, I shout, "I didn't sleep with anyone last night." My voice barely projects over his loud, angry grunts. "I haven't had sexual contact with anyone but you in over a year."

His onslaught on the bag halts, but he remains facing away from me, allowing my eyes to absorb every muscle, dip, and curve of his sculptured back.

When he eventually turns to face me, my pupils enlarge. His stare is unnerving, but even with his eyes showing his anger, I see a small amount of reprieve forming in them.

"Say it again," he requests, his voice hoarse from the harshness of his workout.

"I haven't had sexual—"

"Not that statement. The one about last night."

Swallowing hard, I repeat, "I didn't sleep with anyone last night."

The hard lines on his face soften, but only by a smidge. "Where were you?"

"I was working."

He can see through to my soul, so he knows I'm telling the truth. He simply delays his interrogation to make me sweat like I did him weeks ago.

"Why didn't you say that this morning when I asked you the same question?"

"Because I was angry with you." Honesty echoes in my tone. "I wanted you to feel what I felt when I saw you with Tatiana."

"I already felt it, Isabelle," he retaliates with a snarl. "When you had your lips on not one but two men *in the same week*." His last four words are shouted.

"That isn't close to the hurt I felt watching you fuck your way through the female population in Ravenshoe."

My annoyance boils when he smirks.

While shaking off my anger before I scream, I pace toward the roller door. "I don't know why I bothered coming."

"Stop, Isabelle."

I ignore his request by increasing the length of my strides instead of halving them. Tears are threatening to spill, and I don't want to give him the satisfaction of knowing he has made me upset.

Without warning, Isaac bands his arm around my waist and twirls me away from the warehouse door, foiling my exit.

"I said stop!" he hisses into my ear.

My anger over everything I've witnessed in his surveillance images and in person over the past five weeks is unleashed when I throw my legs and arms out, endeavoring to get away from him.

Isaac doesn't loosen his tight grip, no matter how hard I fight. He weakens my assault with words instead. "I haven't slept with anyone since you."

"You're a liar!" I fire back. "You had a condom in your wallet. That means you were planning to sleep with Tatiana."

His clutch on my waist strengthens. "Let's get one thing straight. I don't lie, ever!" he rebuts. "And two, I got that condom out of *your* purse. I gave you the benefit of the doubt that you put it in there for me, not Ryan, but you didn't consider giving me the same courtesy?"

My struggle halts when my stupidity smacks into me. I put a condom in my purse that night. I went into the date wanting to spark a reaction from Isaac, so I wanted to be prepared in case my desire for him outweighed my levelheadedness. I didn't think to ask him where he got the condom. I just assumed he had brought it with him.

"Not everything is as it seems, Isabelle, but I haven't been with anyone sexually except you since our weekend away." He laughs as if mortified by his next statement. "I haven't been with *anyone* since you fell at my feet." His tone switches again. It's back to more serious now. "Whether you believe me or not is your choice. I can't make that decision for you."

Once he places me back onto my feet, I scrub my hand across my cheeks to ensure no unnecessary tears spilled, and then I turn to face him.

His handsome face is constricted with angst, and his beautiful eyes are shifting between mine. He's still panting heavily, making his chest rise and fall with every breath he takes, and his glove-covered fists are clenched at his sides.

This is the rawest I've seen him, and it is an equally stimulating and emotional sight.

Although I have deep-seated trust issues from my childhood, I trust Isaac. You can't fall in love with someone and not trust them.

Without trust, there would be nothing.

So as much as my brain is telling me to wait and evaluate the situation once I have a clear and conscious head, my heart has already formed its own decision.

"I believe you." The agitation marring his face softens the instant the words filter from my mouth.

The muscle in his cheek tremors when I cradle his sweat-drenched cheek in my palm. I smile, pleased his body reacts to my meekest touch as robustly as mine does his.

Brazenly, I propel onto my tippy-toes and seal my lips over his. His mouth is warm and inviting and tastes salty from the sweat running over his lips.

When Isaac curls my legs around his waist, a husky moan rumbles up my throat. He's hard, and the natural ridges in his stiffened shaft rub all the right places when I grind against him.

His dominant nature is unleashed when he increases the tempo of our kiss. He takes all the control, and I happily hand it to him.

Unashamed, I grind against his cock in a rhythm matching the lashings of his tongue. Because he's only wearing running shorts, I feel every spectacular inch of his cock through my damp panties.

A familiar tingle twists in the lower half of my stomach as my anger morphs into need.

Isaac plays my body like a musician plays a guitar. It doesn't take him many strums to have me primmed to topple into ecstasy.

Sensing my impending climax, Isaac withdraws from our embrace.

"No," I gasp out breathlessly, my voice whiny and annoying.

Isaac's smirk announces he appreciates my disappointment, but his determination remains steadfast. "Not here."

After placing me on my feet, he yanks my skirt to a modest level before clasping my hand in his.

I struggle to maintain his frantic pace to his car. Acknowledging my fight, he scoops me into his arms before continuing his quest.

When he places me in the passenger seat before latching my belt, the air sucks out of my lungs from the sheer closeness of his striking face.

My god, he's a handsome man. Beautiful yet enigmatic.

My clit throbs when Isaac inhales a vast whiff through his nostrils. The growl he releases when he exhales triples the pleasurable zap and has me squeezing my thighs together.

He watches me beneath hooded lids. His stare is hot and heavy, and I wiggle in my seat.

"Stop looking at me like that, Isabelle, or I'll take you on the hood of my car."

"Please," I beg, unashamed.

Isaac smiles smugly. "As tempting as that offer is, you've been a bad girl, so your punishment is only suitable for behind closed doors."

My cheeks flame as unbridled horniness heats my veins.

After winking at my enthusiastic response, Isaac jogs around the car and slides into the driver's seat. In the process, he slips on a cotton shirt and removes his gloves.

When he cranks the ignition of his flashy car, I barely hold back a faint moan. The healthy purr of his engine adds an exciting thrill to our exchange I've never considered before.

Excitement clusters through me when Isaac revs the engine several times before shifting the gears and tearing out of the driveway.

After fishtailing in the loose gravel, his car whizzes toward the road. Once we're on the highway, he places his hand high enough on my bare thigh that his pinkie finger can teasingly graze my panties but not high enough to subdue my eagerness.

I shift my position, craving more. Needing more. I'm twisted up so tight I'm confident one flick to my clit will have me toppling into orgasmic bliss.

"Not yet," Isaac snaps out before lowering his hand to its original position.

I shift my focus to the derelict buildings whizzing by my window, hopeful the bland scenery will quell my excitement.

It doesn't.

The forty-five minutes on the Wave Runner was pure torture, but this is ten times worse. Isaac's seductive scent is invading every surface of his car, and his index finger is tracing a figure-eight pattern on my inner thigh. I couldn't be wetter.

Just being aware of his sexual prowess has my anticipation of what's about to come overwhelming all rationalism.

I'm so worked up I could cry. But since I know how much Isaac loathes seeing me upset, I harness the wish and hold on for the ride I'm sure will make up for the delay.

After thirty torturous minutes, Isaac pulls his car into the underground garage of his building. With lust energizing the air between us, our elevator ride is intense.

When an elegantly dressed lady enters the elevator in the lobby, her eyes bounce between Isaac and me before they narrow. Unimpressed with my flamed cheeks and wide eyes, she forms her top lip into a snarl.

"Cute dog," I praise, peering at the toy poodle she's cradling.

Huffing, she spins to face the elevator doors. A giggle rumbles in my chest when she covers her dog's eyes. Anyone would swear she caught us in a lewd act, when all she's witnessed is a couple holding hands.

A lewd act is precisely what she gets when Isaac reaches the same conclusion as I do. Before I can blink, I'm spread against the elevator wall, and Isaac's skillful lips and tongue explore every inch of my mouth.

The throaty moan rolling up my chest drowns out our co-rider's loud gasp of disdain. While she frantically stabs the open door button on the elevator dashboard, my hands explore the firm ridges in Isaac's torso and back. I scratch my nails over every delicious asset —his scrumptious ass and rock-hard abs and pecs—before I eventually rake them through his hair to hold his mouth hostage to mine.

When the elevator lurches to a stop on the next floor, I can only assume the old biddy flees like her backside is on fire, but I can't take my focus off Isaac and his sinful mouth to check.

I unashamedly whimper when Isaac inches back a second after the doors snap shut. My disappointment doesn't linger for long. He looks as torn as I do.

After running his finger along my kiss-swollen lips, he says, "If you're going to be accused of something, you may as well do it."

His smirk has me worried I missed the punchline, so we won't mention his quiet ramblings when he walks us down the corridor of the penthouse suites.

32

———

a grunt emits from my lips as I clench black sheets in a white-knuckled hold. Isaac's smug chuckle booms through my pussy before his God-crafted body glides along mine.

Although his mouth is glistening with evidence of my horniness, I'm annoyed beyond comprehension.

I thought the car ride was agony, but this is worse.

Isaac is so in tune with my body he's using it as punishment for kissing Brandon and Ryan.

Until I beg for forgiveness, he refuses to let me come.

Over the past hour, his tongue, fingers, and mouth have teased me to the point of snapping more times than I can count, but mere seconds before my climax topples into oblivion, he withdraws all contact.

It's been hell—absolute agony.

I'd rather be spanked with a paddle than go through this again.

"Not yet," Isaac murmurs before sealing his mouth over mine.

Too sexually frustrated to continue playing his game, I snap my mouth shut and crank my head to the side, denying his kiss.

I'm so annoyed that if his knee weren't between my legs, I'd snap them shut, too.

Isaac raises his lips against my mouth, seemingly pleased he has me rattled. After sliding his hand up my sweat-slicked body, he cups my engorged breast and pinches my nipple between his index finger and thumb.

His talented fingers soon encourage a raspy moan to rumble up my chest.

Isaac slides his tongue inside my mouth when my lips part for a much-needed breath.

I fight with all my might to deny his kiss, but I can't.

It's too scrumptious to ignore.

After weaving my fingers through his hair that's damp at the roots, I pull him onto my overheated body. He swallows my throaty moan when the crest of his fat cock brushes my clit.

I tilt my hips higher, seeking direct contact.

I nearly whine when Isaac inches back before slapping down my hips.

"Not yet," he teases, nipping at my lips with his teeth.

Once he has my bottom lip tingling from his bite, he rakes his eyes over my naked form. I study him with as much eagerness. It could be the fast track to orgasm I'm seeking. His body alone could make me come just from looking at it.

I mentally high-five my determination to survive the torture when Isaac snags a condom out of his bedside table. While peering at me with lust-crammed eyes, he rests his backside on the balls of his feet before ripping open the foil packet with his teeth.

I watch in awe when he rolls the latex down his cock. It almost seems too small for the enormity it has to protect.

With his condom in place, he tilts my hips high before stuffing a pillow under my ass. A purring moan vibrates my lips when he slowly sinks his cock into my pussy one painstaking inch at a time.

Once I'm full to the brim—but not close to taking all of him—his movements cease.

I assume it is to give me time to acclimate to his girth, but I learn otherwise when several minutes pass with no additional thrusts.

When I wiggle my hips, wordlessly begging for him to increase the tempo, he grips my hips, dismissing my plea with the same number of words I used to voice it.

Growling, I pop my eyes open and lock them with Isaac's. "Please," I beg, my high tone leaving no doubt about my excitement.

Isaac's lips curl into a heart-fluttering smile before he withdraws his cock to the tip. Pleasure rockets through my womb when he slams back into me with one ardent thrust. I moan, adoring being filled by him once more while also loving his roughness.

When he stills his movements again, I barely hold back a sob. The veins in his neck are bulging profusely, showcasing his arousal, but there's a gleam in his eyes that reveals he can maintain this pace for hours if required.

"I'm not going to beg," I snarl through gritted teeth, certain if I cave now, I'll forever give in to his dominance.

"Yeah, you are." His tone is as cocky as his facial expression.

After rolling my eyes, I shake my head.

He isn't the only stubborn person in this room.

Every claim I've ever given about being an independent and strong woman is upended when Isaac executes an expert roll of his hips.

Pleas for forgiveness spill from my mouth so hard and fast my lips can't keep up with the words they're trying to form.

"Now, that wasn't so hard, was it?"

My begs for forgiveness switch to shallow moans when Isaac increases the tempo of his thrusts. His speed is perfect, and I am racing toward release at a record-setting pace.

I dig my nails into his back as an orgasm waves in my stomach before cresting in my core. My body heats up as his magnificent cock dominates my pussy.

This is brilliant, the best sex I've ever had.

He drives me to the brink, screwing my body as well as he fucked with my mind for the past hour. He claims every inch of me, making me feel thoroughly whole and so sexually satiated I'm exhausted beyond comprehension.

I moan on repeat, incapable of intellectual thoughts, much less words.

Isaac doesn't face the same issue.

"This is mine," he says between grunts. He scans my body with so much possessiveness he activates every one of my hot buttons. "All of this is mine. Say it, Isabelle. Say it, and I'll let you come."

Confident he is a man of his word, I purr without hesitation, "It's yours. All of it is yours. I'm yours."

Isaac thrusts into me deeper, rolling his hips at the exact spot that drives me crazy. Shudders wreak havoc with my frame as a second climax wavers on the edge. My muscles tighten and prime for release, knowing they're moments away from bliss.

As he showcases his sexual prowess in a way no amount of light could ever shadow, I purr like a pussycat, loving the sensation bristling the fine hairs on my body.

"Oh. Oh. *Oh.*" My veins thicken with lust as a fiery warmth spreads across my skin, coating it with a thin layer of sweat.

"Eyes on me, Isabelle."

Isaac's husky demand reveals I'm not the only one caught off guard by the brilliance of our exchange.

He is as taken aback as I am.

My eyes pop open when his thumb circles my pulsating clit. It is the final push I need to sing the praise of ecstasy for the second time tonight.

Isaac's name roars from my throat when I free-fall over the edge. My orgasm scorches through my body like an out-of-control wildfire as my nails bend harshly into his back.

The spasms of my orgasm inspire Isaac's release. He fills me to the hilt seconds before spurts of cum explode from his cock, and my name rips from his throat.

Once every drop has been freed, his hooded eyes collide with mine. "You are mine," he says before sealing his mouth over mine.

He kisses me so passionately the walls of my vagina clench around his still-convulsing cock, begging for round two.

"Every inch of you is mine, Isabelle."

33

While groaning a long and tedious grunt, I flutter my eyes open. My muscles are weary, and my temples are throbbing from the lack of sleep I've gotten the past two days, but I'll happily accept this type of delirious exhaustion any day of the week.

When I scan the room, I realize it's as bland and uninviting as it was months ago. The walls are void of any paintings or pictures, and no knickknacks adorn the bedside tables.

When I roll over and snatch my satchel from the bedside table, I wince. It isn't a bad pain—more of a reminder of what Isaac and I did numerous times earlier this evening.

What Isaac said the last time we were in this room is undoubtedly true. You don't have any doubts when you've been bedded by Isaac Holt. If every muscle in your body aching isn't enough of a sign, the mass surge of adrenaline running through your veins hours after the event is a surefire indication.

I screw up my nose when I fire up my phone and see it's ten o'clock at night. As much as I'd like to sleep until next week, I can't go back to bed now unless I want to be awake in the middle of the night.

After scampering out of bed, I snag Isaac's shirt he was wearing this afternoon off the floor. I ensure the coast is clear before raising his shirt to my nose and sucking in a huge whiff of his smell.

A shiver runs through my body when his delicious aroma invades my senses.

I have a second sniff before skimming my eyes over the room, seeking the clothes we discarded when we fumbled from the entryway to the bedroom while undressing.

When my hunt comes up empty, I pull Isaac's shirt over my head, remove my unruly hair from the collar, and then exit the room.

My flightless steps are weighed down with panic when, "Hey, Isabelle," sounds through my ears.

I shoot my hands down to the hem of Isaac's shirt while silently praying it has enough pull to hide my private parts.

Hugo chuckles at my panicked response. I'm glad he can see the humor in the situation—not. I'm not wearing any panties, and although Isaac has a few inches on me in height, meaning his shirt hits the middle of my thighs, I doubt he would appreciate a member of his team seeing me like this.

I freeze like a statue when Isaac exits the kitchen with a glass in his hand. His smoldering eyes run down my body before they suddenly shoot to Hugo, who's sitting in direct line with my crotch.

When Isaac's eyes return to me, I swallow harshly before scrambling back, intimidated by his glare.

"Stop, Isabelle."

Unlike at the warehouse, this time, I immediately halt, rendered motionless by his pinning gaze.

While smirking at my passiveness, he glides toward me, his steps as striking as his handsome face.

He stands so close that his whiskey-scented breath fans my lips when he says, "As ravishing as you look right now, I don't like other men eyeing what's mine." Although his warning could be mistaken as intimidating, his tone doesn't reflect that. "There are clothes in the closet for you. Go get dressed, and then I'll take you home."

I stalk back to his room, ignoring my disappointment that he already wants to take me home. I'm barely two feet away when he calls my name.

My heart beats at an irregular rhythm when I crank my neck back to face him. It grows wilder when I spot the dominant gleam brightening his eyes as he says, "From now on, anytime you leave my room, you're only to wear my shirts."

My brows squeeze together as I hesitantly nod.

Didn't I just get reprimanded for doing precisely that?

I shrug off my confusion and head for the hidden walk-in closet. My bewilderment intensifies when I enter the expansive space. The collection of suits and polished shoes that was here months ago has been removed, replaced with a handful of dry-cleaning bags and unopened boxes.

My toes dig into the plush carpet as I saunter further inside. When I spot over a dozen Jimmy Choo shoe boxes underneath a handful of designer dresses, my breathing turns laborious.

I allow my love of Jimmy Choo to overrule logical thinking.

A squeal emits from my lips when I pry open the first box. After lifting them from their box, I absorb every perfect stitch and exquisite design of a pair of Kia 110 boots, but my excitement is squashed when I see they're a petite size six.

Even on a non-humid day, my size eight hoofers will never squeeze into a six.

After giving them a final hug, I place them back into their box before selecting an outfit.

Once I've changed into a fresh set of clothes, I return to the living room. My pulse quickens when Isaac's eyes lift and lock with mine. The dominant gleam I spotted in them earlier triples when he absorbs the white-wash jeans and light-pink cashmere sweater I chose from the selection of women's clothing in his closet that was my size.

All the designer dresses were too small for my generous breasts.

As I glide past a grinning Hugo, I mouth an apology for the awkward predicament I placed him in earlier.

"It's all good, Izzy. I saw more the night you climbed over the privacy partition."

I snap my eyes to Isaac when he growls at Hugo's taunt. His jaw is quivering, and his hands are fisted at his sides.

"I'm joking," Hugo assures us as his humored gaze flicks between Isaac and me. "You know me, boss, I never water another man's turf."

While continuing to glare, Isaac downs a generous nip of a brown liquid inside a whiskey glass in one swallow. After running the back of his hand across his mouth, he sets the glass on the coffee table, then rises from the white leather sofa.

Although Hugo's expression shows his apprehension, he's the first man I've met who doesn't cower from Isaac's infuriating glare.

Hugo rubs his hands together, pretending he can't feel the tension in the air. "So, where are we off to?"

Isaac's words are for Hugo, but his eyes are for me when he answers, "Your services won't be required again until Monday morning."

I smile when Hugo vaults off the sofa, his excitement at a weekend off all over his ruggedly handsome face. "You don't need to tell me twice. You've got my number if you need me."

He bolts for the door so fast air glides over my forearms.

Once the penthouse door slams shut, I drift my eyes to Isaac and jest, "You need to give him more days off."

He doesn't grace me with a reply, but a smirk tugs his full lips higher. "You ready?"

Smiling, I nod.

———

My brows join together when Isaac turns left at the Remington Avenue T-intersection instead of right.

"My apartment is that way?"

He's been to my apartment on three occasions, so I'm somewhat surprised he has forgotten the directions.

I never expected a man with Isaac's astuteness to be forgetful.

His grip on the steering wheel tightens before he confesses, "We're not going to your apartment."

I arch a brow. "You said you were taking me home."

"No, I said I'll take you home." He drifts his eyes from the road to me. "I didn't say whose home we were going to." Excitement slicks my skin with sweat when he clarifies, "I'm taking you to my private residence."

In a nanosecond, my eagerness slips, and anger takes its place.

"Where did we just leave if that isn't your home?"

Isaac's lips twitch, but he returns his eyes to the road, ignoring my question with the skill of a nark.

Every second he delays answering me intensifies my anger. It brews in my gut until I can't hold it back for a second longer.

"Was that your fuck pad?"

Isaac's eyes snap to mine. Although his glare could cut through diamonds, I don't back down.

"Was that your fuck pad?" I ask again, sterner this time.

He works his jaw side to side before saying, "I don't call it that, but I guess some people could see it that way."

"How many women have you slept with in that bed?" I ask before I can stop myself. "Actually, don't answer that. I don't want to know. I already feel sick."

I'm not lying. My stomach is threatening to spill at any moment. I also have an overwhelming desire to take a shower.

I've never felt as dirty as I do right now.

"Take me home," I request, fighting to ignore the moisture looming in my eyes.

"I *am* taking you home."

"No..." I breathe out the agitation making my voice snarky. "Take me back to *my* apartment."

Isaac's grip on the steering wheel firms so much that his knuckles go white. "No, Isabelle. You are mine. Which means my house, my bed, my rules."

I glower at him, too stunned to form a response. I fought Alex tooth and nail not to become a commodity, but Isaac is making me precisely that.

I'm not a possession.

Nobody owns me.

"Don't look at me like that, Isabelle." Isaac's tone is low in warning.

I turn my eyes to the star-filled night as the first tear trickles from my eye. Anger is burning through my veins, but unfortunately it isn't hot enough to dry my tears that everything my uncle worked for is being so poorly disregarded.

Not even a heartbeat later, I shoot my hands out to brace the dashboard when Isaac slams on the brakes and yanks his car to the side of the road.

After unclasping my belt, he drags me across the center console until I sit side-straddled on his lap. His nostrils flare with every breath he takes as his remorseful eyes dance between mine.

The pain maiming my heart fades when his thumbs clear away my tears. Not a word spills from his lips, but he doesn't need to speak to convert his thoughts. His begging eyes tell the entire story.

His beautiful gray irises are my biggest weakness. They're the gateway to his soul, the key to unlocking the real Isaac Holt. Although he is known for being cold-hearted and ruthless, his eyes relay an entirely different man. They're my greatest ally in unearthing the man behind the enigma.

Once my tears have settled, Isaac presses his lips to mine. Even upset, I melt into his embrace, incapable of denying his affection.

His kiss is scrumptious and sweet, and it clears the turmoil swirling in my stomach in less than a second.

He kisses me until I'm breathless and the windows of his sports car are covered with fog.

While rubbing my kiss-swollen lips with his thumb, he filters his eyes over my face and says, "I shouldn't have taken you there, but I needed to be sure you were mine before I fully let you in."

Tears form in my eyes so fast they sting, but this time, they're from happiness, not hurt.

Isaac is a highly private man, so for him to accept me into his life has my heart enlarging so much it's close to exploding.

Shocked by my unexpected response, Isaac eyes me curiously.

I'm certain I look ridiculous with tears flooding my cheeks while a huge grin is spread across my face, but my response can't be helped.

I'm too happy to hold back my excitement.

After slapping my hands on either side of his cheeks, I place a sloppy kiss on his stern mouth. I feel him smirk against my lips before he takes our kiss from playful to teasing.

In seconds, his talented mouth has me wishing we weren't in the tight confines of his car but determined to make the most of it.

I meet the lashes of his tongue stroke for stroke as my hands slither over the contours of his chest and abdomen.

I'm about to tackle his belt when a stern tap hits his driver's side window.

"Move along." A male police officer in a fluorescent yellow vest waves us along.

When Isaac lowers the foggy window, the officer's glare weakens. "Oh, good evening, Mr. Holt. I'm sorry. I didn't realize this was your vehicle," apologizes the handsome African American officer.

"That's okay, Jimmy. It's new." Isaac scans my face before boldly winking. "I've only taken her out a handful of times."

I return his needy stare, certain he's no longer talking about his car.

When his cock twitches against my backside, I'm one hundred percent confident in my assumption.

Even with his big cock digging into my ass, Isaac checks in on the officer's family. "How are Marisha and the kids?"

I'm shocked he can engage in conversation without alluding to his aroused state. I'm fighting not to writhe, and I can hide the effects he has on my body. Isaac isn't so lucky.

The officer smiles. "They're good. Bobbi just made the varsity team."

When he floats his eyes to a car approaching on the other side of the road, I swivel my hips, vying to alter Isaac's flawless composure.

Although his cock stiffens to a mouthwatering thickness, his flow of conversation doesn't falter in the slightest. His tone remains neutral, and he doesn't respond to the raging boner sending my thoughts into a tizzy.

After Isaac bids the police officer farewell, two minutes longer than I would have liked, I flop onto the passenger seat.

Once my belt is latched, Isaac pulls his car back onto the road, waving to Jimmy on the way by.

A shiver of excitement and, if I'm being honest, a tremor of fear run through my body when Isaac murmurs, "You'll pay for that tease later."

34

My breathing stills when I absorb the impressive private residence in front of me. When Isaac enters a security code into the black box at the edge of the driveway, a black wrought iron gate creaks as it opens, exposing a curved path that weaves up to a beautiful brick house at the top of a hill.

The manicured gardens are well maintained but have a classic bachelor design with manly hedges and a collection of potted plants.

Isaac drives up the pebbled driveway before stopping in front of his remarkable mansion. When I step out of his car, the first thing I see is a beautiful arched window on the third floor.

Each window in the mansion is either a circular or curved design, but the only window on the third floor is a perfect half-circle.

Upon noticing the direction of my gaze, Isaac says, "That's my bedroom." The sexy purr of his voice ignites my senses. "At night, you can see the whole of Ravenshoe from my bed."

"It's beautiful. A fitting castle for a prince."

He chuckles. "There's nothing princely about me."

I shrug. He may not be a prince charming, but not every girl wants a prince. Some want a brainy geek. Others want a rock star. I want an alpha male who makes me scream his name at the top of my lungs while the most earth-shattering climax rips through my body so hard I see fireworks.

With my composure slipping, I try to get our conversation back on track. If I want this to work out, I need to occasionally participate in activities with Isaac that don't involve sex.

"How long have you lived here?"

He curls his hand around mine and walks us toward the curved glass doors at the front of his mansion. "I've owned this house for nearly three years." He stops when we reach the front door and peers down at me. "This is my private residence."

I smile, loving that he's inviting me into his private sanctuary.

My grin doesn't ease Isaac's inner turmoil.

"I don't think you understand what I'm saying. This is my *private* residence. I don't let anyone come here. Hugo has only been here a handful of times."

Oh.

"So anything you hear or see behind these doors has to stay behind these doors." He motions his head to the front door. "I share enough of my private life with the public. I'm unwilling to give them more of myself than I already do."

"I understand."

When a broad smile spreads across my face, making my cheeks ache, he angles his head and arches a brow, silently questioning why I look like the cat who caught the canary.

"You *like* me." I overemphasize the word "like."

He *pffts* at my immaturity, but the faint curve of his lips reveals his true reply.

He can't refute my claim.

The inside of Isaac's house is as spectacular as the outside, with beautiful antique furniture, luxurious materials draped over arched doors, and priceless paintings adorning the walls of each room.

My impromptu private tour of his private abode ends in his large black-and-cherry-oak kitchen.

After releasing my hand, Isaac heads for the refrigerator. "What would you like for supper?"

With one hunger more rampant than any I've had, I answer, "You."

Isaac pops his head out of the industrial-size refrigerator. He stares at me for several long seconds before he says with a smirk, "You'll be dessert, but first, I need to feed you to make sure you can keep up."

I chew my bottom lip, hoping it will lessen the intense fire building in my womb, before I wipe his smug grin from his face with my tongue.

After a frisky wink, announcing he understands my battle, Isaac says, "Being Saturday, our options are limited. It's either Catherine's lasagna or chicken parmigiana."

I take a moment to ponder which meal sounds more enticing.

My brain is in such a lust-filled fog I can't decide which I'd rather eat.

Sensing my reluctance, Isaac decides on my behalf. "Lasagna it is."

He places two containers of lasagna into a convection oven, hits the reheat button, and then pulls two china plates down from a cupboard next to the oven.

He places the plates on the island before removing two sets of cutlery from a drawer beneath.

Even watching him do something as simple as setting a table is an exhilarating experience.

Once the island is set for an intimate dinner for two, he gestures for me to join him. A girly squeal spills from my lips when he lifts me to sit on a high-backed barstool. Flashbacks of him doing the same six months ago in the business class lounge rush to the forefront of my mind.

"Can I ask you something?" I ask, my tone apprehensive.

Isaac freezes for the quickest second before replying, "Can we eat before commencing an interrogation?"

With his jaw tighter than it was seconds ago, he removes his jacket and slings it on the beautiful wooden bench before tackling his cufflinks.

Once they're undone, our eyes lock and hold for several electrifying minutes.

There's no doubting the sexual connection between us, but something much greater draws us to each other.

And I'm not the only one willing to acknowledge that.

I grin when Isaac says, "One question."

I have a hundred questions I want to ask him, but I settle for one that will strengthen our bond instead of fraying it. "What was your first thought when I tumbled at your feet at the airport?"

Relief washes over his face before he smirks. "You continue to surprise me every day, Isabelle."

I mockingly cock a brow. "Why, what type of question were you expecting?"

He smirks again before moving for the convection oven signaling our meals are ready. "To be honest, I thought your fall was a ruse to gain my attention. Over the past few years, I've become accustomed to the tactics women use to secure my attention." He removes the lasagna from the oven before placing a generous serving on my plate. "But the instant your big, beautiful eyes looked up at me, I knew it wasn't a ploy. You were truly embarrassed and seemingly unaware of who I was."

"I didn't know who you were until I arrived in Ravenshoe..." I stop talking, wondering if I've revealed too much.

Slowly, I raise my eyes from my plate of lasagna. Seconds feel like minutes as we undertake an intense, chemistry-filled stare-down.

I grin in victory when Isaac breaks the connection first. He nods before returning to the refrigerator. "I guess I allowed my reputation to get the better of me." He pulls out a bottle of red, checks the label, then continues. "I'm certain everyone in Ravenshoe knows who I am, but you've humbly reminded me there's an entire world outside of Ravenshoe that doesn't know about an arrogant businessman named Isaac Holt."

"Their loss."

His chuckle has my mind wandering far away from the food in front of me.

Forever diligent, Isaac says, "Eat, Isabelle. You'll need your energy."

He isn't joking. Once we finish dinner and two glasses of wine, Isaac has his dessert on the very counter we ate on.

Then in the shower, and in his monstrous four-poster bed.

By the time we're preparing to sleep, the sun is already rising over the horizon.

Isaac emerges from the bathroom. He has disposed of the used condom and has a washcloth in his hands.

Even though I am sexually satiated, the pulse in my neck still thrums when he cleans me with the washcloth.

Once all the residue of my climax is removed, he slips back in between the sheets and pulls me in close to his fit and enticing body.

A moan tickles my throat when my soft curves mold into his ridges.

I moan again when Isaac says, "Stop moaning, or neither of us will get any sleep."

"Is that even possible?" I say through a yawn, certain he can't be ready for another round so soon after round three.

My eyes bulge when his rapidly stiffening cock digs into my backside. "Does that answer your question?"

After biting my bottom lip, I roll over to face him. The tension turns palpable when he saves my bottom lip from my teeth while saying, "You're going to be the death of me."

35

"I didn't even know there was a muscle there," I mumble to myself.

Every muscle in my body is throbbing. Don't get me wrong. It's a good pain I'd happily choose to feel every day, but I'm suffering soreness in areas I didn't know housed muscles.

After working my neck side to side to relieve the kink that formed there from sleeping on Isaac's drool-worthy pec the past several hours, I climb out of bed.

Unsurprisingly, I'm once again waking up in an empty bedroom.

I feel like a zombie, so I have no clue how Isaac can live off such little sleep.

This room is more adeptly decorated than the room in Isaac's fuck pad. The color theme is burgundy and a charming steel gray. His bedside tables have pictures and knickknacks, and the ceiling isn't mirrored.

I guess the mirrored ceiling in his penthouse apartment should have been my first clue that it wasn't his primary residence.

"Wow."

The view from his bedroom window is remarkable. I was so focused on Isaac last night that I didn't pay any attention to the scenery. From this vantage point, you can see nearly the entire down-town area of Ravenshoe.

I smile while sliding my arms into the sleeves of Isaac's blue business shirt he was wearing last night.

Once I have the top three buttons done up, I pull my hair from the collar and exit the room.

I wander around for almost twenty minutes before locating Isaac behind a mahogany desk in an office.

He's seated in a black leather chair, swiveled around to face an arched window behind his desk. He's talking to someone on his cell. From his tone and demeanor, I'd say it's a business associate or a staff member.

I prop my shoulder on the doorjamb, intending to watch him in silence, but forever vigilant, he senses my presence before I get my fill.

My breath hitches when he pivots around to face me. He's wearing dark-washed jeans and a fitted white shirt. To add even more allure to his sexiness, he's also barefoot.

As I absorb the sexually satisfying visual of a casual and laid-back Isaac, he studies me with just as much eagerness.

When he notices I'm wearing nothing but his shirt from last night, he flashes a panty-clenching smile.

"Yes, I'm here," he snaps down the phone when his perusal of my body interrupts the flow of his conversation.

My pulse quickens when he gestures for me to join him. While fiddling with the hem of his shirt, I pad into his office. When I reach his desk, he pulls me down to sit in his lap. Yearning ripples through me when his cock digs into my ass.

I'm not surprised when he continues with his call. More turned on. His authoritative tone never falters, not even when he slips his hand under my shirt to tweak my nipple.

"Henry, enough stalling. I don't care what it costs. Just get it done." He disconnects his call, not giving Henry the chance of a reply.

Too curious for my own good, I ask, "Was that the Henry I met when we went away for the long weekend?"

"Yes," Isaac answers as his gaze becomes more hooded. Since he's no longer holding his phone to his ear, he has an extra hand to explore my body.

Any further interrogating is left for dust when he starts to massage my shoulders.

I moan, adoring the release of the tension sitting there, but Isaac hears it as something else. "Are you sore?"

"A little."

A groan rips from my throat when he withdraws his talented fingers from my neck. He stands, taking me with him before he exits his office at the speed of a bullet.

I grin when he places me on an expansive marble vanity in the main bathroom. It turns into a full-toothed smile when he commences drawing a bath.

After squirting bath products into the fast-running water, he faces me. Although his eyes expose his hunger, something brighter is sparkling in them.

My breathing slows when he pulls his shirt over his head in one fluid movement before he undoes the button on his jeans. Once his jeans and boxers are removed, he shoots his hands to the buttons of my shirt.

I'm a big girl. I can undress myself, but I'm too busy drinking in his magnificent body to do something as mundane as remove my clothes.

Isaac's words are drenched with cockiness when he asks, "See something you like?"

I nod. He winks at my unashamed response before he slips his shirt off my shoulders. A triumphant grin stretches across my face when he takes a sharp breath. I'm pleased he finds my body as tempting as I do his.

My words sizzle with sarcasm when I quote, "See something you like?"

He doesn't grace me with a reply, but from the stiffening of his cock, I can make my own assumption.

After assisting me off the vanity, he walks us to the nearly over-flowing bathtub. He slides in first before offering me his hand.

I moan when I join him. The warm water is heavenly to my over-worked muscles.

Water splashes over the tub's rim when I lean against Isaac's torso.

"You're dealing with Catherine tomorrow," he informs me, his warning chopped up with laughter.

I pretend I'm not adoring his happy mood. "Who is this Catherine I keep hearing about?"

If I had an ounce of tension left in my shoulders, he clears it away when he massages them again. "She's my..." He stops mid-sentence, piquing my curiosity. "Trying to give Catherine a title is like trying to give Hugo one. They're both all-rounders. I'd say Catherine is a housekeeper, personal assistant, shopper, and grandma." My heart warms when he says "grandma."

"So she isn't someone I should be worried about?"

Isaac chuckles. "No, Isabelle. She and her husband celebrated their fortieth wedding anniversary last month." He shifts my position until I have an unimpeded view of his handsome face. "You don't have *anyone* to be worried about."

Smiling, I rest my cheek on his pec muscle before categorizing every striking feature of his face.

The longer I admire, the more Isaac's jaw muscle spasms.

"What?" I question when the tension reaches a breaking point.

"Do I have anyone to be worried about? Because I'm already aware of the impression you made on Ryan, so I was wondering if there is anyone else I should be informed of."

My breasts flatten on his chest when I roll over to face him. My heart skips a beat when our eyes collide.

I knew a jealous Isaac would be as sexy as an angry Isaac.

"As handsome as Ryan is—"

Water splashes over the tub's rim when Isaac clenches his fist so fast it creates a ripple.

"Let me finish my sentence before you get all tense." Jealousy is blazing through his eyes, but it isn't scary enough to stop me from saying, "As handsome as Ryan is, no one makes my body ignite the way you do. No one ever has, and no one ever will. You've ruined me for any other man." I slide my body along his until we meet eye to eye. "No man could ever compete with someone as incredibly gorgeous as you. Not even Kellan Kyle."

Stealing his ability to reply, I seal my lips over his.

He smiles against my mouth before he returns my kiss with the same amount of intensity I'm bestowing.

It starts slowly, but like every time we're together, it builds in urgency.

I drink him in, tasting, licking, and absorbing every delectable portion of his mouth as the bathwater cools.

When his raspy moans spur on my boldness, I slither my hand down the ridges of his six-pack before palming his cock.

I stroke him for several minutes before circling my hand around him and sliding my thumb over the rim of his cock.

My seamless and somewhat frantic pumps soon have him chasing release.

I'm right there with him.

When the head of his cock brushes the entrance of my pussy, his raspy grunts spur on my pursuit.

I adjust my position so the crown of his cock stabs into my pussy with each stroke I award him.

Each pump has him inching into me more and more.

First an inch.

Then two.

I'm almost at the point of taking him entirely bare when he senses how badly my resolve has slipped.

Isaac's heavy-lidded gaze pops open before he calms the speed of my pumps by placing his hand over mine. "As much as I want to plunge into your pretty pink pussy, we need a condom."

The throaty deepness of his voice spikes a severe bout of recklessness. "I'm on the pill."

He stiffens for the quickest second before pinching my chin and forcing the alignment of our eyes.

When I stare into his beautiful eyes, reluctance reflects at me. Except it doesn't center around him. It is solely focused on me.

"Are you sure, Isabelle?" he asks a short time later. "Because once I make you mine, there's no turning back. There will be *nothing* between us again."

I answer him with actions instead of words. After removing my hand from his cock, I slam down—hard!

Water splashing onto the marble tile echoes around the room, along with Isaac's gruff moan. "Fuck, Isabelle."

The sting of his fingers when he stills my hips adds to my excitement.

After forcing our exchange into an intermission so I can adjust to the sheer girth of him, he alters my position so I can take more of him without additional pain before he clutches the rim of the tub in a white-knuckled hold.

Over time, I increase the tempo of my thrusts, encouraged by his provocative moans.

"You feel so good."

He pumps into me three times.

"So tight."

He almost drives me to the brink of hysteria when he fucks me so relentlessly that the world blurs and stars form.

"So fucking wet."

A moan tears from my throat when he adjusts the tilt of his hips. Our new position allows almost every inch of his fat cock to stuff inside me.

I purr his name when he slithers his hand between our connected bodies and rubs my clit in a circular motion.

His thumb toys with my clit while his cock commands every inch of my pussy.

"Oh..."

I want to say more, but I can't.

Lust has stolen my words.

My nails dig into Isaac's shoulders as I fall into orgasmic bliss. As a climax cascades through my body, my moans reverberate throughout the bathroom.

Its shudders are so strong, even I'm surprised by their intensity, but they don't slow Isaac down. He continues driving into me, fucking, claiming, and marking me until I come for the second time.

The sensation rendering me into a sticky, speechless wreck augments when cum rages out of Isaac's cock several blistering minutes later.

I clench around him, greedily sucking at his cock, milking every drop of his cum I want coating the walls of my pussy.

Several body-shuddering minutes later, I collapse onto his sweat-glistening torso. I'm exhausted and gasping for air.

After sinking back into the tub, Isaac runs his hand down my frazzled hair. Even with the temperature of the water beyond chilled, the heat radiating off our bodies is enough to keep us warm.

My heart flips when Isaac's lips tickle my temple as he murmurs, "That was a first."

Once my heart rate settles, I peer into his sparkling eyes. "That was a first for me, too. I've never had sex in a bathtub."

He stiffens, and his cock, still nestled inside me, softens. "I meant it was my first time without a condom."

Although I should be mad he brought up previous sexual conquests during our exchange, a smile still curls on my lips.

I slip off his semi-erect cock while saying, "I'm glad I was your first."

Isaac's jaw tics so profusely I hear it over the sloshing of the bathwater when I step out of the tub. "Isabelle..."

His angry snarl usually makes me freeze in fear, but not this time. I wrap a towel around my sexually satiated body, pretending I'm not the least bit fazed by his tempered growl.

When Isaac stands from the tub, I can declare without doubt that a jealous Isaac is by far the sexiest Isaac I've ever seen.

Although I could continue to tease him, I let him off the hook by admitting, "It was also my first bareback ride."

After my tease in the bathroom, I spend the next two hours paying the repercussions for my actions.

Isaac's stamina truly astounds me. I've never met a man with so much self-control in the bedroom. I lost count of the number of orgasms that ripped through my body this afternoon.

I was left sated, delirious, and unable to move. So much adrenaline was running through my body that I felt drunk even though I hadn't had a drop of alcohol in the past week.

Thankfully, Isaac let me rest most of the afternoon, only waking me when it was time for dinner.

We've spent the last hour eating homemade tacos and talking in his living room.

I've loved every moment I have spent with him, whether in the bedroom or hanging out.

Only thirty-six hours have passed since we left the abandoned warehouse, but it feels like a lifetime.

"I'll be back in a minute."

When I nod, Isaac collects our empty plates from the coffee table before heading to the kitchen.

After placing my phone where our plates once lay, I glance at the pictures proudly displayed on the mantel above the fireplace. Over two dozen photos of various people in different poses are displayed. Their ages range between each picture, but one gentleman appears more often than anyone else.

When Isaac returns, I ask, "Who is this man?"

His lips arch up when he notices the photo I'm holding. "That's my brother, Nick."

When he removes the frame from my hand, his smirk enlarges to a full smile. Mine drops as my brows lower. The teen in the photos is handsome but has no features similar to Isaac's. Isaac has brown hair, gray eyes, and a light olive complexion. The man he is claiming as his brother has blond hair, dark-blue eyes, and pasty-white skin.

And don't get me started on how Isaac's persona demands respect and authority, whereas his brother's seems a little roguish and cheeky.

Noticing my odd expression, Isaac chuckles. "He's my brother. There's no doubt in my mind."

He places the photo back onto the mantel before facing me. Air snags halfway to my lungs just from the sheer closeness of his handsome face.

I'll never tire of seeing his tempting features.

Isaac returns my focus to the land of the living. "Do you have any siblings?"

Grimacing, I shrug.

Isaac eyes me curiously but remains quiet, patiently waiting for me to decide if I want to respond further.

When reluctance hangs an invisible noose around my neck, he sits on the sofa before offering for me to join him. My unease drifts away when he interlocks our hands and lowers me to straddle his lap.

After settling my nerves with some big breaths, I say, "I have siblings, but half of them probably doesn't remember me, and the other half doesn't know I exist."

When my voice cracks at the end of my confession, Isaac runs his thumb over the veins protruding in my hand. "You don't have to say anymore." He locks his eyes with mine. "But I'm ready to listen when you feel comfortable sharing."

I smile, grateful he isn't going to push me. Knowing he won't force me out of my comfort zone makes me want to share stuff with him that I've never shared with anyone.

"My mom fell in love with the wrong man." My voice is barely a whisper when my family's shame is exposed. "My father was already married and had a handful of kids with his wife and multiple mistresses when they met. He promised her a lavish life if she'd give up her current lifestyle and become his mistress. She readily agreed because she grew up living well below the poverty line and was only seventeen." Air whizzes from my nose. "Instead of a life of luxury, she got an endless list of false promises."

I cough to clear my throat before continuing. "She got pregnant with me not long after they got together, and that's when her life spiraled out of control." I try to rip off the Band-Aid in one fell swoop instead of in little tidbits. "My father preferred to have sons, and since I was born a girl, he despised me on sight. His hate saw my mom's life spiral. She overdosed when I was six."

Isaac's thighs stiffen, but he continues to dutifully listen.

"My father didn't want me, and his wife didn't know I existed, so I was... umm... he... ah..." This is harder than I could have ever predicted.

When I wipe under my nose to ensure the contents inside don't spill, Isaac says, "That's enough for tonight."

He wipes away a handful of tears I couldn't hold back before he kisses my eyelids. His gesture is kind, almost loving, and it causes a sudden shift in the air.

Sexual tension builds as lust hisses and cracks.

When it grows too great to ignore, I roll my hips, desperate to discover if his cock is thickening beneath me.

It is.

I adjust my position before rocking my hips again. My pace is slower than the ones we've been using over the past two days, but fire-sparking at the same time.

Goosebumps break across my stomach when Isaac slips his hand under my shirt. Although his touch is as light as a feather, it's robust enough to gain my body's full attention.

His slow but sensual pace heightens my senses, making sure I pay careful attention to his every move.

A moan vibrates my lips when he kneads my breasts before he rolls my nipples between his fingers. A roaring sensation darts through my body, only stopping when it clusters in my needy pussy.

Isaac stands, taking me with him, before he places me on a white fur rug in the living room. He guides me backward until my back molds into its soft fibers, and then he slips my shirt over my head.

Once it's removed, he requests for me to place my arms above my head and intertwine my fingers. When I do as asked, he uses my shirt to secure my hands together.

"Keep them above your head."

I display my trust by nodding without pause for thought. My pulse quickens when Isaac tugs off his shirt, and then it thrums when he stands before me barefoot and wearing nothing but jeans undone at the button.

I greedily take in his magnificent body as if it's the first time I've sampled it.

Once his jeans are discarded on the floor, he undoes the three buttons on my jeans, then slides them down my legs, brushing my needy clit on the way by.

His mission to strip me bare continues until I present before him as naked as the day I was born.

Confusion swamps me when he exits the living room.

I have no reason to fret.

Not even thirty seconds later, he returns with two pillows. My libido surges when he places one under my head and the other under my backside.

"Your eyes are never to leave mine, Isabelle."

Unable to coerce words through the lust curled around my throat, I nod.

After gracing my stomach and thighs with gentle nips and

caresses, Isaac's attention shifts to the areas throbbing for his devotion.

He blows a hot breath over my clit before spearing his tongue between the folds of my pussy and poking it inside.

He eats me like he's starved and will never get enough of my taste. He fucks me with his mouth so well I will never again deny the feelings that have been bristling between us since day one.

Watching him worship my body is an exhilarating experience that has me free-falling into ecstasy more times than I can count.

I come over and over again until I'm on the brink of delusion, and my body is a hot, sticky mess.

With my body super lax from sexual exhaustion, Isaac places a final kiss on my drenched pussy before he climbs up my body. A familiar tingle builds in my stomach when his swollen crown braces the entrance of my vagina.

Even exhausted beyond comprehension, my body can't help but react to his closeness.

I arch my back and moan when he slowly inches inside me. The sensation is amazing. I am filled to the brim.

"Eyes, Isabelle."

My eyes snap to Isaac's as a long, salivating moan rumbles up my throat. Our bodies are joined in the most intimate way, and the visual heightens my senses even more.

Isaac's muscles flex with every thrust, and each precise pump sends jolts of pleasure to my tightening core.

Sometime later, I wriggle my hands, fighting against the restraints binding them together. The urge to run my hands over Isaac's sweat-slicked body is so overwhelming I can't hold back my desire for a moment longer.

When Isaac frees my hands, I run them along his bulging biceps before raking them down his sweat-drenched back and gripping his glorious ass.

With every pump, the pleasure overtaking me grows. I moan his name when a long and intense orgasm lights up my body. I shudder in ecstasy, growling his name on repeat as fireworks detonate.

"One more," Isaac requests through panted breaths barely a second after I've returned from orgasmic bliss.

He adjusts our position so my knees hug his hips and my breasts squash against his smooth pecs.

I'm exhausted beyond comprehension, but nothing can hold back my glee when Isaac says, "Choose your pace, baby."

I am unable to move since my legs feel like Jell-O, so he rocks his hips upward, gliding his cock in and out of my pussy.

"Like that?"

I don't grace him with a reply. I groan a long, purring moan as warmth flames my skin. A bead of sweat runs down Isaac's cheek as his perfect rhythm has me desperate to chase my next climax.

If I weren't already close to the brink, his dirty mouth soon has my orgasm teetering on the edge.

All his comments about how much he loves fucking me, how good my pussy feels wrapped around his cock, and that he could fuck me for years and never get enough have my next climax building at a rapid pace.

I'm not the only one on the verge of release.

Isaac's cock thickens as his sprint for the finish line ramps up.

Spurred on by his impending climax, I increase the tempo of our thrusts. I match his grinds pump for pump. I suck at his cock and tighten the walls of my vagina around him, desperate for him to find release with me this time.

Our pace turns so wild that only skin slapping skin echoes around the living room.

"Fuck, Isabelle, you get even tighter when you're about to come."

His words push me over the edge. I shake and moan as fireworks explode in front of my eyes. Isaac's name tears from my throat in a rumbling scream as I quiver through a blinding orgasm.

My climax has no end in sight when I feel the sting of Isaac's teeth on my shoulder. It is closely followed by hot spurts of cum as he erupts inside me.

37

My eyes flutter open when Isaac scoops me into his arms and strides through his impressive mansion. I snuggle into his sweat-slicked chest, loving that he can carry me with such ease.

Once we reach his bedroom, he continues his fast pace until we're at the double shower in his master bathroom.

He turns on the faucet, not once relinquishing me from his hold or making me concerned he might drop me.

When the water is warm, he steps us into the shower. The spurts of the hot water flowing from the showerhead revive my overtired muscles within minutes.

Once the ache has lessened, Isaac places me back onto my feet.

In silence, he squeezes body wash onto a shower puff and spreads it over my body.

Once he washes away the suds, his pampering shifts to my hair.

My heart swells from witnessing a side of him I don't think many people have had the pleasure of experiencing.

The ruthless businessman has succumbed to a mere man who is lovingly nurturing a person he cares for.

"You really, *really* like me," I mumble, my voice hoarse from the number of screams I released.

His fingers freeze in my hair as he lowers his eyes to mine. "Why do you think I forced myself to stay away from you?"

He acts as if he didn't ask a question by returning his focus to shampooing my hair. His thick, powerful fingers have goosebumps breaking out across my skin, but they do little to stop my mind from running away on me.

I know why I had to put distance between us, but I wasn't aware Isaac was fighting a similar battle. How many months have we wasted fighting an urge greater than us both?

I grow worried I mumbled out loud again when Isaac expels a sharp breath.

My quiet ramblings aren't the cause of his sigh. A burden too heavy for him to continue carrying alone is the perpetrator.

"I'm not a good man, Isabelle. I tried to stay away from you so I could protect you." Before I can form a reply, much less articulate it, he silences me by squashing his index finger against my lips. "It would have been safer for you if we'd never met, but now that I've claimed you as mine, I can't give you up. But I promise to protect you and never let anyone hurt you."

His pledge adds more suspicion to a theory that's been running through my head over the past few months.

Realizing this may be the only opportunity to ask a question that's been haunting me for weeks, I blurt out, "What did Col Petretti say to me in Italian the night we left your club?"

Isaac stiffens before his gaze shifts to the side. Although he could be perceived as looking at my face, I know he isn't. He's glancing past me. How do I know this? His gaze is so hot that when it leaves you, you experience the loss of its heat.

Before any lies can spill from his mouth, I remind him of the promise that brought us together. "Don't lie to me, Isaac. You said you never lie."

He snaps his eyes back to mine. The loving man mere minutes

ago shampooing my hair has been replaced with a man whose gaze alone would have the most brutal men shivering in their boots.

As he clenches his fists, he answers, "And you will soon become one."

My brows pull together as confusion bombards me.

Why did such a simple statement create such an adverse reaction from Isaac that night?

It's only when the first part of Col's sentence filters through my mind do I understand Isaac's reaction.

You're exquisite. You have the face of an angel... And you will soon become one.

My heart constricts as more truths smack into me. "Is that why you went on all those dates? So Col would think I wasn't any more significant to you than a woman keeping your sheets warm that night? You were protecting me?"

"That was my plan, but even Col could see"—he stops mid-sentence and swallows hard—"whatever this crazy thing is between us. The instant I retaliated to his threat, he knew you were more than a random one-night stand."

I try to hide my smile. I give it my best shot, but the smallest one creeps across my lips before I can stop it.

Isaac stares at me, seemingly dumbfounded by my odd response to having my life threatened.

I shouldn't be grinning, but hearing him admit there's something "crazy" between us makes it impossible not to respond with giddiness.

My glee is bitch-slapped out of my reach when Isaac says, "Col has been spotted several times the past four weeks in Ravenshoe."

Hugo's station outside my apartment over the past few weeks makes sense now.

"You have Hugo watching me?"

The tic in his jaw becomes prominent when he says, "I won't let Col hurt you, Isabelle."

"I know that." My tone is confident. "I'm more worried about why

Col wants to hurt you. Why does he have a vendetta against you, Isaac?"

Awkward tension plagues our gathering, but I'm grateful that Isaac keeps the communication lines open. "He blames me for his daughter's death."

"Why?"

Quicker than I can click my fingers, the barrier he uses to protect himself mentally rises before my eyes. Remorse floods his face as his beautiful eyes turn dark and stormy.

No words escape his lips as he washes the shampoo out of my hair and steps out of the shower. Even with the tension thick enough to cut with a knife, he still dries me with a lush towel before carrying me into the central part of his room.

Once he places me on the mattress, he walks to a cabinet of tall drawers at the side of his massive walk-in closet.

My heart breaks for him when the cause of the devastation on his face makes sense. Not only does Col blame Isaac for Ophelia's death, but so does Isaac.

I can't comprehend why he thinks a traffic accident is his fault.

"Thank you," I whisper when he dresses me in one of his T-shirts.

When our eyes lock, for the quickest second, he forgets his grief. A smile tilts my lips when he cradles my cheek to wipe away a droplet of water from my drenched hair.

When I lean into his embrace, wanting to offer him quiet comfort, he pulls away like my touch scorched him.

I hate that more than anything.

I stalk him as he moves around the room, preparing it for an undisturbed sleep. Even though my urge to know everything is hounding me to probe him for answers to the questions muddling my mind, my heart knows now isn't the time to drill him.

He needs comfort, not an interrogation.

Once he dons a pair of cotton sleeping pants that hang low enough I can tell he's commando underneath, he slips into his side of the bed.

Like a sucker who gets off on being rejected, I crawl across the mattress, nuzzle into his side, then rest my cheek over the area his heart sits.

Blood surges through my veins when he doesn't repel my loving gesture this time around.

We sit in silence for several minutes, but it isn't a bad thing. The smell of our intermingled scents reminds me of a perfect way I can comfort him.

When my hand slithers over the ridges of his stomach, my heart flutters. His muscles contract with every minute move I make.

"Isabelle..." Isaac groans when my fingertips skim the waistband of his sleeping pants, his tone warning that I'm treading in uncharted waters.

Determined to ease his turmoil and also desperate to taste him for the first time, I kiss his unshaven jaw before dropping my lips to his chest.

When I tug on his erect nipple with my teeth, he releases a throaty moan. His levelheadedness is slipping as fast as my horniness is climbing.

Needing the focus to stay on him, I shoo his hand from underneath my shirt before saying, "It's my turn to play."

I lift my eyes to his in anticipation of an intense stare-down.

I get that and so much more.

He's undoubtedly angry, but instead of panicking about his narrowed glare, my libido feeds off it.

"Please," I beg. "Just one night."

I don't want him to relinquish his dominance forever.

Just tonight.

Shockwaves rocket through me when he smirks for the quickest second before he adjusts his pillow. Once he scoots up the bed and leans his back on the headboard, he glides his hand down his body, granting me access to do with it as I please.

My wish to taste him should inspire a humiliating minute of clumsiness, but somehow, I don't fumble like a newborn giraffe learning how to stand when I slide down his body.

My movements are effortless and graceful—almost sophisticated.

When I kiss each muscle of Isaac's six-pack, he groans, and wetness pools between my legs. I drag my heavy breasts over his rapidly stiffening cock before fisting the waistband of his sleeping pants and connecting our eyes.

I watch him over the rise and fall of his chest as I slowly guide his pants down his thighs. When his cock springs free, my insides clench. It's beyond perfect. Long, thick, and veined.

Incapable of waiting a second longer, I moisten my lips before stretching them over the broad crest of his cock. My cheeks hollow from the pressure I apply when I suck him into my mouth.

"Yes, Isabelle," Isaac moans, his anguish forgotten. "Suck me hard and fast, baby. Make me come in your pretty little mouth."

While moaning about his sinful request, I run my tongue along the vein feeding his cock, absorbing his delicious taste.

By paying careful attention to the changes in Isaac's breaths, I soon work out which method of sucking produces the most intense reaction.

Once I get the perfect combination of suction and speed, he fists the sheets, and his eyes snap shut.

"Eyes," I babble through a mouthful of cock.

Isaac's eyes narrow, but he doesn't respond to my playful taunt with words. He keeps his eyes locked with me as requested as I suck, lick, and stroke his cock.

His gaze is hot and heavy and crests my excitement to a never-before-reached level.

Knowing I can cause a crack in his usually impenetrable shell is thrilling. It sends a shiver of euphoria scuttling through my veins and makes every fine hair on my body bristle.

Over and over again, I draw him to the back of my mouth, only occasionally triggering my gag reflex.

The longer my blow job progresses, the more my climax builds. Pleasing him orally feels as good as when he has his head buried between my legs. I am moments from climaxing.

Isaac's hips buck off the bed when I increase the strength of my sucks. My jaw aches, but watching him unravel will far outweigh any discomfort I could endure.

Even if I don't come, I won't care.

That's how much I am enjoying giving him head.

As Isaac's grip on the sheets tightens, his thrusts become more urgent. He's so close to release there's no stopping the train now.

A short time later, when the veins on his cock throb, I draw him into my mouth until the crest of his cock hits the back of my throat, and my gag vibrates his knob.

"Fuck, Isabelle," Isaac roars as spurts of salty cum pump onto my tongue and slide down my throat.

I swallow eagerly, loving the ability to taste his release.

Greedily, I milk him with my hand, relentlessly pumping his cock until every last drop of cum is expelled into my mouth.

After licking my lips to gather any spillage, I crawl back up his body and rest my head on his sweat-glistening torso.

His heart thrashes wildly as he comes down from his brutal climax. I smile, glad I can render him so mindless his grief is forgotten for a few minutes.

It is the same for me. Although I didn't orgasm, Isaac's hand running down my hair, smoothing the frazzled pieces back into place, has me feeling the safest I've felt in a long time.

It also has me spilling secrets I've never shared with anyone. "My uncle who raised me isn't really my uncle." Isaac stiffens when I confess, "I was sold to him when I was six."

His grip on my hip tightens so much pain shoots through my hipbone. "Isa—"

"My father hated me so much he didn't care who bought me," I interrupt, needing to finish before I chicken out. "He just had one requirement. Whoever was the highest bidder had to pay for me in cash."

When Isaac's teeth grinding together shrills through my ears, I pop my head off his chest and peer into his tormented yet still beautiful eyes.

"My uncle was a good man. He saved me from a life of misery. If it weren't for him, who knows where I would have ended up."

My confession eases some of the angst in his eyes, but it does little to loosen the tightness of his jaw, so I'm forced to say, "One question."

Isaac smirks. It isn't his usual panty-wetting smirk, but I'll take it over the devastation in his eyes.

"Did he...?" He doesn't need to finish his question. He doesn't need to. His terrified expression speaks volumes.

"No, Isaac. God, no. He wasn't that type of man. He wasn't a monster. He *never* touched me like that. I promise." Isaac expels a relieved breath when I continue. "He treated me as if I were his daughter." My brows stitch as pain strikes my chest. "Well, as a father would a daughter if he were anyone but Vladimir Popov."

When Isaac's breathing ceases to exist at the mention of my father's name, I realize he's heard of him.

38

Gripping the marble vanity bowl, I lift my eyes to the vanity mirror. My face is white and gaunt, and my pupils have sunken. The dark circles plaguing my eyes make it look like I haven't slept in over a year, but an illness is the cause of my appearance. The chaotic mess of confusion in my head makes me look sick.

Being immersed in Isaac's world over the past forty-eight hours made me forget the bureau is investigating him. When I'm with Isaac, I only see him. Everything else is a blur of white noise, but now that the dreaded Monday morning has arrived, reality has come to painfully bite me in the ass.

After my confession last night, Isaac remained quiet. I knew he was awake even though I couldn't see his eyes. He ran his hand along my arm for nearly an hour before he slipped out of bed and snuck out of the room. I considered following him, but after recalling Cormack's advice weeks ago, I left him alone to contemplate.

Isaac is a guarded man, so I wanted to give him time to process my blurted confession in privacy. It isn't every day the woman you're sleeping with acknowledges being the daughter of a well-known mob boss.

That type of revelation would rattle even the strongest man.

Isaac's apprehension of my confession last night made me wary of advising him that I'm a federal agent. Although legally I cannot disclose that I am an agent to anyone, morally, it's the right thing to do.

My heart wants to be truthful with Isaac, but my head is warning my heart that it isn't the smart thing to do.

My heart-and-head fight continued well into the early wee hours of this morning.

After many silent deliberations, my head eventually overruled my heart.

The reason my head won isn't what you might think. It's because I don't believe Isaac is the man his FBI file portrays him as. So I've made it my mission to ensure his investigation is handled fairly. Once it's closed and Isaac is acquitted, I'll make sure his file reflects the true Isaac Holt.

Once he learns I defended his integrity the entire time, he will forgive me for deceiving him.

At times, government departments can be unjust. My childhood reflects that. My uncle was undercover in the Popov family for nearly five years before I was auctioned.

Once I was old enough to understand, he explained that he initially tried to have the sale canceled legally, but since the bureau didn't believe I was a valuable enough asset for him to break years of cover for, the auction went ahead as planned.

My memories of Tobias at the time are vague, as I was so young, but the image of his huge smile and roguish face when he'd bring me and my brother groceries will always have a special place in my heart.

My mom was unfortunately addicted to meth. The urge for her next fix was greater than her desire to feed and look after her children. Since she graced my father with a son a year after I was born, he arranged for a family member to assist her in raising his children.

Although Tobias wasn't related by blood, he was still addressed with the title of uncle. Any male with a close connection to the *family* was classed as uncle, even if he wasn't a blood relative.

Tobias was the man my dad tasked with looking after me and my little brother, Enrique. He said I was just shy of my first birthday when he came into my life. He gave me the nickname "Rabbit" because I was nothing but skin and bones.

That nickname stuck until the day he was killed.

Since the FBI refused to help, Tobias went against their strict protocols. He mortgaged his family home in Tiburon and overdrew every credit card to ensure he had enough cash to buy me.

His bid was successful, and we left Las Vegas the same day.

When news of Tobias's abandonment surfaced through the FBI, he created the ruse that he was in a relationship with my mother while undercover and that Vladimir had found out about his indiscretion, meaning he was shunned from the family.

The bureau believed him, and he was demoted to a new task force.

With the help of Regina, I was issued a birth certificate stating I was the daughter of Tobias's deceased brother, Abraham, who had died three years earlier.

For the last nineteen years, I was raised by Tobias and his дедушка—grandpa in Russian—in the house Tobias mortgaged to bid for me.

To this day, the FBI is none the wiser of my connection to the Popov family.

My gloomy thoughts are interrupted when a heated gaze ignites every nerve in my body. Isaac is leaning on the doorjamb of the primary bathroom, watching me with hunger in his hooded gaze.

I shake my head. "No, Isaac."

Our rigorous physical activities this morning have already stretched my time thin. I'll be late to work if I don't leave within the next thirty minutes, and I don't see a man with a stamina like Isaac's understanding the word "quickie."

Isaac chuckles while entering the bathroom. I act like my heart isn't beating a million miles an hour at the pleasure of drinking in how his tailored three-piece suit showcases his body.

I continue my fruitless attempt to hide the dark circles plaguing my eyes with the compact foundation I carry in my purse. It is a shade too light since my skin is blessed with the hue of ecstasy, but it's the only makeup I have access to, so it will have to do.

My heart flips when Isaac kisses my freshly shampooed hair before snagging his toothbrush from the ceramic holder on the vanity.

Every hair on my body bristles to attention because of his closeness. His cock scorches my ass when he dampens his toothbrush under the running tap, and a tiny shudder flows through me.

Even after being sexually satiated numerous times in the past forty-eight hours, I can't stop my body from responding to him. The more I have him, the more I want him.

I stash my compact back into my purse and grab the spare toothbrush from its holder before joining Isaac in brushing my teeth. He remains quiet, but I don't need to look at him to know he's watching me. The heat of his eyes is an obvious sign.

Intimacy fires in the air as we brush our teeth side by side. Although there's a double sink, Isaac spits his toothpaste into the one in front of me, aware every brush of his body against my arm heightens my senses.

Two seconds later, I nearly choke on the mouthwash I'm gargling when he tugs open the towel curled around my body. As he draws in a sharp breath, he assesses my body. From the bulge his trousers are straining to contain, I'd say he appreciates the visual of me standing before him naked.

Since I'm not strong enough to ignore the tension for a second longer, I spit my mouthwash into the sink before turning around. "You have twenty minutes."

His lips crimp into a mouthwatering smile, making my body quiver and my heart thud in my throat.

Returning his smile, I throw myself into his arms and seal my mouth over his minty lips.

Over thirty minutes late, I scamper into the office as fast as my quivering legs will take me. I should have known a man with stamina like Isaac's wouldn't know the definition of a quickie.

Even Hugo, driving like a maniac and taking every shortcut he could find, couldn't get me back the hour I had lost in the bathroom earlier.

I shoot my eyes to Alex's office as I scramble for my desk. I sigh in relief when I spot him behind his desk, peering out the window.

After plopping into my chair, I fire up my computer before throwing my purse into the bottom drawer of my desk.

A girly squeal erupts from my lips when I raise my gaze. Brandon sneakily moved to my desk, undetected.

"Holy crap, you scared me."

He smiles and wiggles his brows. "Sorry, Izzy. I just thought these might stop you from another one of Alex's famously long tirades for being late." He gestures his head to the eight cups of steaming hot coffee he's holding.

"I love you. I love you. I love you." After leaping out of my chair, I kiss his cheek.

His face turns the brightest shade of red. "That's okay. I'd do anything for you."

As he hands me the two crates of coffee, Alex pivots around. Our eyes lock and hold for several terrifying seconds. Seconds feel like hours anytime his stern blue eyes reprimand me. His gaze is so troubling that a sweaty mustache forms on my top lip.

My breathing returns when his eyes snap to the coffees, and his lips curve into a smile.

"I owe you big time," I whisper to Brandon before dispensing the coffees to each recipient, ensuring I drop off Alex's black coffee first.

***

By the time lunch rolls around, my neck no longer feels the ache from Isaac's fingers digging in when he arched over the tub this morning.

It's from scanning hundreds of documents into the geriatric copy machine in the dingy, cramped supply closet.

Alex wants a digital copy of my uncle's hand-scribbled notes and files, meaning thousands of documents must be manually scanned into the FBI database.

In a larger task force, this assignment would take a couple of days, but using an ancient copier that only scans one page at a time, it will take weeks, if not months, to complete.

I'm still rubbing the kink in my neck when the supply closet door creaks open. My breathing levels when Alex enters the cramped room. The air turns stifling when a thick stench of awkwardness suffocates us.

After offering him a quick, unassured smile, I focus on scanning the documents. Alex clears his throat before he goes to the corner of the room to gather some camera equipment. Because of the lack of space, his hand accidentally connects with my backside as he passes by me.

After gathering a digital camera with a long zoom lens, he walks to the exit. I pull in close to the copier to ensure he can glide by without bumping into me.

Upon exiting the door, he spins around to face me. "You can make up your late arrival by either skipping your lunch break or staying back later tonight," he advises, his tone stern.

Swallowing harshly, I nod.

Obviously Brandon's ruse has been unhatched.

39

Two hours later, Brandon discovers me sitting on the floor in the supply closet. He offers me a reassuring smile before making his way into the room. An appreciative grin forms on my mouth when he sits next to me before handing me a club sandwich and a bottle of OJ from Harlow's bakery.

"I heard you had to work through your lunch break."

"Yeah. I think Alex is more watchful than either of us perceived." I run the cuff of my blouse under my eyes to ensure I don't have raccoon eyes from my mascara running down my face.

Once the smears are on the sleeve of my blouse, Brandon asks, "Why are you crying?"

I hand him the photo I'm clutching in a shaky hand. "Ophelia Whitney Petretti was only nineteen when the car she was driving was struck by a B-double truck that veered onto the wrong side of the road. She was killed on impact."

Brandon's eyes snap down to the photo I found of Ophelia in Col's file. Ophelia was beautiful. In the picture Brandon holds, she has light-brown shoulder-length hair with caramel highlights. Her eyes are so light in color, they're nearly transparent, and she's smiling brightly, even with the tip of her pointed-up nose red from a sprinkling of snow landing on it.

A smile curls my lips when Brandon tugs me close, offering quiet comfort. "I read the police report on her accident over the weekend. It's always sad when you hear of *any* life being taken too soon." Even with him offering me comfort, he sounds hesitant. I guess it's hard for him to understand the reason for my tears since no one knows of my association with Isaac.

I'm genuinely upset that Ophelia's life was cut short at such a young age, but my tears aren't for her. They're for Isaac.

Once I dove into more of Col's file, I discovered several handwritten notes my uncle had scribbled on napkins from a diner called Buck's.

Ophelia was a waitress at Buck's Diner for over a year before she was involved in the accident. All the notes were about Ophelia and a young man Tobias had spotted her with on numerous occasions over three months.

From the timeline of the napkins and some more detailed reports, it appears Isaac and Ophelia were a couple for nearly six months before she passed away.

I hesitantly hand Brandon a second photo. It's a picture of Isaac and Ophelia together. It is time-stamped a few hours before she was killed in the traffic incident. Isaac is wrapping a scarf around her neck. He's smiling in a way I've never seen, and his beautiful, entrancing eyes stare into hers. Nothing but love and admiration radiates from his face.

"Isaac and Ophelia were a couple?" Brandon asks, shocked. His eyes flare with a glint I don't recognize when I nod. "You have to tell Alex you've unearthed the connection between Isaac and Col." His volume dips a smidge. "This will get you off coffee and filing duties in an instant."

He jumps up off the worn carpet, eagerness beaming from him in invisible waves. I accept the hand he thrusts out in front of me. His sharp yank on my arm pulls me off the ground and has me crashing into his firm chest.

Not wanting him to get the wrong idea, I step backward and run my hand down my blouse to ensure it didn't rise during Brandon's eager lift.

Once everything is in place, I turn my attention back to scanning the documents into the old copier. "I don't have time to write a report on their relationship." My eyes roll at my dim excuse. "This scanning will take months as it is." I twist back around to face Brandon, who is eyeing me curiously. "You spent your whole weekend going through Col's file. Eventually you would have discovered these photos yourself." My expression mimics his confused state. "If you're willing to type up the report, I'll let Alex believe you discovered the connection."

"I don't want to take your credit, Izzy."

"You're not taking my credit," I interrupt. "You're helping me out. I'm snowed under here." I gesture to the mountain of papers I still have left to scan. "This isn't even a small dent in the boxes left in the conference room."

Brandon remains quiet as his concerned eyes shift between mine.

After what feels like a lifetime but is more like minutes, he agrees to compile the report to present to Alex. "But you'll get the credit for finding the connection between Isaac and Col," he says before walking out of the supply closet.

I drag my palm over my sweat-drenched neck. Leading a double life is a lot harder than expected. My heart is pounding just from sharing a snippet of Isaac's personal life.

Although I feel guilty, either way, this secret would have been unearthed eventually. If it weren't by me, Brandon would have found it.

Once my high heart rate is back under control, I scarf down the sandwich and OJ Brandon brought me before recommencing with the scanning.

I'm famished since my breakfast was burned off during my impromptu romp in the bathroom with Isaac this morning.

A short time later, Brandon's head pops back into the room. "Your phone has been vibrating nonstop for the past thirty minutes."

I frown, lost as to who would be contacting me with such urgency.

While mumbling a quick thanks to Brandon, I hurry past him and head to my desk. Since I've spent nearly five hours crammed in a small office, my body screams in protest at every step.

My throat works through a hard swallow when I peer down at my phone. There are over a dozen missed calls and text messages from an unknown number and a handful of messages from Harlow.

My brows tack closer with every message I read.

> UNKNOWN NUMBER:
>
> Isabelle, I'll meet you at Harlow's bakery at 1 p.m. sharp.
>
> Isabelle, where are you?
>
> HARLOW:
>
> Did you know Isaac was meeting you here for lunch today?
>
> Jesus, Izzy, the veins in Isaac's neck are about to burst.
>
> UNKNOWN NUMBER:
>
> I've been waiting for nearly an hour.
>
> HARLOW:
>
> Will you hurry up? Isaac is scaring my customers away ;)
>
> UNKNOWN NUMBER:
>
> You will be lucky if I let you come for a week after standing me up. Call me as soon as you get my messages.
>
> HARLOW:
>
> He's gone, but you have some explaining to do, young lady… PS an angry Isaac is sexy as fuck.

I smile when I read Harlow's last message.

If she thinks an upset Isaac is sexy, wait until she sees a jealous Isaac.

I bounce my eyes around the room. Other than catching the eye of Brandon, the rest of the team's focus remains on other tasks, so I send Harlow a quick message telling her I'll pop into the bakery later this afternoon and explain everything.

Once I have the crumpled business card Isaac scribbled his cell phone number on months ago in my hot little hands, I scamper back to the supply closet.

I nearly lose the grip of my phone while dialing Isaac's private number since my palms are slick with sweat, fretful Isaac will uphold his threat of not letting me orgasm for a week.

Isaac connects our call before one full ring sounds through my ear. "Isabelle."

Although his tone is clipped, my name rolling off his tongue sends an excited thrill through my body.

"I only got your messages now," I blurt out.

A length of silence crosses between us.

"Because I was late this morning, my boss made me work through lunch," I explain, my tone getting edgier.

It's technically Isaac's fault I arrived late, so if anyone should be punished for my tardiness, it should be him.

"A simple message advising me you could not attend lunch would have been appreciated. Then I wouldn't have been spending the last two hours panicked something horrible had happened to you."

My heart clutches. "I'm sorry." Moisture dampens my eyes. "I left my phone in my desk drawer, but I promise I'll carry it with me at all times from now on."

I'll say anything to relieve his worry. I don't want to be responsible for more concern in Isaac's life.

Another stretch of silence fills the void before Isaac says, "Hugo will pick you up outside your office building at six o'clock."

Before I can reply, he disconnects the call.

Hating that I've upset him, I pull my phone down from my ear and return a message to the unknown number.

ME:

I'll make up for our missed date tonight.
Dessert is on me. ;)

A short time later, my phone dings, indicating I've received a text message.

ISAAC:

Dessert IS you, Isabelle.

Warm slickness pools between my legs... until my phone dings again.

ISAAC:

But that doesn't mean I'll let you come.

Pouting, I shove my phone into my pocket and spend the next two hours miserably scanning documents before going to Harlow's bakery for the afternoon coffee run.

While Harlow prepares the coffees, I give her a rundown on everything that happened over the weekend, skimming over the parts of the story I uncovered immorally.

She fans her cheeks during the more heated parts of our conversation, and giggles when I make out I loathe Isaac's dominance.

Once I've finished spilling every sordid detail, my jaw muscle is exhausted from how much I shared.

"I'm so glad you guys have finally gotten your shit together." Harlow hands me the two crates of coffee she finished preparing. "I'll text Cormack later to see if we can schedule a double date sometime next week."

I freeze. I can't risk being seen with Isaac in public until his investigation is finalized.

"Why don't we have a more intimate gathering? I could cook dinner at my place?"

Harlow glares at me like I've grown a second head.

"I could *try* to cook us dinner," I correct.

Harlow's giggles echo around her nearly empty bakery. "We'll work something out."

After rolling my eyes, I wave goodbye as well as I can while carrying two full crates of coffee before exiting the bakery.

40

———

At precisely six o'clock, Isaac's town car pulls up to the curve in front of the building where my office is housed. I scan the area, ensuring no one is watching, before opening the passenger-side door and slipping into the front seat.

"Hey, Isabelle," Hugo greets me in his usual friendly tone before pulling the car into the dense commuter traffic.

After securing my belt, I reply, "Hey, Hugo," trying to mimic the long drawl of his rugged voice.

He chuckles at my taunt. My smile freezes halfway when my name rolls off a tongue that has made me quiver more times the past seventy-two hours than I have in the entire span of my sexually active life.

I twist my head to the back of the car so quickly that I nearly give myself whiplash. My mouth waters when I spot Isaac in the backseat. He's removed his jacket and tie, and his shirt sleeves are rolled up to the elbows.

Even with his handsome face marred by an angry scowl, he looks scrumptious enough to eat.

After unlatching my belt, I throw myself over the partition more eagerly than I did weeks ago.

Hugo slaps my backside when it's thrust in his face during my unladylike maneuver.

Isaac's face remains stern during our playfulness, but I see the slightest curve on his lips that gives away his true feelings.

He's happy about my eagerness.

"Hi," I greet him, plopping into the space next to him.

My teeth menace my bottom lip as my eyes absorb his handsome face. He appraises me with as much eagerness while pushing a button on the console of the back passenger door.

I swallow to relieve my dry throat as my eyes flick between Isaac and the rising privacy partition.

Once the barrier is in place, Isaac demands, "Remove your clothes, but leave your panties on."

Heat blemishes my cheeks as my eyes stray to the partition.

"Hugo can't hear or see anything," Isaac assures me.

I lick my parched lips before doing as instructed. If our time together has taught me anything, is that Isaac rewards submissiveness.

Once my clothing is removed, Isaac slides down the zipper on his trousers. My eyes widen when he releases his cock from his briefs before fisting it.

When he slides his manly hand up and down his thickened shaft, slickness builds between my legs. His seamless pumps have a fire raging out of control in my pussy.

"Tonight, you're not allowed to touch me." His husky voice adds more excitement to the sexually satisfying visual playing out in front of me.

Furthermore, if watching Isaac please himself is my punishment, I'll happily accept it. I'm confident watching him crumble into ecstasy will have me toppling into orgasmic bliss with him.

My breaths increase with every stroke to his magnificent cock. He glides his thumb over his knob, gathering a sticky bead of pre-cum pooling at the top from raking his eyes down my naked body.

I groan when he slides the droplet down his shaft, using it as a lubricant to increase the quickness of his pumps.

Over time, the urge to touch him overwhelms me.

I thought the visual alone would satisfy my need for contact.

It doesn't.

Although Isaac's hooded gaze hides his inner battle, they also relay he's fighting the same struggle.

He wants to touch me as badly as I'm dying to touch him.

"Are you wet, Isabelle?"

Unable to speak through the lust clutching my throat, I nod. I'm beyond wet. I am drenched. Every spring in my body is coiled, prepared to snap at any moment, but my desire to touch him is more rampant than my wish to climax.

The heat in the interior of the car turns stifling when Isaac continues his pursuit of his climax. Although the visual of him stroking himself is one I'll forever cherish, not touching him is nearly killing me.

One touch. That's all I want.

I need to feel my skin on his.

I pout when Isaac slaps away my hand before it gets within an inch of his cock.

"Please let me touch you," I shamelessly beg, no longer capable of fighting the urge to run my fingers over him.

I need to feel him, touch him, taste him.

I need it more than I require my next breath.

"I wanted to touch you today." A bead of sweat glides down his cheek as his strokes quicken. "Even just your lips on mine, but I was denied. Now, I'm denying you the same opportunity."

"That isn't fair." My voice is nearly a sob. "I got reprimanded for being late to work because *I* gave in to *your* pleas this morning."

My anger boils when he shrugs.

Fuming with rage, I scoot across the cold leather seat.

Isaac's hand that isn't pounding his cock grips my ankle to drag me back next to him.

Ignoring the pleasing zap jolting through my body from his touch, I stab my stiletto into his thigh.

I'm so angry tears well in my eyes.

"You're being cruel," I yell. "You're taking your anger out on the wrong person…"

I stop talking when a blob of moisture splashes my cheek. My tears are more from the emotionally draining day I had going through Ophelia and Isaac's private life than Isaac teasing me, but once my tears start flowing, I have no chance of reeling them back in.

The instant Isaac sees my glistening cheeks, his frantic pumps stop. In seconds, I go from being seated on the dark leather seat to being cradled in his firm chest, and my knees hug his hips.

His cock braces against my damp panties as his thumbs rub away my tears.

"Please don't cry," he mutters so softly I can barely hear him.

My faint sobs turn into a moan when he slips my panties to the side and enters me in a slow, mouthwatering thrust.

His eyes never leave mine as he undoes the buttons on his dress shirt and flattens my palms on his sweat-slicked torso. Without a word spoken, he permits me access to his body as his cock demands the attention of my pussy.

The fire in my belly gains in intensity with every kiss, caress, and pump he does. It is a wonderful, blissful time that sees me coming undone in a shamefully quick few minutes.

When an orgasm sweeps through my body, igniting my senses like fireworks in a pitch-black sky, my anger is forgotten.

I let the shivers of climax carry it away as I hope my touch eases Isaac's grief.

Although I'm barely coherent by the time my shakes lessen, Isaac continues with his slow, soul-stealing pace. He guides his cock in and out of my pussy as his eyes remain locked on mine.

He makes love to me.

After a while, my name tears from his throat in a seductive purr as hot spurts of his cum line the walls of my pussy.

Exhausted—both mentally and physically—I rest my head on his sweat-misted chest. He stays quiet but maintains physical closeness by keeping his semi-erect cock surrounded by my heat.

After a small amount of time, my blinking lengthens until my eyes eventually flutter shut.

By the time Isaac wakes me, the night sky is pitch black. Not even the moon illuminates the sky. It is hidden behind a scattering of dark clouds from a storm brewing on the horizon.

I glance at my watch in confusion. The standard thirty-minute drive to Isaac's private residence took over two hours.

Isaac unearths the delay when he says, "I asked Hugo to take the long route home."

I sigh when he withdraws his still-firm cock from my pussy, my body sad about the loss of his contact. I love that he kept us connected for so long. I can see it becoming a regular occurrence for us.

Isaac smirks at my response before snagging his suit jacket from the car's floor. I must have kicked it off the seat during my tantrum earlier.

My heart skips a beat when he wraps his jacket around my shoulders and secures the buttons so my private parts are covered.

After cranking open the passenger door, he exits the vehicle. My lips tug higher when he leans back in to offer me a hand. Once I've excited, my eyes dart around his property.

I exhale loudly when I don't see Hugo anywhere.

Although I'm fully covered, I don't want him to see me like this.

Not a word spills from Isaac's lips over the next forty-five minutes.

Instead of the rough and abrupt enigma I experienced earlier this evening, he's the caring, nurturing man I encountered during the weekend.

He heats us a generous serving of chicken noodle soup and makes my heart swell when we eat our meal by using the same spoon.

Once our dinner is consumed, he carries me into the shower and pampers my body and hair before placing me on my side of his bed.

I say "my side" as he always puts me on the same side whenever I sleep in his bed.

I smile when he joins me in bed before spooning me, interlocking our hands, and wrapping them around my waist.

My hips naturally swivel when I feel his cock straining against my backside.

He scoots back. "Not tonight. You need sleep."

His rumbling laughter vibrates through my bursting-at-the-seams heart when I murmur, "You really, really, *really* like me."

Then it bursts open when he replies, "Maybe."

arlow's brows etch high into her hairline as she asks, "How many?"

I bite my bottom lip before raising three fingers into the air.

Harlow gasps so loud air blows onto my face. "In a row, or did he take a break in between?"

"Isaac doesn't break between orgasms." My cheeks heat as I dash my eyes around the half-full bakery to ensure no one is paying attention to our conversation.

I return my eyes to Harlow when she says, "I thought guys need time for... you know... down there to pump back up."

I cock my brow before tilting close to ensure the lady seated next to us doesn't have a coronary from my question. "Cormack has never fucked you so hard that once he came, he kept going until he climaxed another two times?"

Harlow's pupils dilate to saucers. "Honestly, no, he hasn't. But that's because I have a hard enough time keeping up with his sexual prowess as it is. By the time he does come, I'm so exhausted, I can't keep my legs in the air."

Our giggles are interrupted when the lady next to me touches my arm. "Make sure you hold on to those two fine gentlemen." Her sparkling eyes flick between Harlow and me. "It's rare to find a guy who can pop a cork on a champagne bottle, let alone find your G-spot."

As mine and Harlow's mouths gape in sync, we watch the elderly lady in awe as she puts on her light-teal trench coat.

She's easily in her eighties, if not older. Every hair on her head is a beautiful strand of silver, and even a full face of makeup can't hide the heavy set of wrinkles that come with age.

"Suck them dry for every orgasm they're willing to give," she advises before exiting the bakery with an extra spring in her step than when she entered.

My eyes remain planted on the door she exited for the next several minutes. I'm stunned into silence.

It's obtuse of me to think only young couples can enjoy vigorous bedroom activities. I don't believe it would matter if I were twenty or ninety, I'll never stop enjoying Isaac's bedroom antics, so why would I expect it to be any different for her?

My head emerges from the clouds when Harlow mumbles, "I think I'm in love."

"She was pretty cool. I can only hope to be as rocking as her when I'm her age."

I return my attention to Harlow. When I see the panic smearing her face, I realize she isn't talking about her elderly customer. She's referencing Cormack.

"Then why do you look so worried? Love isn't supposed to make you stressed."

My grim expression grows when I realize how poorly my double standards are.

No matter how much my head tries to deny it, my heart has already fallen in love with Isaac. I've loved him from the moment I laid eyes on him.

I'm just too terrified to tell him.

The past four weeks have been a crazy, lust-filled blur. Every waking moment I'm not at work with Isaac I've spent sleeping in his bed, eating his food, or snuggling on his lap while he makes business calls.

Because of his busy schedule, our sleep patterns are at opposite ends of the spectrum. Before I was in the picture, Isaac never came home until after three in the morning, but because he knows I'm waiting for him, he generally ensures he's home no later than ten o'clock.

His business is most likely suffering because of me, but I love that he's willing to make sacrifices to ensure he has the time to see me.

It's another reason I fell in love with him so quickly.

I haven't had any struggles hiding my relationship with Isaac for the past month. Other than Harlow and Cormack, everyone is none the wiser that we're a couple.

Isaac wants to ensure Col never finds out who I am. I agreed with his plan, knowing I couldn't risk Alex or the surveillance team finding out about our relationship.

Although the secrecy adds intrigue to our relationship, I look forward to the day I can declare we're a couple. I can't wait to go on double dates with Cormack and Harlow and not need to look over my shoulder whenever I slip into his town car each evening.

After shrugging off my confusion about my relationship status, I return my focus to Harlow's dilemma. "Does Cormack feel the same way?"

Her glossed-over eyes drop to the tabletop. "I don't know." She exhales a nerve-cleansing breath before returning her beautiful eyes to mine. "I may have accidentally declared my love during an intense orgasmic experience."

Smiling, I wiggle my brows.

"Shut up." She slaps my arm. "It was more the fact he didn't say anything back. I know he heard me, as he stopped thrusting, but not a word seeped from his lips. Not even a thanks."

I giggle at the last part of her comment. "One, you would have been mortified if he said thanks."

She grins while nodding.

"And two, maybe he thought you said it in the heat of the moment. Have you said it to him outside of the bedroom?"

She shakes her head. "I'm too petrified he won't say it back."

My heart squeezes from her panicked tone. "If he didn't say it back, would it change your feelings about him?"

Her lips quirk as she contemplates my question. "No. I'd still love him."

"Well, there you go. That's the answer to your question. You have to tell him." Not giving her the chance to reprimand me on my double standards, I thrust my hand toward her. "Hi, Kettle, my name is Pot."

Harlow and I spend the remainder of my lunch break discussing our plans for Thanksgiving.

Isaac invited his dad; his brother, Nick, and Nick's fiancée, Jenni, for dinner. Thankfully, he also arranged for a catering company to prepare the feast.

He asked if I'd like to make the meal, but I had to decline.

I'm not going to lie; my ego took a beating when I admitted that I struggled to make mashed potatoes, let alone a full meal.

While being honest, I'll admit I am both nervous and excited about meeting Isaac's family. Worried because I want them to like me. Excited because it's a step forward in our relationship.

Although we've only been official for a little over a month, it's been a crazy whirlwind affair that makes it seem so much longer.

One I'd happily experience again and again.

As I walk back into my office, a commotion of laughter gains my attention.

After placing my satchel in the bottom drawer of my desk, I saunter to the window that has captured the other agents' attention. "What's going on?"

Brandon's eyes stray to me. Unlike the other agents, they reflect concern, not amusement. "Megan Shroud."

He continues speaking, but I don't hear a word he utters. All I heard was Megan Shroud, and then my hearing is muffled.

Panicked something horrid has happened to Isaac, I rush to the window and barge agents out of the way to get a clear view of Isaac's nightclub.

Fear clutches my heart when I spot the gigantic bouncer who usually mans the club's front door carrying a screaming Megan in his arms. Her legs and arms thrash as she fights to free herself from his firm hold, and her face has turned the color of beets.

He ignores her screaming pleas to be put down, only stopping to dump her next to a yellow car she's been photographed in numerous times.

As soon as he releases his hold, Megan charges toward the entrance of Isaac's nightclub. She doesn't get far. The bouncer wraps his arms around her waist again, thwarting her endeavors to enter the premises.

"Why isn't someone calling the police?" My words quiver with fear. "She's clearly unstable and not just a threat to the public. She's also a threat to herself."

Michelle's eyes rocket to mine. The amusement brightening her usually bland eyes changes to remorse, but the other agents continue to watch the spectacle unfold without concern for anyone's safety.

"Alex, you need to call the police."

I place my hand on his arm to emphasize that he knows it's the right thing to do in a situation like this.

His stern gaze shoots down to my hand resting on his arm, and his brows stitch, but he maintains his hard-ass stance. "Isaac made his bed. Now he has to sleep in it."

Although he denies my request, he shoos the agents away from the window and then lowers the blinds, blocking their live drama sitcom for the afternoon.

My eyes lock with Brandon. His face is marred with as much concern as mine, but he is also at a loss on what to do.

Urged on by panic, I remove my bureau-assigned weapon from the second drawer of my desk, and after scanning the room, I secure it to my ankle.

Because the other agents are too busy discussing the scene they just witnessed, no one pays me any attention—except Brandon.

He gestures his head to the corridor, requesting me to join him outside. I nod before lifting my finger in the air, needing a minute.

I need to make a phone call before I do anything.

Unsurprisingly, my call goes straight to Isaac's voicemail.

My lips quiver as I begin to speak. "I know it's early in our relationship, but I wanted you to know that I love you, Isaac," I whisper into my cell.

I silence my phone and store it in the pocket of my trousers.

After ensuring no one is watching me, I make a beeline for the corridor. When Brandon notices I've entered the hall, he stops pacing and moves to stand in front of me. "I'll follow her."

I ensure we're alone before I reply, "They'll know you're gone. They won't notice me, as I've spent the last four weeks in the supply room scanning documents." His brows pull together as panic clouds his gaze, but I continue speaking before he can announce his worry. "Nobody ever comes in there looking for me but you. Cover for me, and I'll owe you big time."

He runs his hand over his head. He's quiet, but I still catch part of the cuss words he murmurs under his breath.

After a few big breaths, he places a set of keys into my palm. "It's a blue BMW coupe half a block down."

I rush toward the exit of the building before gratitude for his trust washes over me. After pivoting around, I dart back to Brandon. He balks when I sling my arms around his neck and whisper my thanks for his support into his ear.

He returns my hug with so much force he squeezes the bejeebus out of me.

"Be careful, Izzy," he pleads, his eyes relaying his genuine concern.

Nodding, I rush out of the building.

42

Megan fights the bouncer for nearly twenty minutes before she gives in and walks back to her compact yellow car. Her steps are slow, and her shoulders are slumped in defeat.

When I stab the key into the ignition, Brandon's car roars to life, startling me. Its engine is bigger than I'm used to driving. Plus it's a stick shift. I was taught to drive an automatic, but this is the only car I have access to, and I will not lose the opportunity to follow Megan because I can't drive a stick shift.

The instant Megan pulls her car onto the road, I merge Brandon's car into the heavy traffic. Several motorists honk, annoyed I pulled out without signaling.

Metal grinding together roars through my ears when I forget to push in the clutch before shifting the gearshift.

"Shit. Sorry, Brandon."

My knuckles go white from my determined hold of the steering wheel, and I feel like I'm about to have a heart attack, but even when I', riddled with fear, my urge to protect Isaac outweighs my panic.

Other than my heart madly beating, I make the drive across town in silence. I follow Megan close enough that I won't lose her in traffic, but not close enough for her to become suspicious.

When she pulls into a rundown motel on the outskirts of town, I park Brandon's car along the curb at the front of a McDonald's restaurant.

A large droplet of water splats on the windshield, followed by another and then another. In no time, my view of the motel is clouded by a sheet of water.

I pull my jacket over my head to shelter myself from the rain before peeling out of Brandon's car. Once the street is clear of traffic, I dart across the road and seek cover under the rusted motel awning.

My fear surges when Megan emerges from a room two doors down from where I stand. Because she's so focused on mumbling under her breath, she doesn't notice me hiding under the awning.

While I stand by, helpless, she jumps into her car and dangerously reverses out of her spot. Her vehicle whizzes out of the motel parking lot so fast she'll be long gone by the time I scamper back to Brandon's car, so I survey the area instead.

Because of the rain, most guests have congregated inside. I veer for the room Megan just exited. My steps are so nerve-wracking my legs shake uncontrollably.

Once I'm sure no one is watching me, I try to jimmy the lock.

"Come on."

After two long, panicked minutes, I still haven't picked the lock. This latch is more technical than the locks I trained on.

Desperate to gain entrance, I ram the door as hard as possible with my shoulder. Pain shoots up my arm, and tears sting my eyes, but my hit is successful. The door swings open with only the tiniest creak.

After I dart my eyes around the area, I enter Megan's room, closing the door behind me. It is spotlessly clean with the pungent aroma of bleach. From the two stars on the sign hanging at the front of the motel, I would say it's Megan keeping this room so hygienic.

The bed has been perfectly made to where you could bounce a

nickel off it. She's replaced the standard motel bedding with a more elaborate love heart quilt, and a crib is set up next to the bed.

Is Megan pregnant?

Oh god, please don't let it be Isaac's baby.

Snubbing the queasiness swirling in my stomach, I head for the only desk in the room. My fear that Megan is pregnant surges when I spot several textbooks on pregnancy and medical procedures stacked on a crumbling shelf above the desk.

After grabbing a wad of tissues to cover my fingerprints, I yank down the first lot of books. A picture slips out of a pregnancy pamphlet from an obstetrician's office in Ravenshoe.

My breathing halts when I flip the photo over. It's an ultrasound picture of a distinguishable fetus.

With the baby's face so prominent, Megan must be over six months pregnant, which is surprising considering she didn't have a bump on her svelte frame.

I swallow to eliminate the lump in my throat before slipping the photo back into the pamphlet and then placing it in its rightful spot on the shelf.

Ignoring my hammering heart, I appraise the spotless room. Other than a bed, desk, chair, and baby crib, the room is empty, so I go to the only other door, excluding the entrance door.

"Holy hell."

Every surface of the bathroom is covered with a range of different photos. Most are of a heavily pregnant female with strawberry-blonde hair. In multiple images, her eyes are gouged out, and trails of blood streams down her legs.

When I move deeper into the room, I spot photos of a blond man who appears to be in his early twenties or late teens.

When my eyes adjust to the flicking fluorescent light, air traps in my throat. The man in the photos is Isaac's brother, Nick. Although I've never met him, I recognize him from the numerous pictures Isaac has of him on his living room mantel.

Does that mean what I think it does? Is Megan after Isaac or his little brother, Nick?

After yanking my phone out of my pocket, I collect digital evidence in case these documents get destroyed before the investigation team arrives.

Some photos have "I hate her" and "She must die{" scribbled over the female's face and torso.

Once I've taken numerous pictures, I walk back into the main room. My heart stops beating, closely followed by my steps when Megan enters via the main entryway, her attention focused on a glossy magazine.

Her grin makes my stomach lurch.

I sink back, praying she can't hear my ragged breaths.

As my lungs struggle to fill with air, the burn of their fight warms my chest. Realizing the only safe place to hide is behind the shower curtain, as noiseless as possible, I climb into the tub and plaster my back to the sparkling white tiles.

I close my eyes and try to calm my breaths since the hiss of my panicked lungs echo around the outdated but spotlessly clean bathroom.

Not long later, Megan enters, increasing the smell of bleach and plunging the room into a muggy, uncomfortable heat.

"I'm waiting for you, my love. We'll be together soon. You just have to be patient. Wait for me."

I adjust my position so I can get a better view of her. A torn-out magazine page is in one of her hands, and a roll of duct tape is in the other.

She rips off a large section of duct tape and sticks a paparazzi image of Nick and his bandmates onto the wall solely dedicated to Nick and cardboard hearts.

Seconds later, her fidgety movements halt as her manic eyes dart around the bathroom. I press my back to the tiles and keep as still as possible. I don't even breathe for the fear she may hear my inhalations.

After several terrifying seconds, Megan exits the bathroom as quickly as she arrived. When I wheeze in a shaky breath, my burning lungs relish the fresh air, even if it is riddled with toxic bleach.

Another twenty minutes pass before Megan leaves the motel again. I rush out of the room as fast as my quivering legs can take me, my eyes widening when I cross paths with Megan in the corridor of the motel. She's carrying a bucket of ice.

A sigh spills from my lips when I realize how close I came to having my escape foiled.

Dangling on the front of the ice machine next to Megan's room is an out-of-order sign with instructions to use the ice machine one floor above.

If that ice machine had worked, Megan would have busted me exiting her room.

By the time I park Brandon's car outside of our office building, my heart is still pounding out of control. Although I'm relieved that Megan isn't targeting Isaac, I'm beyond panicked at what Isaac's reaction will be when he finds out that she is threatening his brother.

The entire drive back to the office, my mind replayed Isaac's statement from months ago.

What about for someone you love? You wouldn't get your hands a little dirty for someone you love?"

Isaac undoubtedly loves his brother, and deep down in my heart, I know he'd do anything in his power to protect him.

Anything at all.

Brandon's eyes lift when I walk back into the office. He gulps before he rushes my way. "I should have never let you go alone." He pulls me into his chest and squeezes me tight.

I inch back before asking, "Did anyone notice I was gone?"

I dart my eyes around the office. Surprisingly, the usually bustling space is relatively quiet for the late hour.

"No, they've been too busy with the local cops versus FBI turf saga that happens in every town we go to." Brandon's voice gains a hint of arrogance. "A local detective arrived on the scene not long after you left. Alex is worried he's going to quote 'piss all over my investigation' unquote."

My heart swells, pleased Isaac sought legal help to deal with Megan.

Over the next three hours, Brandon assists me in compiling the longest report I've ever filed. We want to ensure we've dotted every i and crossed every t so the report cannot be dismissed.

Once the report is perfect, we head to Alex's office to share our findings.

"Are you ready?" Brandon asks.

After a quick exhale to calm my nerves, I briskly nod.

Alex's head lifts from some reports when he hears Brandon's curt tap on his office door. When he permits us to enter, Brandon gestures for me to go first.

Once we gain Alex's full attention, Brandon hands him the extensively noted documents and several printouts of the photos I took in Megan's bathroom.

The more Alex's eyes wander over the report, the closer his eyebrows become. "How did you get these photos and information?" he asks, surprised.

"I followed Megan to a Motel 6 on the outskirts of town."

I wait to be reprimanded for going out in the field unassigned.

Astonishingly, no negative remarks leave Alex's mouth. "I'm impressed with the caliber of this report." His eyes dart between Brandon and me. "First thing in the morning, I'll have two agents assigned to Megan."

"Really?" I interrupt in surprise.

As a grin stretches across Alex's face, Brandon squeezes my hand and mouths, *Good job.*

I'm on a high for the rest of the day, but my happiness falters when I slide into the back of Isaac's town car at six o'clock, and Hugo tells me, "Unfortunately, Isaac is indisposed tonight. He asked me to take you back to your apartment."

43

I probably shouldn't have told Isaac I loved him over the phone. If I had waited and done it in person, I would have been able to gauge his reaction by reading his face or staring into his enthralling eyes.

Now, I have the misery of wondering if my message was the cause of his sudden change in routine the past four weeks or if he really is indisposed for the night.

What does "indisposed" mean, anyway?

"Are you sure you don't want to come inside? It's getting a little chilly out there."

Half of me is being friendly, whereas the other half wants to probe Hugo until he spills the beans on where Isaac is tonight.

"For the fourth time, I'm okay out here," Hugo replies from his station outside my door.

He's sitting on a wooden chair that's part of my dining table set.

After the first hour ticked by, I gave him one of the cushions from my sofa, as his bottom would have to be sore sitting on the firm seat.

A smile tugs my lips high when Hugo drones under his breath, "I prefer my nuts attached to my body."

"And here I was thinking you were the first guy I've met who isn't scared of Isaac," I reply sarcastically. "I guess tonight I'm being proven wrong."

Hugo works his jaw side to side before rising to his feet. I try to hide my smile when he glares at me, but I can tell he knows I'm goading him just from the gleam in his eyes.

"Do you remember what happened the last time you had a man in your apartment?" he asks, wiping my smile off my face. "So, since it isn't me who will be punished for denying Isaac's request, I guess I can come inside."

Excitement and fear tremor through my body at the same time.

Trying to pry information from Hugo is like drawing blood out of a stone—impossible!

After two hours, I give up and toddle off to bed.

After tossing and turning for nearly an hour, I give up my endeavor of sleep and pull my phone off the bedside table.

My nose screws up when I see it's a little after two in the morning. I haven't received any messages or calls from Isaac all day today.

Even though it has only been a month, my bed feels cold without him.

Deciding I can't dig my hole any deeper than it already is, I send a message to Isaac's private cell.

> ME:
>
> I miss you. I'm lonely and cold without you.

I lie in silence, staring at the phone's screen, waiting for it to ding with a message.

After twenty minutes, my eyes grow weary.

I don't know how long I've been sleeping when I'm awakened by someone slipping into my bed.

I stop reaching for my gun when Isaac whispers, "Don't scream, it's me."

"What time is it?" I ask to hide my panic that I almost pulled my gun at him.

"It's nearly dawn." My heart rate quickens when his lips brush my ear. "I only just got your message."

I want to ask which one—the one that said I missed him and I'm cold, or the one I declared my love for him.

Before any words can spill from my lips, Isaac silences me by kissing me.

It is lush, deep, and passionate. Every lash of his tongue and nip of his teeth has my heart enlarging.

While raking my hand through his luxuriously thick hair, I pull him closer and deepen our kiss. Our relationship could be construed as only being based on lust, but it's the affection we display during sexual contact that proves even if the passion dampens, something greater will still tie us together.

Isaac tweaks my nipple until it's a stiff peak, every roll increasing the tingles in my pussy. "Could you come just from me playing with your nipples?" he asks when my pants of ecstasy purr throughout the room.

"Uh-huh." I'm not the slightest bit embarrassed. "I could come just by looking at you."

He emits a sexy growl that has my thighs trembling before he makes the situation between my legs worse by adjusting my position so his rapidly hardening cock can grind against my clinging panties.

He grinds against me until my panties are soaked through and I'm on the verge of begging.

Then, he finally gives in to the tension bristling between us.

After tugging off my panties, he lines up his cock with the entrance of my pussy, connects his eyes with mine, then drives home.

I still for half a second before arching my back and moaning.

I'm so full. So very, *very* full.

"Eyes on me, Isabelle."

When our eyes collide, he screws me into oblivion.

Isaac fucks how predicted when we knocked heads. His body is a machine built for pleasure. Every pump is perfect, and every hip flick is timed. He plays my body like a musician would an instrument, and I'm soon lost in the throes of climax.

Not long after the revitalizing shudders of a third orgasm rocket through my body, my alarm clock on my bedside table starts hollering.

Not adjusting the speed of his seamless pumps that have made me a sticky, incoherent mess, Isaac grabs my alarm clock, yanks its cord out of the wall, and then throws it across the room.

It shatters into pieces when it hits the wall with a thud.

Surprised, my eyes missile to Isaac. His eyes display his exhaustion, but they also announce his determination.

He's the most possessive I've ever seen him, and he reveals the reason when he says, "I don't care if I have to fuck you for twelve hours straight. You're not leaving this bed until I hear those words come out of your mouth in person."

Without warning, an intense, core-clenching climax rushes through my body. My back arches off the bed as my nails drag down Isaac's back so harshly I'm certain I've drawn blood.

Isaac lessens my purrs of ecstasy by sealing his mouth over mine, stealing every breathless moan with his tongue.

Once my shakes lessen, he rolls over, keeping his big cock hilted in me during the process. The change of position means he can enter me deeper with every thrust.

When I lean back, my nails stab his thighs. I ride him hard and fast, overcome with the chase of my next release. My speed is relentless and unforgiving. Although my pussy is swollen from hours of sexual contact, my body is still hungry, craving, and needing more.

It won't matter how many orgasms ravish my body, the chase never ends when I'm with Isaac. I want to unravel him, to have him exposed and as open to me as I am to him.

I want him raw.

"Eyes, Isabelle," Isaac demands when orgasm shivers through my body.

After releasing my grip on his thighs, I lean forward and entrap his mouth with mine.

My kiss is selfish and starved, as if I haven't tasted his mouth in months when it has only been mere minutes.

"Oh god," I purr in a grunted moan when the sensation darting through me becomes too much to bear. It is closely followed with, "I love you, Isaac."

Upon hearing my declaration of love, a flare darts through Isaac's eyes before his hot cum coats the walls of my vagina.

Even though he doesn't return my words, his actions make my heart swell, and a violent climax shreds through me so hard and fast that my vision blurs.

A leisurely hot shower, more orgasms than I can count, and access to an endless supply of cosmetics have me walking out of my room with an extra spring in my step.

I smile when I spot Isaac in my living area. When I rented this apartment, I thought the living room was adequate, but having a man like Isaac sitting in it dramatically depreciates its size.

It isn't the room's fault that a man with an aura like Isaac's suffocates the space, making it appear smaller.

Noticing that Isaac is on a call, I enter the kitchen and pour a cup of coffee from the pot Isaac brewed earlier.

Isaac's eyes lift to mine when I return to the living room. His expression is stern, but it still causes excitement to run through my body.

Not waiting for permission, I dump my phone and mug onto the coffee table, then straddle his lap. His conversation never falters, but his cock stiffens.

I feel sorry for whoever he's talking to. His tone is clipped and furious, his grumpy mood bouncing off him in invisible waves.

I press kisses to his unshaven jawline, hopeful it will cure his surly mood. He smells fresh, as if he recently showered, but his hair is dry, so I assume he's been awake longer than I have.

I tug his ear with my teeth before whispering, "Good morning."

His smirk makes me purr like a kitten. As he continues his conversation, he glides his hand down my back and cups my ass to give it a gentle squeeze.

I return his tease by grinding against his thickening cock.

A thrill of anticipation tightens my muscles when he hisses at my playful tease. Usually, his calm composure never falters. I love that I can spark reactions from him, little flaws no one else has the privilege of seeing.

"I'll call you back."

Isaac disconnects his call, stealing his caller's chance of a reply. His tired, withdrawn gaze studies my face, but not a peep spills from his hard-lined mouth.

"Are you okay?"

He considers my question before nodding.

Although he nods, I can hear his brain ticking over, no doubt overrun with all the information jammed in there.

"Is there anything I can do to help?"

When he smirks a deliciously wicked smile, my insides clench.

"Nah-uh. No. I remember what happened the last time I arrived late to work. That's *not* happening again."

When I attempt to remove myself from his lap, he seizes my wrist before I get two steps away from him. His hot, heated eyes absorb my body before they return to my face.

His desires, needs, and every want are projected from his beautiful eyes, and they all point in one direction.

At me.

"You'll get me fired," I say, as if the possibility of me getting fired wouldn't be the best thing that could happen to our relationship.

"Good afternoon, Izzy," Hugo greets while rolling down the window of Isaac's town car.

I hand him a cup of coffee and a white bag stuffed with freshly baked goodies. His eyes bulge when he spots the scrumptious treats Harlow has supplied him with.

"She threw a couple of extra treats in the bag for you."

Since I found out Isaac has Hugo shadowing me, I added Hugo to my morning and afternoon coffee orders. I've tried numerous times over the past few weeks to tell Isaac I don't require Hugo's services during working hours, but Isaac is adamant that if I'm not with him, Hugo will be with me.

Hugo must be bored out of his mind sitting in a car for at least eight hours a day, so if there's anything I can do to ease his boredom, I'll do it.

Coffee and cakes might not be much, but it's better than nothing.

Hugo gestures his head to the clouds forming on the horizon. "If this storm ends up brewing, wait under the awning of your building, and I'll pull up at the front."

"All right." I smile. "I'll see you in a couple of hours."

When I enter the foyer of my office, my heart stops beating. Agents are running in all directions, gathering bulletproof vests and holstering pistols onto their waists.

Brandon races for me just as quickly. After yanking the coffees out of my grasp, he dumps them into a waste bin in the foyer before pulling a bulletproof vest over my head. "You need to get your vest on."

"What's going on?"

He doesn't grace me with a response. He continues adjusting the straps of my bulletproof vest before handing me my bureau-issued revolver, which I usually store in my desk drawer.

"We have a five-minute window. Move in quickly, secure the target, and move out. This needs to be done fast and with minimal fuss," Alex yells over the buzz of activity.

"Who are we arresting?" I ask anyone who might be listening.

Alex ushers the agents out the double-glass doors while shouting, "Let's go. Move, move, move!"

Brandon and I shadow our colleagues out of the building at a frantic pace. My heart plummets to my stomach when we race across the street and storm into Isaac's nightclub.

"Get on the ground!" is yelled over and over again by numerous agents. Their screeching roars through my ears so loudly they overtake my frenetic pulse.

Riddled with fear, I adjust my position to improve my view.

With every shaky step, I pray we aren't here to arrest Isaac.

A sharp ache stabs my chest when the image of Isaac standing in front of a handful of agents with their guns drawn comes into my peripheral vision.

Isaac's livid eyes glare at Alex. His nostrils are flaring, and the tic of his jaw is noticeable, even with me halfway across the room.

"Get on the ground," Alex sneers, directing his gun at Isaac's head instead of his chest.

My heart constricts as time stands still.

"Please get on the ground," I silently chant.

Isaac's infuriated gaze shifts sideways. I can't breathe when our eyes lock and hold for several terrifying seconds, but I wordlessly plead for him to get on the ground before Alex or one of the other agents shoots him.

Even with numerous guns pointed at him, Isaac's dignified stature beams out of him. His eyes never relay his fear. They merely convey his anger and disgust.

"Please get on the ground." My appeal is more a plea than a demand.

The agents surrounding Isaac grow panicked when he storms away from them. His long, powerful strides as he rushes my way quicken my pulse, but this time, fear, not euphoria, is responsible for its spike.

After holstering his gun, Alex attempts to tackle Isaac to the ground.

Isaac's pursuit to reach me is too strong for Alex to overcome. His determination is unnerving and once again solely focused on me.

My legs quiver when I raise my gun to Isaac's erratically panting torso. Tears well in my eyes so fast they burn from the sudden rush of moisture.

"Please get on the ground," I beg, my nerves so rattled my gun shakes.

I don't want to do this, but someone will shoot him if he doesn't listen.

Since this unit is trained to shoot to kill, I'd rather he be shot by me than someone who won't care if they take him down permanently.

Isaac's delicious scent engulfs me when he stops an inch from my face. The barrel of my gun digs into his suit-covered chest as he furiously glares at me. His eyes are the darkest I've seen them—desolate and broken.

My heart cracks from the utter hurt reflecting from his beautiful gaze.

When gunfire booms around the room, I panic that my worst fear is coming to fruition.

"The next one won't be a warning." Alex's tone is as vicious as the tautness of his face.

With my heart in my throat, I stare at Isaac, wordlessly begging for him to surrender before Alex makes true on his threat.

"Please," I beg as a tear splashes on my cheek.

For the quickest second, remorse flashes through his squinted gaze. He seems torn, unsure if he's coming or going.

He's not the only one.

Fear clutches my throat when Isaac suddenly drops to his knees. Even though I didn't hear a gunshot, I scan his body, seeking an entry or exit wound.

I sigh upon discovering he's uninjured.

With his eyes fixed on the floor, Isaac places his hands behind his head as Alex instructs from across the room. Alex is the only one not bristling with confusion about my exchange with Isaac. You'd swear he knows that we've previously met.

The cracks in my heart enlarge when Alex instructs me to arrest Isaac. I shake my head, but Alex refuses to take no for an answer.

"Now, Agent Brahn!"

Through the blur of tears, I holster my gun and place my hand on Isaac's tense shoulder before whispering, "I'm sorry."

When I lower him onto the floor, the thump his defeated body makes when it hits the floor adds more nicks to my already crumbling heart.

In an instant, several male agents scurry toward us. My heart shatters more when they pin him to the ground with their knees. Despite the pain they inflict on Isaac, however, he remains completely motionless.

Not a noise seeps from his lips as he's cuffed and read his rights. His gaze only leaves the ground when I push back one of the agents using more force than needed to arrest a man who isn't resisting.

Isaac's eyes are livid and broken. They appear almost soulless.

And that is precisely how I feel when he says, "If you're going to be accused of something, you may as well do it."

To be continued in *Unraveling an Enigma*
Out now!
We also get inside Isaac's head from here on out!

Join my author page for updates on the next installment in the *Enigma series*.
https://www.facebook.com/authorshandi

Join my READER's group:
https://www.facebook.com/groups/1740600836169853/

Hunter's, Hugo's, Cormack's, Hawke's, Ryan's, Rico's, Regan's, and

Brax's stories have already been released. Brandon, and all the other great characters of Ravenshoe will be getting their own stories sometime during 2020/21.

Join my newsletter to remain informed:
subscribepage.com/AuthorShandi
If you enjoyed this book, please leave a review.

ALSO BY SHANDI BOYES

<u>Perception Series</u>

<u>Saving Noah</u> (Noah & Emily)

<u>Fighting Jacob</u> (Jacob & Lola)

<u>Taming Nick</u> (Nick & Jenni)

<u>Redeeming Slater</u> (Slater and Kylie)

<u>Saving Emily</u> (Noah & Emily - Novella)

<u>Wrapped Up with Rise Up</u> (Perception Novella - should be read after the
Bound Series)

<u>Enigma</u>

<u>Enigma</u> (Isaac & Isabelle #1)

<u>Unraveling an Enigma</u> (Isaac & Isabelle #2)

<u>Enigma The Mystery Unmasked</u> (Isaac & Isabelle #3)

<u>Enigma: The Final Chapter</u> (Isaac & Isabelle #4)

<u>Beneath The Secrets</u> (Hugo & Ava #1)

<u>Beneath The Sheets</u>(Hugo & Ava #2)

<u>Spy Thy Neighbor</u> (Hunter & Paige)

<u>The Opposite Effect</u> (Brax & Clara)

<u>I Married a Mob Boss</u>(Rico & Blaire)

<u>Second Shot</u>(Hawke & Gemma)

<u>The Way We Are</u>(Ryan & Savannah #1)

<u>The Way We Were</u>(Ryan & Savannah #2)

<u>Sugar and Spice</u> (Cormack & Harlow)

Lady In Waiting (Regan & Alex #1)

Man in Queue (Regan & Alex #2)

Couple on Hold (Regan & Alex #3)

Enigma: The Wedding (Isaac and Isabelle)

Silent Vigilante (Brandon and Melody #1)

Hushed Guardian (Brandon & Melody #2)

Quiet Protector (Brandon & Melody #3)

Enigma: An Isaac Retelling

Twisted Lies (Jae & CJ)

Bound Series

Chains (Marcus & Cleo #1)

Links (Marcus & Cleo #2)

Bound (Marcus & Cleo #3)

Restrain (Marcus & Cleo #4)

The Misfits

Russian Mob Chronicles

Nikolai: A Mafia Prince Romance (Nikolai & Justine #1)

Nikolai: Taking Back What's Mine (Nikolai & Justine #2)

Nikolai: What's Left of Me (Nikolai & Justine #3)

Nikolai: Mine to Protect (Nikolai & Justine #4)

Asher: My Russian Revenge (Asher & Zariah)

Nikolai: Through the Devil's Eyes (Nikolai & Justine #5)

Trey (Trey & K)

The Italian Cartel

Dimitri

Roxanne

Reign

Mafia Ties (Novella)

Maddox

Demi

Rocco

Clover

Smith

RomCom Standalones

Just Playin' (Elvis & Willow)

Ain't Happenin' (Lorenzo & Skylar)

The Drop Zone (Colby & Jamie)

Very Unlikely (Brand New Couple)

Short Stories - Newsletter Downloads

Christmas Trio (Wesley, Andrew & Mallory -- short story)

Falling For A Stranger (Short Story)

One Night Only Series

Hotshot Boss

Hotshot Neighbor

The Bobrov Bratva Series

Wicked Intentions (Katie & Ghost)

Sinful Intentions (April 25)

Devious Intentions (June 13)

Deadly Intentions